# HOLDING TESS

## The McKenna Brothers, Book Two

## MARIELLA STARR

Published by Blushing Books
An Imprint of
ABCD Graphics and Design, Inc.
A Virginia Corporation
977 Seminole Trail #233
Charlottesville, VA 22901

Holding Tess
Mariella Starr

ebook ISBN: 978-1-64563-516-1
Print ISBN: 978-1-64563-517-8
v2

## Prologue

Tessa Foster's eyes snapped open when a hand hit the hospital door. She sat up, and her feet hit the floor. She'd been trying to catch a few minutes of sleep during an eighteen-hour shift in the emergency room of Dell Seton Medical Hospital. Working at the Del Seton had been a natural progression for her after completing her college and medical school at the University of Texas at San Antonio. Dell Seton was part of the university teaching hospital.

Nurse Trent stood in the open door. "Incoming, three-vehicle collision," she said in her calm voice.

"Casualties?" Tess said without looking up as she pulled on her sneakers.

"Vehicle one, four teenagers in transport, three girls, one boy. Minor fractures, not critical," Nurse Trent said in clipped, shorthand sentences. "Vehicle two, victim one, male adult, in critical condition. He has been Life-flighted to the Military Medical. Don't ask why the Life-flight doctor made that decision. I don't know. The female is incoming here. She has broken ribs and possible internal injuries. Vehicle three, two adults. Male with chest injuries, possible broken ribs. Female with leg fractures. Three small children in seat restraints, and appeared to be unharmed. The kids were taken to Dell Children's Medical Center to be checked out. Social services have been notified. All victims are in-bound."

"Alert everyone, and get the patient information ASAP. If those parents are awake, they're going to be asking about those kids," Tessa said, over her shoulder. She was already at the door, sprinting past the nurse toward the ER ambulance intake.

This was her life. It was busy and chaotic. When she had a chance to take a deep breath, she knew it was exactly what she had wanted. Tess had been working toward her goal since she'd been twelve years old. She also knew it was time to make changes and move on.

She was going to miss Dell Seton, but it was time for her to make a change. Working full-time in an ER was her life, with no time left over for anything else. She needed more. Now, because of an unexpected financial windfall, she could take those next steps. If she could decide on what she wanted to do next.

Tess's family had imploded years ago, due to divorce and selfishness on the parts of both her father and her mother. Her parents were two immature people, who had brought children into the world and had promptly decided their personal needs, and desires were more important. Her mother was on her way to husband number five, and the majority of her relationships hadn't made it to the altar. Her father had never remarried. He did regularly have live-in girlfriends, half his age, and sometimes younger. The live-ins didn't last long enough for Tess to learn their names.

As far as she was concerned, Tess's family consisted of her and her sister Lauren, three years older. Lauren was divorced and had fivecount themfive daughters, all under the age of nine. The three youngest were identical triplets. Her divorce had been one caused by abandonment, but she had survived it. Now her sister was stronger for it, ran a successful business, and was taking on life on her terms.

There had been a half-brother from her mother's second marriage. Jeremy had been diagnosed with severe autism. Somewhere hidden within his mind, had been a child they couldn't reach. Tess had tried. She had worked so hard to reach him, visiting him several times a week. Non-verbal, he had died four years earlier of peritonitis caused by a ruptured appendix. He had never cried, never shown any indication of pain.

Tess looked around the emergency room at the doctors and nurses who all performed miracles to preserve life. She was proud of being one of them. The latest accident victims would all live. They might hurt for a while, but there would be no amputations, paralysis, or life threatening after affects. It had been a good shift, and she didn't have that many left before her contract would expire. She wasn't going to renew it."

———

Micah McKenna stepped onto a three-level deck overlooking a lake and sat to enjoy his first cup of coffee of the day. He was an early riser, loved the early hours when he was at odds with the rest of the world. Well, at least the small portion of the world he claimed as his own.

While most people were sleeping, his mind was active and creative. The music, the lyrics, and now the images, they came to him in the pre-dawn hours, long before most people were awake. From the first time, as a child, when he had discovered that he could sneak out of bed and get something done, he'd been hooked.

Micah got more done before seven a.m. than most people accomplished in a full day. His parents had shaken their heads and tried to get him to conform to more normal sleeping hours. He had never understood why. There was so much to do, and he didn't want to waste his time sleeping!

His parents had finally given up in defeat and allowed him to get on with his projects as long as he didn't wake his brothers. Micah was past the thirty-year mark now by two years. He knew his body rhythms were firmly set in place.

Micah was rarely a multitasker. He could kick himself into high gear; it just wasn't his preferred way of getting things done. He concentrated on one thing at a time and gave it his full attention. When he was finished, it was time to move on to the next task. He was a deliberate man. Study the situation, calculate the challenge, and go after the results required. He'd been accused of being an overachiever. Maybe he was, but he could live with the accusation. It was, after all, a finely tuned family trait.

After inhaling the last drops of his coffee, Micah went inside to refill his cup. Careers and interests, of which he had too many, were tidily aligned into time frames of what needed to be done first, second, and so forth.

Over the last couple of years, his life and his priorities had changed drastically. When two of his best friends and fellow musicians had died in a car accident, Micah had suddenly become a father. Juggling, a talent he'd never wanted or needed had suddenly become a way of life. It was a talent he'd discovered most parents possessed.

He and his daughter, Katie, were the only full-time residents at the McKenna Lake property. His family had vacationed there for years when he and his siblings were children. When the property had gone on the market, he and his two younger brothers had purchased it. At the time, he had no idea it would become his permanent residence.

When his long-term relationship without the ties of marriage had imploded, his lake cabin had become a sanctuary. Now it was his permanent home. The breakup, with his ex-girlfriend, had turned into a nasty situation. It had taken almost as long as the relationship itself to sever the ties, both personal and financial, during long and drawn-out litigations.

Carla had been the one who had insisted there was no reason for marriage. She was the one who had decided they should keep their finances separate. Carla had also been the one who had deceived him. When he had objected, she'd fought a vicious and dirty battle to take him for everything he was worth and ruin his reputation. Carla Mancuso hadn't succeeded, although she had made his life hell for the last couple of years.

The McKenna lake property had been a recreational retreat before it had been purchased by the family. There was a main lodge and nearly a dozen cabins of various sizes. Most of the old cabins and buildings were rundown and neglected. Micah had claimed one of the nicer cabins. The small five-room house had met his temporary needs when he took a break from work. It hadn't fit his needs when he decided to live there permanently. The original two-bedroom, one bath log cabin was now a recording studio. He'd had the structure moved off its foundation, and had built a new home to his specifications. Now his new home was a mountain retreat, minus the mountains. Inside it was state-of-the-art with the latest technology and fixtures, as was his music studio out back.

He'd decided to build a new house right after his relationship had imploded. That had been the year before he'd become responsible for a two-year-old child. The lake house was their permanent home.

The house project had kept his mind and body busy during trying times. He'd learned a lot about the trades in the process. His home was a masterpiece of stone, natural wood, and glass that would equal any million-dollar chalet in Aspen. Micah had visited Colorado, loved to ski, but he was a Texan. He'd traveled all over the world as part of the I-35 band. There were many beautiful places, but he was a Texan in his heart.

He'd been taking his sweet time with the construction of his new home. He hadn't been in a hurry. Then in the blink of an eye, he had become responsible for a child. He had been suddenly submerged in a different kind of adulthood.

Micah looked over to the large folder, still lying on the kitchen counter. It held copies of the legal termination of his association with Carla Mancuso. They hadn't been married, but the split had been more vicious than most divorces. Their split had never been about feelings or their relationship. It had been about money. He'd earned it. She wanted it.

He still owned the townhouse he had shared with Carla in Austin. He'd listed the property for sale several times. He had also taken it off the market because of her interference. He would sell it now.

The gut-wrenching shock and pain of what she'd done had lessened over time. Any feelings he'd had were gone. Her betrayal could never be forgotten or forgiven.

Micah picked up the envelope and took it to his office, and filed it in the back of a bottom drawer of a file cabinet. That part of his life was over, and he was done with it.

The lake property had become his retreat and his home. It was a place where he could live and not be bothered or harassed. Raised in a house full of love, noise, and chaos, Micah had learned at an early age to value quiet solitude.

Micah and his daughter were the only full-time inhabitants of the lake property. His brothers appeared now and again. His parents spent a couple weeks at the lodge in the summers.

The three older McKenna brothers, who were I-35, the band, had a nine-year difference from the oldest to the youngest. Four more children had been added to the family, adopted when they'd lost their parents in a car accident. Now, Micah had twin sisters who were almost twenty-one, a fourteen-year-old brother, and a little sister who was eleven. The McKenna family had always been tight. They were bound together by love and strong beliefs in family values.

Micah and his closest brothers had been straining against those close ties for a while. It was difficult for parents to let go when their children became adults. He enjoyed his separateness, yet he was a McKenna. He was still part of the band, I-35. He was invested, as were his brothers, in the music studio, headed by their father. Micah was also the CEO of a successful music production company he owned.

His position in life was that of a father, son, and brother. He was the problem solver. He was Micah.

## Chapter 1

Hard Rock turned to the loudest volume on an old boom box was interrupted by the rhythmic crack of an ax splitting wood. Set-up, step back, and swing. The repetitive action was almost cathartic, but a large pile of split firewood was proof that Micah McKenna wasn't only a pretty boy, rock star. He looked strong, fit, and lean because he was a man who knew how to work with both his mind and his muscles.

He'd had a haircut recently. Shorn close to his scalp at the sides and back, it looked lighter than his medium brown. She knew those lighter blond tones weren't from bleaches. Micah spent a lot of his time outdoors.

Tess Foster preferred it longer, but he only let it grow because he hated someone, anyone messing with it. He claimed it gave him the heebie-jeebies and would shudder at the idea of sitting in a stylist's chair. She called it a phobia, but Micah shrugged it off or gave her that look that was a warning. She knew that look. He was thinking about smacking her ass. She'd been able to spot it since she was about twelve-years-old.

About twice a year, Micah would appear with his hair short

and neat. It sent his agents and managers into a panic. He didn't give a damn. His jawline looked like he was using clippers on it rather than shaving. She liked the neat but scruffy look. Tess liked looking at Micah, she always had.

Tess didn't call to him. She didn't want to startle anyone swinging an ax. In loose, ill-fitting hospital green scrubs, Tess Foster looked amorphous. At five-foot-nine inches, she was anything but shapeless. Because she was slim, with somewhat delicate facial features, people tended to think she was smaller and more fragile. She delighted in ruining their preconceptions. Tess took the time to enjoy watching her friend.

Micah turned and noticed her. He grabbed his ax and locked it in a wooden box that was attached to a tree. He threw a few pieces of freshly split wood into a pile and walked over to her.

"Hey, kiddo, I didn't think they let you doctors escape, except at ungodly hours of the night, like vampires!" He swung his arm around her and nudged her toward the stairs. Then, he backed off with a look of disgust. "Whoa, I hate to tell you, Tess, but you stink!"

"I know," Tess admitted with a grin. "I was sent over to the night clinic at Columbus Hospital because they were short-staffed. I was on my way home when I was the first responder to a car accident on the interstate. It was a mess!"

Micah winced, and Tess knew what he was thinking. She put an arm around his waist and squeezed as they took the deck steps together. "It wasn't fatal. The woman driving did take a hard whack to the head. There were three little kids in the car from three to ten. The two little ones were in excellent car seats, and they weren't hurt. The older boy was about ten and small enough that he should have been in a restraining seat. He wasn't badly hurt, a broken arm that I could diagnose. The mother was flown by Life-flight to Austin Trauma. The kids were sent by ambulance. I was able to get family information from the older boy, Tyler. He was a sweet kid. His arm was hurting, but all he could think about was his little sisters and his mother. His dad and grandparents were going to meet them at the hospital when I left the scene.

"As the first responder, I was in the dirt trying to do triage until the ambulances arrived. I'm covered with mud, blood, and thanks to the three-year-old, vomit. I thought I would stop here and see if I could get a shower and maybe borrow some clean clothes before I take this exhausted body home to sleep."

"Sure," Micah said, giving his friend a push toward his bedroom. "Take your stinky self to my room and jump in the shower. All I have that will fit you will be sweats."

Tess stripped out of her sticky hospital greens and stepped into a luxurious bathroom. She had seen the bathroom before but had never had the opportunity to use it. After determining, what knob controlled what, she turned on all the massage jets and stepped into her idea of pure luxury. She grabbed a bottle of shower gel, sniffed, and smiled. It wasn't the usual fruity, flowery smell of what she bought that was on sale at the supermarket. This shower gel smelled slightly spicy, a little musky, and definitely like Micah.

"Tess!" Micah's voice was loud outside the bathroom door. "Throw your scrubs out, and I'll toss them in the washer!"

Tess stepped from the shower and cracked the door enough to toss her soiled clothing onto the hardwood floor. "Can you make coffee?" she asked.

"Is the sky blue?" he answered.

"Micah!" Tess opened the door a little wider. "Don't touch the blood or the vomit! Those clothes will need a cycle of cold washing and a second cycle with hot water and a disinfectant if you have any. Wash your hands thoroughly with a strong soap, even if you don't touch anything nasty," she ordered authoritatively.

"Yes, ma'am," Micah drawled over his shoulder as he headed toward the laundry room.

Twenty minutes later, Tess left the bathroom wrapped in a long terrycloth robe she'd found behind the bathroom door. She slid onto one of the kitchen bar stools and watched as the man she respected above all others, finished making a grilled ham and cheese sandwich, and poured soup into a bowl.

"I thought you might be hungry."

"I'm starved," Tess admitted, and she took a healthy bite of the sandwich and spooned in the soup.

Tess cocked her head and looked around. "Where's Katie?"

"School and a sleepover tonight. There seems to be a lot of that going on as the school year ends. I think she has three or four sleepovers planned for the upcoming weeks. I'll go get her tomorrow evening."

"So, you are here, all by your lonesome?"

"I am most of the time," Micah said. "I get a lot done, and I enjoy the quiet." He pointed his finger at her sternly. "Do not try to set me up on a date again!"

"I apologized for that! Don't be hypersensitive."

"I'm not," he said, placing another half sandwich on her plate and taking the other half to eat himself. "I don't need to find a *nice girl*."

"That's a quote from your mother."

He grinned. "It is, and six aunts and countless others. I don't want anyone pushing me into dating again."

Tess's eyes crinkled with humor.

Micah gave a loud sigh. "I don't mean to jump on you, Tess. You know I love you, but I get tired of the endless advice. I signed the final papers last week. All connections or perceived connections to Carla have been severed, personally, and professionally. Emotionally, I was done a long time ago. She's the one who has dragged the crap out for so long."

"Do you think it will end the harassment?"

"It better. It's been almost five years. She spent the first year trying to wheedle her way back into my life, and the last four tormenting me. She and those weasel lawyers were warned by the judge. They will be charged with a half-dozen criminal charges if they persist. She's claiming bankruptcy and trying to get out of paying her legal team. Carla told the judge she has a job in London, and she has received her work visa. She is supposed to be gone for a couple of years. Good luck to her."

"I pity whoever hired her," Tess exclaimed.

"Don't be nasty, she's gone, and it's over," Micah scolded.

"Nasty?" Tess queried with outrage in her voice. "A bitch like her gives all women a bad name!"

"Behave," Micah said mildly. "Summer is almost here. What's on your agenda next?"

"I'm still looking into it. My contract is over next week, and the hospital seems to be trying to squeeze every hour left in me. The Head of Administration is not pleased that I have decided not to renew my contract. I haven't decided what I want to pursue next. I wouldn't mind getting a fellowship to advance my knowledge of cardiothoracic surgery, or maybe it's time to join an established medical practice."

"I have applied for an eighteen-month fellowship working with Dr. Kirby Frost at the National Naval Hospital. He's heading a program studying abnormal brain dysfunction in children. His office contacted me, which was a real coup for me. His group has been reading the results of the papers I have published on our findings using music to stimulate autistic children. He was impressed with our website."

"Not *ours*, it's your website," Micah corrected. "My brothers and I haven't had anything to do with your results."

"The three of you write the songs and the music," Tess protested. "The parents get the results! It's big, Micah. Really big!"

"All we do is write little rhymes about getting dressed and combing hair and set them to music."

"The parents have been getting positive results, so don't belittle your part of it!" Tess insisted. "Sully's not around to help much anymore. You have come through every time I have asked for anything, even if you had to pawn it off on Coyote. I know parents would genuflect to you if they knew who was writing those little *rhymes* as you call them. We could never reach Jeremy, but part of me wants to keep learning and trying to help other children. Another part of me is telling me that joining a practice makes more sense. I would, at last, have time to have a life outside of medicine."

"So, I'm in flux. I may be going to the Naval Hospital in Bethesda, Maryland. I have the first interview scheduled for next month. There will be a series of interviews. Dr. Frost is known for taking his time in interviewing and hiring."

"What happens if you don't get the fellowship?"

"There are others. Dr. Dennison is in charge of a research program at Goldsbury Children. I'm considering the idea of joining a practice. However, most of my ER experience would go to waste in a mainstream clinic."

Micah shook his head. "Your experience could never be a waste. Like today, you were driving and boom something happens. You probably saved lives. You do every day."

"Maybe I need something different," Tess said with a sigh.

"This doesn't sound like you. You have planned every single class, and study program since you entered college at sixteen."

Tess finished her sandwich, took her mug of coffee, and moved over into the living room. She flopped on the couch, propping her bare feet on a trunk that served as a coffee table.

"I'm tired," Tess said finally. "I'm especially tired of working in a 'for profit' environment. I know hospitals have to make a profit, but I'm sick of my decisions being second-guessed by accountants.

"I haven't had a life for the past twelve years. I've been busy with full-time school and part-time jobs. I haven't had a date in two years! Every time I make one, an emergency comes in that I can't leave. I love being a doctor, but I can't continue at this pace. If I want a life, I have to remove myself from the ER department."

Micah looked at her with a furrow between his eyes. "What's going on?" he asked, sitting beside her and offering her an open bag of chocolate cookies.

Tess smiled as she snagged a cookie and took a bite. "Exhaustion, and a big wake up call. I fell asleep at the wheel."

"What!"

Tess nodded. "I must have been partially cognitive. I managed to pull off the road, so I didn't crash or hurt anyone else. I was awakened two hours later by someone knocking on my window. They thought I'd had a medical emergency. It's time to take a break."

"When was the last time you had a vacation?" Micah asked.

Tess shook her head. "No time, and even if I had the time, there was no money. I'm good at running an ER department. It's a specialty very few can handle. It has paid the bills and paid down a lot of my student loans, but it's time for a change."

Micah looked away, and his jaw stiffened. "This really pisses me off. Why didn't you say something? I could have helped!"

"Micah, unless a medical student comes from a wealthy family, the average debt coming out of training is in the three-hundred-thousand range. My student debt was less than that, and you have helped many times. I know you'll deny it, but it's a fact!" Tess exclaimed. "It is what it is!"

"You'll get the fellowship if it's what you want," Micah said, taking a deep breath to release his frustration. "You've had offers before, and if they don't hire you, it is their loss. Doctors are like celebrities, most of them start believing their press, and that leads to having God-like egos."

"Watch it, big guy. I am a doctor," Tess reminded him with a poke in the ribs.

"I know, and I'm, well, whatever I am. Neither of us is tripping over our egos, I hope. I try to overlook that you are the most stubborn person I've ever met. I still love you," Micah said, grinning.

Tess leaned over and laid her head on his shoulder. "I know, and I overlook that you are sometimes the biggest macho dork I have ever known."

"Hey, that is a politically incorrect pronoun and a highly insensitive insult. Besides my brother, Coyote still holds the title for dork," he teased.

Tess smiled and gave another tired sigh. "You are still my Micah."

Tessa grabbed the remote, looking over the program guide on a huge widescreen television over a fireplace that doubled as a mirror when not in use. She didn't find anything interesting, and she turned it off. She tucked into Micah, and they sat together, enjoying his fantastic lake view. They didn't need words to feel comfortable with each other.

Micah looked down, enjoyed the view for a few seconds, and raised his eyes upward. "Uh, Tess."

"Hmm," Tess mumbled.

"Not that I don't enjoy a peek, but the robe is coming apart," Micah said.

Tess looked down and realized that she was exposing one of her breasts. She looked into Micah's face.

"Enjoying it?"

Micah smirked, ready to make a joke when he realized that

Tess's eyes weren't smiling but intense and sultry with an invitation. He lowered his head and kissed her, first hesitantly, and when she responded hungrily, his mouth matched hers. One taste of her, and he wanted to savor and feel again.

They surfaced, and Micah stroked a gentle hand over her cheek and drew her against him. "Do you want this, Tess? Can we do this?"

Tess's fingers tugged at his shirt. "Yes, and yes."

He took possession of her mouth again. Even as she melted against him, he hesitated until she unzipped his jeans and freed him. She stroked him, and it was a flashpoint. A fever ignited that shattered his hesitancy as he touched, kissed, needed, and took what was offered. He needed so badly that he throbbed, but Micah held back, and Tess made the decision for him.

She straddled Micah, lowering herself over him, enveloping him in the wet heat of an identical passion. She rode him and rode him until she was gripped with sensations that swamped her as her body shuddered, tightened, and finally broke from release.

He pushed her to lay on the couch, and he drove into her with long slow strokes, igniting the fever again as he kissed and stroked and suckled.

Tess's legs wrapped around his waist. He thrust harder, faster, and finally pitched forward as he spilled his release and held onto that moment, wanting it to last longer.

Micah could feel his heart pounding, and he took several deep breaths to calm down. His first coherent thought was, "What the hell have I done!" His second was… "Hold on, we are adults, it was consensual." Then it was… "Dear God! I just had sex with Tess!"

Tess's reaction was a deep breath of pure satisfaction. Finally, finally, she'd had her way with Micah. She'd been in love with him half her life. He had never noticed her as anything beyond being another kid that he felt responsible for watching over. She wasn't surprised when he pushed away from her.

With a shove, Micah rose in a sitting position. Tess had somehow been relieved of the borrowed robe, and she was perfectly comfortable although she was naked. She smiled when he grabbed a throw pillow and laid it over his naked lap.

"Jesus, Tess, I didn't even get my pants and boots off!"

She watched him in amusement. "You're blushing."

Micah knew he was, but he shook his head in denial. "Men, don't blush."

"If that's true, I need to take your blood pressure because you might be headed for a stroke."

Micah took a deep breath because he thought having a stroke might be a real possibility. His jeans were pooled around his ankles, and he was sitting bare-assed naked on his couch. He was sitting beside a gloriously naked woman, but it was Tess! She'd been his brother Sully's best friend since he'd been a teenager. Oh yeah, and they had just had sex! Fantastic, hurried sex, and it had been over way too soon.

"Tess, what did we just do?"

She turned to him, and this time she wasn't smiling as her eyes searched his. "Micah, if you apologize for what just happened, I will smack you so hard you will land into tomorrow."

He pushed the throw pillow away and yanked her over into his lap again. He laid a kiss on her, a long, hungry one. He distanced himself a few inches as he stroked her naked breasts. "I wasn't going to apologize. I was going to suggest that if we are going to do this… let's move it into the bedroom."

Tess pushed back, looked into his eyes again for a long moment, then stood and offered him her hand. Micah took it and made a grab for his jeans with the other tugging them to his knees. Tess started laughing, and so did he. With a final tug of both hands, Micah dragged his jeans onto his hips and hooked the button. He lifted her, and she wrapped her legs around his waist as he carried her to his bedroom.

Hours later, Micah stretched and pulled Tess against his body. "Tired?"

"Exhausted," Tess mumbled, but she opened her eyes. "It was so worth it. I feel like that little boy in Oliver Twist... May I have more, please?"

He chuckled. "Yes, you can, but being a doctor, you know more about the male body than I do. After that marathon, I need to refuel and to rest a while before having another go. Besides, I'm hungry."

"Me, too," Tess agreed. "Plus, I should be going."

"Stay," he said, placing an arm over her to hold her in place.

Tess turned over and looked him straight in the eyes. 'Should I?"

"Yes. We have started something. I don't know where it will go, but I am not willing to let go of it. How's your schedule for the next twenty-four hours?"

"Twenty," Tess corrected, looking at her watch. "I have a twelve-hour shift starting at one tomorrow. I'll need an hour or so to go home. I need to check my mail and messages, and find something clean to wear, before heading to the hospital."

Micah grinned wickedly. "Do you mind if I make a suggestion on how we spend the next nineteen hours?"

---

Micah waved and watched as Tess backed her little compact car from his driveway, and drove along the gravel road until she was out of sight. He gave a tug on the loose sweats he was wearing and gave a hitch to his private parts. Like every male on earth, they all did it when members of the opposite sex weren't around. Sometimes a man just had to rearrange the junk.

It had been a long time since he had made love until he was sore and exhausted. He and Tess had been on a twenty-plus hour marathon of sex, sex, and more sex in every way possible.

The only time they hadn't been having sex was when they were napping, and that was only to gain enough strength and energy to start over again. Tess had been insatiable. He shook his head and grinned because he hadn't been able to get enough of her either.

Micah McKenna had definitely jumped off the celibacy wagon! He had lost count. They'd made love on the couch, the bed, in the shower, on the bedroom floor. Hell, they'd had sex against the wall and on the kitchen counter. He would never be able to look at his house in the same way again.

When Micah's cell indicated an incoming text message, he knew by the tone that it was his younger brother. Coyote's message was short. *Need?*

Translated, it meant Coyote was heading north and wanted to know if Micah needed anything. It was a courtesy call, as the lake was sixteen miles from the nearest town with a Gas and Go convenience stop. Twenty-five miles from a grocery store. Coyote split his time between the two campuses of the University of Texas in San Antonio and Austin. He had to drive near the lake property, on his way to Austin.

Micah texted: *Usual.* His younger brother was under a standing order to pick up milk, bread, and fruit. It was a no-brainer.

Micah then looked around and headed for his bedroom. He had to get his house in order. Coyote only had one speed—fast. He would be lucky to have an hour to get rid of any and all evidence of his and Tess's sex orgy. He yanked the sheets off the bed, stopped in the bathroom for the dirty towels, and made his way to the laundry room. With one large load started, he went to his bedroom with clean linens for the bed.

He opened the bedroom windows and the double doors that led to the deck that ran the full length of his house. He sprayed an air freshener around the room. He grabbed clean clothes and headed for the shower—another place that was going to hold very fond memories. This time, he needed a lot of hot water and maybe jock cream.

When he had completed his mental list of chores, Micah grabbed his keys. He had to go get his daughter. If he wasn't there when his brother arrived, he knew Coyote would make himself at home. His brothers had the keys.

## Chapter 2

Coyote McKenna, officially named Harrison Riley, only on his birth certificate, turned off at the private entrance to the family property. It was a massive compound, although the family referred to it as *the Lake*. He was driving faster than he knew was wise, but he was in a hurry. He was in a hurry because he was habitually late. He buzzed the gate with his remote and braked when he skidded on the gravel-topped dirt road.

His passenger, a small waif of a girl, smiled at him, and he grinned back. Macy was going to be a great surprise unless his brother had read his e-mail messages, which was doubtful. Unless Micah was involved with a project, he pretended e-mail, and cell phones didn't exist. Even though his brother carried a phone, it was almost always kept on silent or vibrate. He would check incoming calls, but was more likely to ignore them. For a man who understood technology, and used it proficiently, his older brother hated being at the beck and call of his phone. Micah had his incoming ring tones identified by musical tunes, so he knew which calls he would answer immediately.

Macy McKenna, their younger sister, was a ballet dancer in the Royal Ballet of London. She had studied ballet in Paris for three years before moving to the London Ballet Company. At almost twenty-one, she had lived and studied in France and now England, for the last five years. Her stringent training regime and travel schedules made it difficult to plan visits. Her trips home to the States had been rare. Most of her family contact was done when she or her brothers were on tour, and they managed to make their paths cross or through their electronic devices.

Coyote drove his Jeep into the driveway of Micah's house. The lower half was framed in natural stone, the upper half, what wasn't in glass, was cedar naturally aging into hues of gray and brown. He parked slightly off to the side so his vehicle couldn't be seen from the windows that framed the entire front façade of the house.

"Duck down, and let me take a cooler in first. Give me a couple of minutes to get Bubba's attention and come in," Coyote suggested.

"Are you sure my coming here won't be an imposition?" Macy asked. "Maybe we should have asked him first."

Coyote shook his head. "Sissy, it's Micah. He is not going to throw you out, and even if he did, Sully's house is around the next curve, and the lodge is empty. Pick a place and move in. Only the folks, Sully, and Micah have laid claim to their houses, and all three of them have been rebuilt extensively. Don't get any ideas of calling *dibs* on the boathouse and tower because that is mine!"

She nodded and moved her left leg carefully as she slid lower into the seat. She was small, so it was easy for her to hide behind the seat.

Coyote jumped from his Jeep, grabbed a large cooler, and hauled it up the steps to the front door and let himself in. He looked around, but he didn't see his brother. He carried the cooler into the kitchen and set it on a large slab of polished natural stone that was the countertop for the kitchen island.

"Hey, Micah, you home?" he shouted so his voice would carry to the loft area.

There was a sound of a door closing, and Micah appeared from the hallway. At six foot one, Micah was tall but he always felt small when he stood next to his younger brother. As they aged, it was apparent to everyone that they were siblings.

At six-foot, five-inches, Coyote had won the family lottery on height. They both had the same shape to their eyes, the same jawline, and their facial features were similar. Both were good-looking men. Sully was the only brother that had taken after their dad with blond hair and blue eyes. Micah and Coyote had their mother's brown eyes and brown hair.

Coyote had been tagged early on as the rebel of the band. He had cultivated a wild and crazy persona in public. Hair that hung to his waist was part of that image. He never let it loose except on stage. Now, as usual, it was hanging neatly down the back of his shirt in a long ponytail.

"Quiet, you big lug! I finally got Katie to take a nap. You wake her, and you can deal with her," Micah warned.

"Fine by me," Coyote exclaimed, raising the lid of the cooler. "I've got Mom's Meals on My Wheels for you."

"Great, what did she send?" Micah asked, diving into the cooler.

"I don't know. Mother Dearest said if I opened the coolers before I got here, she was feeding me haggis the next time I came for dinner!"

"Ouch! She was ticked off," Micah laughed, his mouth curving into a smile.

"It was only brownies," Coyote complained, shaking his head in disgust. "It's not like you're a starving nation or something!"

"It was a triple batch of fudge-iced brownies, Bubba,"

Micah complained in a growl. "You ate a whole triple batch, and you didn't leave me any!"

"They weren't intended for you," Coyote sniped at his brother. "They were supposed to be for Mom's precious grand-daughter, and you don't want her eating sweets anyway!"

"Yeah? Well, thanks to you being a hog, neither of us got any," Micah complained.

"You seriously need to learn how to cook," Coyote exclaimed.

"I cook," Micah, protested eagerly exploring the contents of the cooler.

"Smearing something on bread does not qualify as cooking!"

"I can do more than that," Micah said. "Admittedly, it's not generally safe when I do, but I haven't set the fire alarms off lately."

"You say that like it's a major accomplishment," Coyote winged back.

"I'm taking baby steps, little brother, the nearest fire station is twenty-five miles away. Safety first! I do appreciate our mother's love of cooking."

"Who makes these deliveries, Lamebrain… me! You owed me the brownies. Man! She sent lasagna," Coyote moaned as he pulled labeled containers from the cooler. "When did I lose my status as a starving college student?"

"Years ago when she figured you were going to be a professional student," Micah said.

"Fudge cake and enchilada casserole," Coyote grumbled. "I'm coming to dinner every night next week!"

"A one-hundred-and-twenty-mile round trip for dinner seems a little excessive, don't you think?" a female voice said from behind them.

Micah jerked around. A smile of surprise and joy crossed his face. "Sissy!" He grabbed the youngest of his twin sisters, picked her up, and twirled her around in a huge hug. He set her on her feet and looked at her with concern on his face. "I shouldn't be doing that, should I? Did I hurt you? I should be more careful!"

"I'm okay, Micah," Macy exclaimed, giving him a long and heartfelt hug. "How are you?" she asked, pulling him down to her five-foot-two-inch level to look him square in the eyes.

"It's over," Micah said softly. "It's done and over."

"Everything?" Coyote questioned, turning to his brother.

"Everything!" Micah repeated firmly.

"It's about time, You should celebrate with a party," Coyote said, taking over the job of storing the food in the freezer. He paused and gave his older brother a hard look "You should have dumped her butt in jail for all the crap she's pulled."

"It crossed my mind many times," Micah admitted. "Fortunately, we've tied everything into a nice and neat package. She has been warned, although it was more of a threat by the judge. She has a job offer to move to England."

"Hey! Why are you dumping Carla on us! Don't forget, I live there!" Macy complained. She did notice that her brother did look better. He had gained weight since the last time she'd seen him. He had taken the break-up of his relationship hard. He had still been reeling from whatever happened between them when Katie had been orphaned. In typical Micah fashion, he had buckled down and taken on the job of being a parent.

Micah had never confided in anyone about what had caused the break-up. Whatever had happened, it must have been really bad. He had walked away from the relationship and removed himself from the public eye. When Katie had been orphaned, he'd made the lake his permanent residence. He'd built a home and taken on the role of father.

Micah was aware of her study of him. He hugged Macy

again. "I'm okay, Sissy. Hey, what is my little sister doing on this side of the pond?"

"You'd know if you ever picked up your phone messages," Coyote said snidely.

"The last I heard, the operation was successful, and you were doing fine," Micah said, ignoring his younger brother.

"The surgery was successful. It was the rest of my plans that were blown out of the water," Macy said. "I'm in San Antonio for a couple of weeks to recuperate from knee surgery. I'm not used to being outnumbered and smothered. I would like to beg a bed from my big brother, for peace and quiet."

"Hey, I offered you a bed," Coyote protested.

"Where?" Micah demanded. "You're never at your pigsty in San Antonio, and the student efficiency you rent in Austin is barely big enough to hold your sports equipment."

"I do not live in a pigsty! I live in comfortable clutter."

Micah ignored his brother's comments and turned his attention to his sister. "My house still only has two bedrooms, but you are welcome. Why aren't you staying with the folks!"

"I've tried it. I've been there two and a half days, and I thought I'd better get out of there before I exploded," Macy answered. She rolled her eyes to the ceiling and blew out a deep breath.

"The folks are driving you nuts," Micah guessed.

She nodded. "Oh, yeah! I know they're trying to help, but, please…" Macy begged, "I don't take very much space."

"I can't offer peace and quiet. I have a rambunctious six-year-old whose volume seems to be stuck on loud. I can't find the mute switch."

"I remember there was a daybed, over by the bookshelves," Macy said, turning around to see if that particular piece of furniture was still there. Since she hadn't visited her brother's home in years, she looked around in awe. "Wow! You said you were doing renovations. This is a new house!"

Micah smiled. "One thing led to another. The old structure was moved. It's a music studio now. The daybed is in the loft. There's plenty of room, but I think I'll give you my room. I'll sleep on the daybed. You shouldn't be climbing stairs that much. The two bedrooms on the first floor are bigger, and each has an en-suite."

Macy did a slow-motion pirouette taking in the spacious home. She hadn't been paying much attention when she'd come in, keeping her eyes on the stone steps so she wouldn't make a misstep. This was a new house, beautiful, and spacious with a lot of windows and light. It was a rustic lodge with all the amenities. There were two staircases, one on each side of the massive main living space, Both of the stairs were made of twisted branches. One was a narrow spiral staircase. The other was a majestic sweeping curve.

"Wow," she repeated, impressed.

"He didn't randomly decide to build a new house," Coyote said, nudging his sister. "He almost burned the old place down. The cabin was moved, but it had to be gutted."

"Hey, I would have had made the changes anyway," Micah claimed.

"Sure you would have," Coyote said, badgering his brother. "Are you guys settled?" He looked from one sibling to another. When they nodded their heads, he sprinted from the room to retrieve another cooler and his sister's suitcases and tote bags.

"Are you sure?" Macy asked again. "I don't want to impose."

Micah pulled his sister into a tight hug. "My little sister does not impose. I'd like to have you around for a while. Do I have to nail your toe shoes to the floor to keep you here?"

Macy smiled and hugged him again. "I'm cleared for eight weeks of medical leave. At the most, I can stay a month, six-weeks maximum. I do have a life in London.

"I will have to schedule physical therapy," she said with a

catch in her voice. "I don't mind telling you, the idea of having my career end at twenty scared the bloody hell out of me. "

"I'll give Tess a call. She can recommend the best doctors for whatever you need," Micah promised. "If athletes can rehabilitate from this kind of injury, you can too. Come on, Sissy, you are just a little bitty dancer, not a big hulking football player."

"Ha! I'll stack my training against theirs any day!" Macy retorted fully aware that her brother was teasing.

Micah grinned and started unpacking the second cooler his brother had heaved onto the kitchen island. "We won't starve. Have you learned to cook?'

"No," Macy grumbled. "I was hoping you had improved."

"No luck there," Micah admitted shaking his head. "I'm absent-minded, and I get sidetracked. I start something, walk away, and next thing I know, the smoke alarms are going off.

"It's safer to purchase meals already prepared and stick with the microwave, the oven, and a lot of timers. Katie is a big help there, she pays attention to the timers. My culinary skills are limited to making coffee, and smearing something on bread. I keep the freezer packed with pre-made stuff that even I can't kill most of the time. Plus, Mom sends over a batch of her home- cooking every couple of weeks."

"You won't starve," Coyote said, opening a second cooler. "She sent extra."

"Coyote!" A whirlwind of bouncing brown curls in a shocking pink tee shirt and yellow jeans burst from the hallway and leaped into her uncle's arms.

"Punkin!" Coyote exclaimed as he caught his niece, and gave her a loud raspberry under her chin.

Katie McKenna giggled and squealed with delight as she hugged him and twisted around, trying to give him a raspberry in return.

Coyote held onto his niece and was doing his best not to

drop the twisting, squirming bundle of giggles. He lowered her to the floor and proceeded to tickle her. She was screaming while he was taunting her by saying, "Say, Uncle! Say, Uncle!"

Katie's response was a high-pitched scream at the top of her lungs. "No! No! No!"

Micah looked on with a mixture of love, pride, and exasperation. "Okay, you two! Break it up! Katie, inside voice, please."

Coyote tossed his niece into the air, caught her, and settled her on his shoulders. She promptly dug both her hands into his hair to hang on, giggling non-stop.

Micah made a motion, and his brother leaned over. He peeled his daughter off his brother's shoulders with practiced precision and plopped her on the kitchen island. "Katie, do you remember Aunt Macy? You've talked to her on Skype, and you've seen her dance online."

"Daddy, I'm not a baby! I remember." Katie turned her attention to her aunt. "We don't get to see you because you live on the other side of a big ocean. Daddy watches you on his computer! We went to see you, and you had black feathers. I fell asleep, and you were gone when I woke up."

"I had to fly out to another performance, and I missed saying goodbye," Macy said. "You were still asleep."

"You were sick," Micah added. "You had an ear infection, and we had to take you to the doctor."

"Do you get to be a black swan all the time?" Katie asked with interest.

Macy shook her head. "No, I only get to be a black swan sometimes. I have to take turns with the other dancers."

"I have a tutu," Katie said with a bright smile. "It's pink and fluffy! My Granny Nana gave it to me. She says when Daddy gets tired of hiding in the boonies, I can take real dance lessons. Nana said it's good for girls to take dance classes, to learn pose, and balance, but it should be only for fun."

"I think that was poise and balance," Micah corrected.

"Ouch," Coyote said under his breath and gave his brother a meaningful look. "Someone's been talking around little people with big ears."

Micah nodded.

"I'm the big ears," Katie told Macy in a matter-of-fact tone. "Would you like to see my tutu?"

"Not right now," Micah intervened. "Right now, I want you to give your Aunt Macy a hello hug."

Katie raised her arms, and Macy stepped into her niece's embrace, hugging her.

When Macy stepped away, Coyote snagged his niece and carried her into the living room. The two of them continued their roughhousing, accompanied by laughter and giggling.

"I'm sorry. I guess Katie doesn't remember much about the performance we saw in Paris," Micah said with a shrug. "She was only four, and at her age, memories are lost quickly."

Macy gave a sigh and a look of regret as she watched the easy way Coyote interacted with her niece.

Micah noticed. "They've been best buds since she was a baby. He's been around all her life. You'll have time to get reacquainted."

"What's ain'ted?" Katie demanded, as Coyote had carried her into the kitchen and was currently dangling her upside down by one foot.

"Reacquainted," Coyote corrected, dropping her gently to the floor. "That means Aunt Macy is going to be around for a couple of weeks. Did you know that Macy is Allison's twin sister?"

Katie frowned. "My friends, Nina and Shelley, are twins. They look alike. You don't look like Aunt Allison."

"That's because we're not identical twins," Macy explained. "We're fraternal twins, which is a little too complicated to explain, but it means we were born at the same time, but we don't look alike."

"Hey, guys," Coyote said, facing his siblings. "I have to go, I have a date tonight."

"I thought you were heading to Austin," Micah said, lifting his daughter from the island and motioning her to the kitchen table.

"No, that was a ruse to get Macy here! Duh!" Coyote exclaimed, shaking his head. "Watch him, Sissy, half the time he doesn't know what day of the week he's in."

Micah only smiled. "Been there, done that, and who cares. Katie will remind me when Saturday comes around, and she doesn't have to go to school."

"Yeah," Coyote grunted in exasperation. "Like it's too complicated to look at the calendar, your watch, phone, or computer for Pete's sakes. What happened to the guy who was permanently attached to his devices all the time?"

"I detached myself," Micah admitted.

"Tomorrow is a Teachers Day, but is it a weekend, Daddy?" Katie asked. "Can I go stay with Granny Nana? She said she wanted me to come for a whole weekend and you promised I could. Remember, Daddy? You said I could!"

"So I did," Micah agreed. "But, I didn't say what weekend, did I?"

"Please, please, please!" Katie begged.

"Let her go," Coyote interceded. "I can drop her off at Mom's. You can get her Sunday when you go to dinner. I have been told it is a command appearance. Everyone is expected. Punkin can keep Mom busy, so maybe she will stop worrying about *you know who*." He waggled his eyebrows at his sister. "Three days of wrangling with Katie will keep her distracted."

"Please," Macy whispered. "Our mother has turned worrying into an Olympic sport!"

"Don't I know it," Micah agreed, and he turned to his

daughter. "Okay, but call Nana first and *ask* her if she would like to have you this weekend. Do not *tell* her, *ask* her," he called after his daughter firmly as she ran from the room.

Katie returned a few minutes later and thrust the phone at her father. "Granny Nana wants to talk to you, Daddy!"

Micah took the phone, answering questions, obviously about Macy, who was standing beside him listening. He disconnected and looked to his pint-sized daughter. "You are going to Nana's for the weekend. Let's get you packed!"

Micah ordered Coyote to get an extra safety seat from the garage and install it in his Jeep. Then, more from habit than anything else, he lectured his younger brother and issued several threats about driving carefully, with precious cargo aboard. Finally, he waved his brother and daughter off. He shut the front door, closed his eyes, and had a single moment of quiet and peace before he reopened them.

"Sissy, it's just us for a couple of days."

"Maybe, not," Macy said, making a face. "While you were packing for Katie, and I was finding my way around your bedroom, I got a phone call from Colleen. Do you remember her?"

"Colleen from two doors down, your bestest, bestest girl-friend in the whole wide world," Micah teased.

"That's the one. Colleen wants me to visit her because she is leaving on a business trip to Hong Kong the day after tomorrow. She's going to be there for two months. If I don't see her now, I won't be able to see her at all."

"I'm not your warden, Sissy," Micah said, gently. "Call Coyote and tell him to turn around and save Colleen the trip. Enjoy your time with her."

## Chapter 3

Tess Foster signed in for her shift at the hospital emergency room and went to get a verbal rundown on what was currently in-house. She was tired, but when you were an ER doctor, exhaustion was part of your daily life. This time what was keeping her awake was thinking of her twenty hours of a sexual dream come true with Micah. She'd been on a sexual buzz since leaving his place.

She'd known Micah since they were kids. He had been the older brother of her nemesis when she had been a kid. She and Sully McKenna had been sworn enemies when they were twelve. She had chased him around like a crazed paparazzi demanding that he give her the inside scoop on being in a local teenage band. At the time, her ambition had been to be a reporter for her school paper. In their late teens, Micah had dated her sister, Lauren.

Tessa and Sully had been forced to spend time together, and they had become friends. Sully was still one of her best friends. He was married now, and he and his wife, Karina, were happily having babies. They had three daughters already, and another on the way.

Micah, as a teenager, had been quiet and shy. When he and his brothers had recorded their first album, he'd been nineteen, twenty-one when two songs hit the charts in the first and second positions. He had been forced from his shell by the adoration from millions of crazed fans worldwide. The vast majority of those fans were female. Micah's leadership in the band I-35 had defined who he was as a person. Micah was the leader of the band, but he had let his younger brother, Sully, take most of the fan attention. Micah had never really caught on that his teenage insecurities had settled into handsome, sultry good looks of a confident man. He also had captivated a fan base of girls and women of all ages, although he considered it a by-product of being in the band.

She'd been jealous of the brothers for a long time. They had parents and a homelife she envied. When she was painfully navigating through the horrible teenage stages, they were the pin-up fantasies of millions of teenage girls.

Tess had gone through every unsightly stage of adolescence known. She'd had the pimples, the braces, and glasses. She had grown a full head taller than most of the boys in her classes, she had been as skinny as a rail. It had taken the boys of her age, two years to catch up. By then, she was known as the girl with her head always stuck in a book.

Micah, who was a couple of years older, had slid into manhood while she was still struggling with hormonal teenage puberty.

The McKenna boys and the Foster girls had lived across the street from each other. She and Lauren had spent a lot of their time at the McKennas' home. Although Micah's dating Lauren hadn't led to anything serious, he had taken on the role of a protective, big brother to both of them.

As far as his world of fame had made him a world traveler, Micah had always been there when Tess needed him. It was Micah who had flown in when she'd called him with the news that her parents were divorcing. He had come to her, let her cry, swear, and whine to him for days. Before Micah had left, he had handed her a cell phone with an international service plan and told her to call, and he meant it. Every time a new phone was released, she could expect the latest, most innovative cell phone to arrive in the mail.

They were involved with each other's lives, although it had been in a remote, peripheral manner. There were long periods when they didn't see each other, but they stayed in contact.

Micah had a strange *'spidy'* sense of when she needed him. They might not communicate for months with their busy schedules. When something happened, though, and it would cross Tess's mind to call him... he would make the phone call to her first. It was like they were subconsciously connected. He might get upset with her, he might be angry at her, but he did whatever it took to help her. Even if he was half a world away, Micah found a way to help.

When she'd been sixteen, a fraternity party she attended had turned into a wild drinking, multiple partner sexual free-for-all. Terrified, she had locked herself in the bathroom. She'd tried to call several friends, but with no answers and her phone dangerously low in power, she had called Micah.

He had called a friend in San Antonio, who happened to be an ex-Marine. Dressed in the uniform of the Marine Corps Police, Micah's friend had entered the frat house, armed and loaded. The Marine had found her and taken her to Micah's parents. Micah had saved her in more ways than one. The police had been called to the party. Most of the party participants had been arrested. Many of them had been expelled, and the University Board of Conduct had suspended the frat house privileges for three years.

When Micah had eventually returned home, he hadn't let her off the hook. He had yelled and lectured her for hours for putting herself in that kind of danger. That had been the time when he had spent most of his time home furious with her. He had also discovered that she was hiding her intellect and playing dumb, so the boys her age would like her. Micah had always seemed older and more mature. He was only four years her senior.

It had been Micah, in person, who rescued her from a bad boy date that had gone very, scarily wrong. He'd blistered her butt for that stunt.

The McKennas had descended from tough, no-nonsense Texan men. She had known and accepted it as fact. In the world of her own feminist leanings, it was odd that they could be such polar opposites. Micah's family, though, with their strong beliefs and love for one another, had been her only glimpse of a loving and functioning family.

Her family had been ripped apart by spiteful anger and petty dysfunction, long before the divorce. Tess hadn't seen her father in several years, and she preferred not to spend time with her mother or any of the younger boy-toy husbands her mother had married and divorced.

For years, Tess had only had her older sister Lauren and the McKenna family to rely on. She considered Sully McKenna and his wife Karina some of her best friends. Micah McKenna, she had come to believe, was her ideal man, although he had been off-limits. He was in a relationship with a woman Tess couldn't stand.

Micah came from a large family of super successful careers. Luckily, she had been allowed to share in a little of it.

Those years—so turbulent for both of them in different ways, had bonded them through technology. Micah was in a relationship that she knew was doomed, although he seemed blind to it. She was dedicated to a long-term goal that many times, she thought was unattainable. They were each other's fallback friend, someone who was there, and steadfast. It had built a strong friendship, hopefully, one that would be unbreakable.

Micah had encouraged her every step of the way as she'd completed college and medical school. He had fought with her and for her many times. When she had been ready to pack it in and quit, he wouldn't let her. She had thrown in the towel once and lost a semester.

When he had found out, he had called, argued, and yelled at her long distance. When he couldn't budge or change her mind, he had flown in from a remote island somewhere in the South Pacific. He'd been there on location while Sully was filming a movie. The brothers were there writing and composing material for their next album.

Micah had come to her. Even after a sixteen-hour flight, he had been livid. He had shown up at her boarding house, taken her to a hotel room, and given her the hardest spanking of her life. Then, he had marched her straight to the registrar's office. He paid her tuition for the next semester and threatened that if she made anything less than a top mark in any of her classes, he would be back, and there would be hell to pay! Several hours later, he had been on a flight back to wherever he had come from.

Micah rarely lost his cool, but when he did, it was a five on the Fujita scale. It was awesome to watch as long as you weren't the target of it.

She had stubbornly refused to allow him or his family to pay for her college. She knew, though, that he had arranged scholarships and grants for her. He denied it, of course, and that was from a man who hated deception and lies. She couldn't prove he was behind the help. Possibly his brothers and his family were in on it, too. He or they had covered their tracks well. Still, she knew in her heart Micah was behind it, and she loved him for it.

Tess figured she had loved Micah for over half her life.

Their lives had been intertwined since she'd been a child, but they had never stepped over the line of best friends. They had shattered that demarcation now, and she wondered if they would survive it.

When a first-year resident shoved a medical file under her nose, Tess stopped thinking of Micah and concentrated on her work. She didn't know where the change in their relationship would lead, and she didn't have time to worry about it. She had work to do, and she never gave less than a hundred percent of herself to her patients.

---

When Coyote returned with Macy the following Saturday evening, Micah was in the backyard, splitting wood again. When Coyote yelled from the top deck, Micah waved, tossed the split wood into a pile, and locked the ax away. He made his way inside gingerly.

"Hey, what happened to you?" Coyote demanded.

Micah moved slowly into the kitchen and sat gingerly in one of the kitchen chairs. "I was working in the boathouse. I turned around and rammed into a wrench someone had left on a bench–right in the gonads," Micah said. "Since I'm the only one working in the boathouse, I can't blame anyone but myself."

Coyote shuddered. "Ouch! You've gotta be more careful with the jewels."

"Hey! Girl, present," Macy complained.

"Sorry," Coyote and Micah both intoned together, but they grinned at each other.

"So, how was your weekend with Colleen?" Micah asked.

"Fantastic. We were like two ten-year-olds again at a slumber party. It was terrific! But then I ruined it by acting like an adult. Tess called and provided a list of contacts for rehab. I called a rehabilitation center, and I contacted my doctors in London. My records are being sent over. The doctors here will have to evaluate the scans and decide on a treatment plan.

"My doctors in London said I should be able to drive three weeks after the surgery, although I don't drive in London, because I don't have a car. It has already been ten days. I have a valid international driver's permit, so I should be able to rent a car to get around."

"We can't trust you to drive here. You drive on the wrong side of the road over there," Coyote reminded his sister.

Macy stuck her tongue out at him.

"I have a Mini Cooper parked in the garage at the lodge," Micah offered. "The American version, with the steering wheel on the left. When you get released for driving, I'll take you driving to make sure you can handle it. If you do okay, you can use it for the rest of your visit."

Macy looked interested, but her cell phone rang, and she went out on the deck for privacy.

"Why do you have a Mini Cooper?" Coyote demanded. "You have a Ford F-250 pickup and a Land Rover. I had to drag you away from a dealer's lot to keep you from buying a Hummer."

"Your point being?" Micah growled.

"You don't like little cars. So, why do you have a Mini Cooper?" Coyote demanded.

Micah looked around to see if his sister was in listening range. "It was an Allison scheme. She wrecked her car and didn't want to admit it to Dad. Of course, she was broke and didn't have the money for a down payment or a replacement. She wanted to borrow enough to get another vehicle. I agreed, but I've been burned by our little sister before. I had the car titled in my name. I told Allison when she paid for it, I'd deed it over to her name. It ticked her off, but she wasn't going to get it any other way, so she agreed. She paid two payments, and I never saw another dime. After several months and a ton of excuses, I confiscated it."

"Man, I wish I'd been there. Finally, someone called her on the crap she pulls. Is she speaking to you?" Coyote asked, grinning.

Micah shook his head. "I'm okay with it. I don't know about you, but I'm tired of Allison's schemes and her attitude. I don't like being played, or conned, and she's pulled both on me. She's the only person I know that has *lost* her purse or her wallet fifty times! Little sister or not, she's supposed to be an adult, and it's about time she got a dose of reality."

"Add me to the list," Coyote agreed. "I'm an easy mark. Turn on the tears, and I cave. Only she has shed those crocodile tears so many times, even I've become immune. Every week it was a new excuse or a new emergency.

"I don't get her attitude. She thinks because we have money, she's entitled to it. It doesn't occur to her that we earned it. I was just a little kid when we started touring. This entitlement thing she has going doesn't work for me. She needs to get her act together."

"I know. When did you see Allison last?" Micah asked.

Coyote frowned. "It's been three or four weeks. I was dropping in to see her at her apartment occasionally. She is my little sister, and I'm supposed to be watching over her. I was two blocks from her place and stopped to see if she was okay. She jumped all over me. Accused me of spying on her for the folks. I suspect she was hiding someone or several someones in her bedroom. I smelled smoke, and it wasn't the tobacco kind.

"I've left a couple of voice and text messages, but she hasn't answered any of them in the last couple of weeks. I'm trying to finish my dissertation. I haven't had a whole lot of free time to worry about our brat of a sister. What little I do have, I don't want to spend it listening to her whining. Should we be worried?"

"Maybe. Does Allison know Macy is on our side of the pond?" Micah asked.

"No, and she's not going to like it. But, hey, as far as I'm concerned, she can stick it up hers," Coyote said.

"That's real nice," Micah chided with amusement.

"I'm tired of playing nice, and being the patsy, and falling for her lies," Coyote admitted.

---

Micah climbed the steps to the three-tier deck at the back of his house. He'd taken full advantage of building a house on a hill. He couldn't take credit for the idea, since the previous cabin he'd replaced, had a similar multi-level deck, although not quite as elaborate. The previous one had been wood, now it was in stone. Awakening at his usual predawn hour, he had decided to take advantage of his daughter still being safely in the hands of his mother.

He'd been working in the boathouse. He needed to finish the job of cleaning the small sail and motorboats that were kept there for family use in the summer. He didn't like working in either the garages or the boathouse when his daughter was underfoot. There was too much potential danger in both places, with gasoline, power tools, and machinery stored in the buildings. The job had taken longer than he expected, but he still had the whole day ahead of him.

He entered his house, and inhaled the smell of coffee and sent a thank you into the universe to whoever had invented coffee pots with timers. He poured himself a large mug and looked around for his sister. She wasn't in the open living area, and he didn't want to check his bedroom in case she was still sleeping. Coffee in hand, he climbed the spiral staircase to a loft area he used as a studio. By his design, half of the second floor was an art studio, and the other half had been left unfinished. Eventually, bedrooms would go in the incomplete section, at least three per his continuously revised blueprints. He found Macy sitting on the floor midway across the expanse of the studio loft, staring at his chaos.

She turned around as he approached, and he saw that there were tears on her face.

He hurried over to his sister and knelt beside her. "Honey, are you okay? Did you hurt your knee climbing those stairs? Are you in pain? "

Macy shook her head. "You did this," she said, nodding her head at canvases of various sizes stacked against the walls. "How could you have this talent, and we never knew about it?"

"I guess because I never had to the time to develop it before," Micah said, sitting on the floor beside her.

"Micah, when are you going to have a showing?" Macy asked.

He snorted. "Never."

"You mean no one has seen them, critiqued, or appraised them?" Macy asked softly.

He shook his head. "Nope, only Coyote, Sully, Karina, and Tess know about them. They also know if they shoot off their mouths, they will be in serious trouble with me! This is private."

"How do you keep Katie from talking about it?"

"We refer to it as *drawing*. Daddy draws," Micah said. "I have sketched and drawn pictures all my life, so even if she does talk about it, no one is going to know the scale has changed," Micah explained.

Macy looked at her brother in awe. "I've known my whole life that you were multi-talented, but this blows me away. This is genius."

Micah snorted again with a doubtful shake of his head. "Sissy, I'm not artsy enough to be a genius. There is only one genius in this family, and that's our whacko brother who has a computer for a brain. I am getting better at it," he said, getting to his feet and helping Macy to hers. "After the split with Carla, I started having problems with insomnia.

"This was Coyote's idea. He was looking at my sketches one day, and the next thing I knew, he'd brought in a whole bunch of art supplies. I started using all those hours when I couldn't sleep painting. I needed something to concentrate on, so I wouldn't feel so pissed off at myself for being blind and stupid for so many years. I was angry and depressed, but worse, I felt like an idiot. Then I was hit with a double whammy with the deaths of Nick and Sally.

"Painting is quiet and calming. You cannot be upset and paint. At least, I can't, and if I tried to paint when I was angry, I had to throw out the results." He handed her his coffee mug.

"How long have you been painting?" Macy asked, taking a sip.

"For the better part of the last four years. What the press calls my *exile*. I burned everything I painted for the first six months or so, half of what I did for the next six. That was while I was trying to decide on a strategy of how to fight lies. Now I'm satisfied with the results, most of the time. I still have a few duds, paintings that just won't work no matter how hard I try. I don't have the skills to figure out why."

"I want to see them, all of them," Macy pleaded. "Please."

Micah shrugged and began to uncover various canvases, one-by-one, and watched his sister's reaction to them. The paintings were mostly of people, children, teenagers, middle-aged, and the elderly. There were paintings of people from all walks of life and many different nationalities. Micah's paintings told stories. The faces showed a life of joy and happiness, or sadness and hardship. Macy cried, laughed, and sometimes she just hugged her brother because she couldn't help herself.

There were a few landscapes, and Macy recognized places where the family had traveled, deserts, and canyons and seascapes. There were a few cityscapes. She was familiar with the park across the street from the school in Paris, where she had begun her professional training. The quaint old hotel where the family had stayed when visiting her at school.

Finally, Micah reached a stack of paintings, and he seemed to brace himself before uncovering them. Two years earlier, he thought doing these paintings would only cause him more pain. He was wrong. Instead, the work had brought him peace and acceptance that despite what life tossed in your path, you had to go on.

"Oh, Micah," Macy cried as she covered her mouth with her hand to keep a sob from escaping.

Micah looked at the first painting he uncovered, and his eyes were sad. His sister pulled him to her, and he hugged her.

"It's Nick and Sally," Macy exclaimed. "I remember them from when you brought the band to France. They were such nice people. Oh, look at that one! They had Katie with them. Silly me! You don't have to look at them, you created them."

"Has Katie seen these?" Macy asked.

Micah nodded. He motioned to an area not far from his worktable. The corner was setup as a play area for a child. "Katie was here when I was working on them. I don't try to hide the truth from her.

"The grief therapist told me I should instill vivid memories of Nick and Sally in Katie. The better job I do of making those memories real to her, the more she will accept their death, and feel safe and loved in my care. Naturally, they won't be real memories for her. She was too young when she lost them to have any memories.

"She calls this stack of canvases, *pictures of my other Mommy and Daddy*. When she wants to talk about them, we have story time, and we talk about Nick and Sally. It's important to me for Katie to know how much Nick and Sally loved her.

"If she wants the paintings when she is older, they are hers.

I don't want her to make a shrine of them. It wouldn't be healthy. It's enough for us to know they are here, and our memories of them won't fade. Two of my best friends gave me the greatest gift in the world."

Macy wiped her hands across her eyes and sniffed. "Did you know they had named you as Katie's guardian?"

"Yes, I was Katie's Godfather, and I knew what was in the will. They were responsible parents. Because both Nick and Sally had lost their parents when they were young, they wanted to make sure their daughter was protected. It's just... Well... no one ever expects the worst to happen! Suddenly I was a parent.

"When that happens, there are only two choices, wing it until you learn what you're doing, or fail miserably. I'm doing what I feel is right for Katie."

"I know you have kept your silence, but whatever happened between you and Carla must have been awful," Macy said. "Then, for Nick and Sally to die so soon after your breakup, it must have been devastating. I know you wouldn't have taken the actions you did unless it was warranted. At the same time, I'm awed that you set your problems aside and took on Katie.

"I want to watch you paint while I am here. I want to see you create these beautiful images. Will you let me? It would mean so much to me to watch my brother produce such beauty."

"It will mean you have to lose beauty sleep," Micah warned his sister with a chuckle. "I usually start painting anywhere from three to four a.m."

Macy puffed her cheeks with air, and expelled it, lifting her bangs. She nodded her head knowingly. "You and Sully are the early birds of the family. I guess I'm going to lose some sleep!"

# Chapter 4

Micah's cell phone rang, and he was glad that he was near the boathouse for privacy. He tried to think of all the things he'd been mulling over for the last week. One look at the number displayed, and his mind went blank. All he could manage was, "Hi."

"I got your messages," Tess said. "Can you talk?"

"Yeah," Micah mumbled and wanted to slap himself in the head. "Tess…"

"Micah," Tess said, speaking over him. "Are you obsessing?"

"Define obsessing?"

"Going over what we did, second-guessing, and worrying it to death?" Tess asked gently.

He pushed his free hand over his barely there, shorn hair. "Yeah, pretty much. We need to talk."

"I guess we do. Hold on…" She had moved the phone away from her mouth, but he could hear her barking out medical orders. "Micah, I have to go. I won't be off until tomorrow at noon. Monday is another long day, but it's my last. I'm going to sleep-in Tuesday morning, and I'll be at your place later." She turned from the phone, and again was addressing another medical issue. "I have to go. Don't worry, we're okay."

Micah disconnected, and he stuffed the phone in his pocket. He wasn't surprised that Tess had been pulled away. He wasn't surprised that she had taken a few minutes from her busy, life-saving routine to reassure him. That was Tess. She was at her best when she was in crisis mode dealing with someone else's problems.

Her expertise was medicine, and she was highly skilled in her field. Her personal issues were something else. She was no longer the youngster who needed reassurance, and sometimes her judgment was a little flawed. He hoped their last encounter hadn't been part of her inability to deal with her emotions.

He couldn't fault her for that. In his personal life, he'd made a colossal mistake, and rather than walking away from it, he had kept trying to fix it. Some problems couldn't be fixed, and he was a witness to that fact.

Somehow, someway, he was going to clear the decks so he could spend one-on-one time with her. Not for sex, although he wouldn't mind a repeat performance. More importantly, he needed to know what-the-heck had changed between them. He had been there when it happened, had been a lusty participant, but he had to be sure she was okay with the change in their relationship.

It was three-thirty in the morning when Micah made a caramel/chocolate latte and a regular pot of coffee. He was very good at making coffee, but it didn't qualify as cooking. Arguing that debate with his brothers, he'd lost. He knocked on his bedroom door before opening it. "Rise and shine, Sissy, I'm heading to the studio to paint."

Macy jumped from the bed and ran into the bathroom, calling to him over her shoulder in her rush, "I'll be there in a second." She made her way to the spiral stairs, where she found her brother waiting for her. She took the offered latte, took a long swallow, and moaned in pleasure. "This is a luxury, I don't get very often."

"No Starbucks in London?" he teased.

"There's one on every corner. If I take in this much sugar and caffeine on an empty stomach before training in the morning, I would be tossing it." Macy hung her camera around her neck and stuffed her cell phone under her tee shirt. She handed the latte back to her brother, needing both hands for the railing. Walking ahead of Micah, she moved slowly and carefully. She had to be careful not to put too much pressure on her healing knee.

Micah walked protectively behind her. The spiral staircase to the studio loft took getting used to. One slip and his sister could ruin her career in ballet permanently. He felt relieved when she reached the top, and he swore under his breath.

"Next time, Sissy use the other stairs. That part of the second floor isn't finished, but there is a connecting door to the studio. It will be easier on your knee and your balance."

He hit a light switch, and bright overhead lights cast an almost daylight effect over the space where he had a workbench and an easel. Although the studio ceiling had massive skylights, it was still dark outside. His worktable resembled a garage tool bench more than an artist's studio table. It was rough and beaten together. It was loaded with hundreds of tubes of paint, and just as many brushes of different sizes and shapes, organized in neat rows. He set a two-foot by four-foot canvas on the easel and tightened it into place.

Micah looked over at his sister and grinned. "I'm not used to anyone watching me, except Katie. This is a little weird. You've had more art training than I have since I've had zilch. I do the best I can to get the results I want."

"There's no right or wrong way to create," Macy said. She

went over to get a bright pink bean bag chair from the play corner, but her brother grabbed it and positioned it at an angle so she could watch what he was doing. She carefully lowered herself into the bean bag and curled into it to enjoy her drink. "If you want to talk, talk. If you work in silence, I'm okay with that too."

Micah nodded, pulled open a drawer, and looked in several folders before he found the photograph he was looking for. He clipped the photo to a white clipboard that was attached but positioned to the left of the easel. He tapped a remote, and Josh Groban's voice flowed from the stereo system. Micah stared at the photo for three full minutes. He stared at the empty canvas for a long time and began to sketch a rough outline of a shape. Then Micah began to mix his paints. He didn't use an artist's palette, but a large flat wooden tray that he set on a high wooden stool beside the easel. He selected a brush and began to paint.

Macy watched and took pictures, both with her camera and her phone. Micah never faltered, never stopped as the form took shape. Four hours later, at almost eight o'clock, she was staring at a painting of a dancer on pointe, and as far as she could see, it looked finished. There was strength, grace, and power in the curvature of the arms and the position of the fingers. She could see the love of movement on the dancer's face and so much more. She was looking at a mirror mirage of herself, but she didn't think she had ever expressed that much emotion while dancing.

Micah stepped away from the canvas and tossed his brushes into a jar of brush cleaner. He cranked his head side-to-side and up-and-down. "That's it for now, Sissy. I'll let this dry a bit and fix a few things tomorrow."

Macy raised her arms, and he helped her to her feet. She wrapped her arms around him. "I am totally amazed."

Micah smiled. "Sorry, it's not exciting, but it keeps me out of trouble."

"You make it look easy," Macy said, trying to stifle a yawn.

"You didn't get enough sleep," Micah said with a chuckle. "Why don't you catch a couple of extra hours of rest this morning? Usually, by now, I am chasing the turbo-charged dynamo around trying to get her to eat breakfast or get dressed. It will be quiet today. Quiet happens so rarely around here, you should take advantage of it."

"I haven't done anything but lie about for hours while you created a masterpiece," Macy disagreed, but she had to stifle another yawn. "Maybe I will return to bed for a couple of hours. Unlike my zombie brothers, I need at least seven hours of sleep. Wake me if you start something new."

Micah shook his head. "This will be it for the day. Go sleep for a couple more hours, and we'll go into Hondo for a late breakfast or lunch before picking up Katie."

"Does Hondo have a western wear store?" Macy asked.

"Sure," Micah answered. "What self-respecting Texas town doesn't? What do you need?"

"Cowboy boots," Macy said, surprising her brother. "My old boots are worn out, and I want a really, spiffy looking pair."

"All right! Texas is lassoing you in again. In that case, we will go to Ferrell's in Lockhart. Ferrell's Leathers carries every major brand of cowboy boot I have ever heard of and plenty of fancy designer labels for the tourists."

They stopped at a small café that he knew had good country-style food. Micah ordered an enormous breakfast of all his favorites. When his sister raised an eyebrow, he shrugged and protested her unspoken censure. "We eat oatmeal, healthy cereals, and we only have scrambled eggs once a week at home. I'm setting a good example for my daughter."

"But, when the cat's away…"

Micah grinned and shrugged self-consciously. "She's more like a kitten, but I admit it. Coyote and I slip away sometimes and splurge, Sully too, if he's in town. I know all about eating healthy. Who doesn't know all that stuff? Practicing it is something else. Sometimes, I want a dose of old-fashioned grease and carbs. I used to get it on the road, but we haven't been touring for a while."

Macy giggled. "I know. I'm just giving you a hard time. I'll keep your secrets."

"You always did, even as a little girl," Micah said fondly. "Have you heard any dish on Sully lately?"

Macy shook her head, thinking of their brother. "He calls once a week, like clockwork. He probably has me scheduled in on his calendar a year in advance, and it's sending him reminders. He stays so busy, I'm not sure how he keeps his head on straight. He is currently in the wilderness of Washington State, and their next stop is New Zealand. He and Karina are expecting their fourth!"

Micah smiled. "I already knew that. They aren't wasting any time, that's for sure. I miss him, but in all fairness, he's had one heck of a tough work schedule for the past couple of years. Dealing with Aunt Lydia's sudden death was tough on them, too. It was unexpected. She hadn't been sick or anything."

"I know," Macy said, and she hesitated before asking. "Is it really over between you and Carla?"

"Yes, and it's about time," Micah said.

"I can say this now, although I would have never said it before," Macy said, honestly. "I never liked her. I know I was just a kid when you started dating her, but I never warmed to her. I overheard her on the phone once, saying that taking on more brats was the last thing the McKenna family needed.

"Why did you take so much crap from her? If it were me or anyone else pulling that stuff, you would have clocked us a long time ago. As much as I disliked the whole disciplinary environment we were raised in, I never met a woman who deserved a trip to the woodshed more than her!"

Micah laughed at his sister's outburst. "We never had a woodshed!"

Macy smiled. "You know what I mean. She was jealous of the whole family."

"I'm a guy, Sissy, but even I figured that out a long time ago. The problem was, and is... Carla can't stop pushing. I tried for years to keep it together, but it's done and over. Even though we weren't married, our split was equivalent to a divorce. A nasty one."

"I have wondered..." Macy began, but she snapped her mouth shut.

"Was I the head of my house?" Micah finished her question. "No. We were more of the mindset that everything had to be discussed, evaluated, and talked to death before making a decision.

"That was a mistake on my part. Don't get me wrong, I believe in the principles of feminism and a woman's independence. Carla wielded those beliefs around like loaded weapons. There wasn't much equality when it came to a lot of the decisions we made as a couple. I gave in way too much.

"I can see now where I went wrong in picking her as a partner. I was trying to build a family. She was calculating career advancement. Sometimes, a firm *No* has a place in relationship accountability, both for the male and female partners. In Carla's case, it should have been a hell of a lot of No's and an occasional sore backside. I won't make that mistake again."

"There speaks my brother, who paddled my backside many times as a child, a true alpha/dominant male," Macy said.

Micah grinned and nodded. "It is who I am, and I won't turn away from my beliefs again. Did you know that Sully and

Karina had the word obedience put in their vows when they married? They were married in Arizona because the state recognizes covenant marriages. They didn't go into their relationship blind. Seeing how great their marriage works, it only highlights the glaring mistakes I made."

"You can't compare the two," Macy said. "Karina was receptive to a D/D relationship. Carla would have had you arrested!"

"True enough," Micah agreed with a grimace. "It wasn't until the relationship crashed that I realized how blind I had been to so many things for so long. I discovered I didn't know her at all. There were so many lies." He took a deep breath. "That's in my past. I am looking forward to a much less complicated future."

Micah drove to the downtown area of the old fashioned, and well-preserved western Texas town. He drove around the block three times, but the closest he could get to the boot store was three blocks away.

Macy insisted that walking was good for her knee as long as she was careful. They strolled along the sidewalk, window-shopping, and enjoying the small-town atmosphere. "Oh, look!" She pointed at a mannequin in the window of the children's boutique dressed in a cute outfit of a pink sundress with matching accessories. "Katie would look adorable in that."

"No," Micah said firmly, shaking his head, and placing an arm around her shoulders to keep her moving.

"Why not?" Macy demanded.

"I called a family moratorium on buying Katie presents," Micah declared. "No one can buy her anything without express permission from me."

"Why?" Macy exclaimed.

"Because I don't want to raise a spoiled brat. The entire family was constantly giving her gifts. It got to the point where every time someone came to the door, she expected a present.

If she didn't get one, she misbehaved very badly, pouting and whining. I stopped the family from treating her like a spoiled princess. I thought it was a much better idea than having to punish my daughter for bad behavior they were causing."

"But it's so much fun to give kids presents," Macy pouted. "You are a big meanie."

Micah laughed. "So I have been told! I am also the one that has to undo the damage while everyone is spoiling my kid. Katie and I had a little sit-down discussion about sharing, and she donated about three-quarters of her toys to one of the church's mission projects. The toys were sent to safe houses where women and children are sheltered and helped."

"Did she understand all that at her age?" Macy asked.

"I kept it simple for her," Micah said. "We used to do the same thing. Once a year, we had to sort through our stuff and either give it to a sibling that wanted it or give it away. Katie is learning to give and to help the less fortunate. She is also learning that not everyone is as fortunate as we are. It's a good thing, Sissy. I would rather my daughter have a few favorite and cherished toys that she appreciates than a houseful of unnecessary junk that she doesn't. I would rather hand Katie a box of crayons and tell her to draw from her imagination, or send her to the backyard with a spade and tell her to dig a hole and try to find China. I don't want her thinking all her entertainment has to come from electronic devices or television. She has an imagination. I want her to use it."

Macy grinned. "So speaks my strict big brother. Only, now she doesn't get any presents or surprises. Is the family going along with this?"

"My daughter is not a deprived child," Micah snorted. "She gets presents on her birthday and Christmas like any other child. Her birthday is in early June, so it's a nice six-month break and gives her something to look forward to. She still gets too many gifts, in my opinion. And, yeah, the family goes along with it because they don't have a choice. I'm the parent, the head honcho, the big Kahuna! I get to make the rules!"

Macy laughed at the self-pleased look her brother had on his face. "Coyote?" she asked with a knowing and questioning tone.

Micah's eyebrows came together. "Yeah, well, Coyote," he complained cheerfully. "He's a tough nut to crack because he was the worst offender. He adores Katie, and she thinks the sun rises just to make him happy. He has stopped bringing her stuffed animals and toys, but he generally has a gumball or a bag of M&M's in his pocket. I have already warned him that if she gets a cavity, he is paying the dentist bill.

"They have a secret little deal going on between them. She thinks I haven't caught on to what they're doing. As soon as Coyote leaves, she disappears and brushes her teeth. Every child has a little bit of a sneak in them, but so far, my daughter's has been harmless."

Micah opened the door to the western boot store and ushered her in. A salesperson instantly zeroed in on Micah, recognized him, and mentally calculated his portion of the commission on an expensive pair of boots for the celebrity.

Micah waved him away quickly. "We're going to look around first." He steered his sister to the ladies' side of the store.

"See anything that catches your eye?" Micah asked.

"Lots," Macy exclaimed. "I want to take my time. Have a seat, big brother. This could take a while."

Micah did just that. Shopping was not his thing. When he shopped, he knew what he wanted. If he couldn't buy it online, he walked in, purchased what he wanted, and the transaction was completed in less than five minutes. He did understand the female rules for shopping. A mother, a long-term girlfriend, three sisters, and a daughter had trained him.

He sat on a bench and pulled a paperback book from his pocket. He was rarely without a book on him. He used to read on his cell or his other devices, but a couple of years back, he'd returned to his love of books, real printed books, hardback or paperback. He liked the substantial feel of them in his hands, and strangely he felt more connected to what he was reading.

This time he spent very little time reading. He was watching his little sister. Macy would always be his little sister, but she had grown into a beautiful and talented young woman.

She examined the boots, stroked the leathers, checked the heel heights, and compared price tags. One pair of boots had caught her eye. A designer style, the boots were a bright turquoise with elaborate stitching in bright colors forming the pattern of peacock feathers and encrusted with sparkling gems. Macy stroked the design, looked at the price tag, and hastily returned them to the shelf.

She walked the length of the store, setting anything that interested her on the floor. Then she walked the aisle again, returning most of the display boots in place as she narrowed her choices to six designs. After she had walked the length of the aisle a second time, she eliminated two more pair and called the salesman over. Micah was impressed. Unlike some other women he knew or had known, his sister wasn't an impulse buyer.

When she sat on a bench to try on the boots, he walked over and raised the peacock boot. He was surprised by the price tag but assumed it was a designer label. When she wasn't looking his way, he motioned to the clerk. He waved the boot and nodded toward his sister.

The salesman took the hint instantly, disappeared into the back, and returned with another box.

Macy looked questioningly at the salesman when he carried the box to her brother. "Did you decide to buy a pair of boots?" she asked.

"No, these are Sissy boots," Micah admitted. "I wear work boots, and I already have several pairs too many. I want you to try these on."

Macy opened the box and started shaking her head. "I can't afford these."

"You like them," Micah stated.

"Of course," Macy admitted. "What's not to like? I can't afford them."

"I can," he said, motioning the clerk away.

"No," Macy said firmly. "Micah, I know what I can afford, and I didn't ask you to bring me here to get you to buy me a pair of ridiculously over-priced boots."

"I know, Sissy," Micah said in a low voice as he moved closer so no one would hear them. "If you had asked me to pay for them or tried to manipulate me into paying for them, it would have ticked me off. If you had done that, I would have busted you for it.

"Honey, you didn't. I know how independent you are, and I can guess roughly about what you earn. I have missed four of your last five birthdays and three of the last five Christmases. Let me do this."

"You haven't missed anything," Macy denied. "Every year, you sent me beautiful gifts."

"It's not the same when I can't see your face when you open your presents," Micah said earnestly. "I have missed you, Macy. Let me do this. Take what I am offering with grace. I'm doing it because I love you, and I want to see you happy."

Macy weighed his words against her fierce streak of independence.

"Besides," Micah whispered with a smirk. "I'm disgustingly rich and terribly stubborn. I can afford to buy my little sister, a pair of boots."

"These boots?" Macy whispered back. "This is an obscene price, and I don't care whose name is on them!"

"While I will agree with you on that point, if you like them, I want you to have them," Micah repeated, and this time his voice was stern. "You know if you don't, I'll be forced to return after you leave, buy them, and ship them to you. I hate shopping. If I have to suffer through another shopping trip, I might have to buy you every pair you tried on. I'd have to make it worth my time and effort of having them shipped."

"You are the only person I know that can turn an offer of a gift into a threat."

"I take my role as the eldest brother seriously," Micah said, feigning a look of indignation. "You've been a good little girl. I haven't had to smack your behind for quite a while."

Macy laughed. "Git," she complained affectionately.

"That's English slang. Translated into American English, what does that mean?"

"Pretty much anything I choose for it to mean. In this case, it means you're pulling rank as my big brother!"

"I can live with that," Micah said, removing a boot from the box. "Try them on like a good girl, and make sure they don't hurt your precious toes."

Macy took the boots tossing her brother a look of exasperation and love. She stretched and kissed him on the cheek. "Thank you! I love you very much too!"

Micah smiled, knowing he had won the battle of wills. "Paid in full!"

They left the boot store, with Micah carrying two boxes. He'd purchased the peacock designer boots and another pair of fawn-colored, soft leather, his sister's other choice. He'd paid for the footwear, but his sister had exacted a price to let him do it. They backtracked to the children's boutique, and Macy spent another forty minutes finding *the perfect outfit* for his daughter.

She quoted his words back to him verbatim. She missed Katie's birthdays and Christmases too, and she was allowed to give Katie a present in person. Micah accepted his defeat with considerably less grace than his sister had shown him. Being a man, he spent ten minutes grumbling under his breath, as he was shown outfit after outfit by his enthused sister.

## Chapter 5

Micah planned his approach and worried that he was rushing the situation. It had been a week of text messages and missed phone calls. Tess's last day had come and gone, and she was still working at the hospital. There was an outbreak of conjunctivitis, and several doctors were quarantined with it. She was helping to fill the void of doctors on duty. He knew she was busy. He also knew he had to talk to her face-to-face.

A slight family hiccup had canceled the command attendance Sunday dinner at their parents' house. Coyote had dropped Katie off at the lake early Monday morning on his way to classes on the Austin campus. He would retrieve her from school and bring her home later. He and Macy would watch her until Micah returned home.

Micah hated deception, but sometimes even he found a use for it. He told his siblings he had a meeting with the movie producers of an upcoming film. They wanted him to do the soundtrack. That part was true. At this time, though, he was reluctant to take on an endeavor that would take the better part of a year to complete. That he was capable of doing it, was a no-brainer. Whether he wanted to do it on their terms was another matter.

His meeting had consisted of a two-hour video conference with the producer and director. Several more meetings and a viewing of completed scenes would be required before he made a final decision. Thus far, he wasn't overly impressed with the producers, or the film.

When he left the lake, he didn't head north toward Austin and his music studio. He headed south toward San Antonio. He hoped to spend the night with Tess and return home the next morning.

Micah wasn't ready to tell anyone about Tess, yet. He hadn't figured out the change in their relationship himself. Parking in the alley beside the building where she lived, he waited. Without prior warning, he expected he might have to wait a while. He'd tried calling, but Tess wasn't answering. He didn't want to think she was giving him the brush-off. Micah was hoping she'd turned her phone off, as she did when she was in surgery, or concentrating on a difficult case, or she didn't want to be bothered.

Luckily, he didn't have to wait very long. Twenty minutes later, Tess's car pulled in and parked. He called her as she was climbing the outside stairs to the second story entrance of her building. It was an addition that had taken the city of San Antonio over a year to approve. The city commissioners were very careful about the changes they approved to Riverwalk properties.

Tess fumbled in her purse after giving a short half-hearted prayer that it wasn't the hospital calling her back. She had finally left her shift after being the primary physician on duty in the ER for the last sixteen hours. She'd done more than her fair share lately, and she was exhausted. She was looking forward to a long, uninterrupted sleep, and she didn't look at the number displayed.

"Dr. Foster."

"Care for company?"

Tess smiled at Micah's voice. "I would love it, but I would be asleep before you could get here."

"How about if I'm already here?" Micah asked, giving his horn a tap, and waving a large bag in his arms.

Tess turned around, smiled, and waited for him to climb the stairs. "Great, Micah, I look like crap, and I am about to fall on my face in exhaustion."

"I can leave, or I can hose you off and tuck you into bed," Micah offered.

Tess pushed the door open. "Is that food?"

"It has to be nuked, but it's from Farinelli's."

"We can nuke."

He grinned and followed her inside.

"You nuke, I'm taking a shower," Tess ordered. "If I don't return in fifteen minutes, it means I have fallen asleep on my feet. If that happens, turn off the water, lock the doors, and go home. Leave the food behind!"

"Are you always this cranky coming off shift?" he asked.

"After the shift I've had, yes," Tess admitted, and she side-stepped as he aimed a swat at her bottom.

Micah took the bags into the kitchen and unloaded them, searching the cabinets for plates and silverware. Tess didn't keep a tidy kitchen. It wasn't dirty but disorderly with clean dishes left in a drainer by the sink and boxes of cereals and pop tarts left on the counters. He opened the refrigerator and found a couple bottles of iced tea. He heated the food containers in the microwave and carried them to the living room coffee table.

The living room was familiar to him as he had been in it many times. Tess's sister Lauren had occupied the apartment with her five daughters, and Tess had lived in an efficiency next door.

Lauren's husband, Chris, had abandoned her after receiving the news that she was pregnant with triplets. In a time of desperate need and panic, Sully's wife, Karina, had offered the apartment to the struggling Foster sisters for long-term occupation.

The gracious turn of the century building, with several others, was part of a property inheritance from Karina's father. Most of the buildings were in the center of San Antonio's famous Riverwalk. The buildings housed restaurants and shops on the first floors and apartments on the upper floors. Sully and Karina still occupied a large, luxury apartment over Farinelli's Italian, when they were in San Antonio.

In the living room, the floor-to-ceiling built-in bookshelves were stuffed with college textbooks, medical books, and journals. Tess's priorities over the past twelve years had been college, medical school, and career. When her sister Lauren had moved from the apartment several months earlier, Tess had migrated over into the larger space. A lot of Lauren's furniture pieces were missing from the room, leaving gaps in the decor. Tess didn't seem to notice such things.

Tess padded into the room, wearing the gray sweats, he'd given her. Her feet were bare, and she flopped beside him on the couch.

Micah handed her the carryout box and watched with amusement as she inhaled three large meatballs before giving a satisfied moan. "God, that is so good. Thanks, I usually get something from downstairs because it's convenient. Kim Ho gives me a discount, but even I get tired of Chinese food after a while."

"Farinelli's has a standing order never to charge you for food," Micah said.

"I know," Tess said, offering him a bite of her food. "I don't like to take advantage."

"Tessa," Micah started to scold.

"I know, I know. Don't start on me," Tess complained. "It's the bane of my existence having best friends who are rolling in dough."

Micah gave her a sharp disapproving look, and she laughed.

"How is Lauren doing?" Micah asked. "I haven't seen her since Christmas."

"Great. The kids are growing like weeds. I miss having them around, but they're really enjoying their new house, complete with a backyard playhouse, jungle gym, and swimming pool. Oh, do you know what Lauren did?"

"Am I supposed to guess?" Micah growled because he hated guessing games. He was lousy at them.

Tess shook her head because she knew he wouldn't. "She paid off my college loans. I would never have asked her to do it, but she did. She said she owed it to me for standing by her during the rough years."

"Stan called and told me that he took Chris to the cleaners, but he wouldn't give me any details—client privilege and all that lawyer stuff," Micah admitted. "I knew she bought a house. We've been playing phone tag, and neither one of us ever seems to be able to connect with the other."

"I can spill the dirt," Tess said with a grin. "Stan Mulclusky, along with the judge and the divorce mediator's recommendations, took Chris down for six-point-two million dollars, and that's after taxes and Stan's attorney fees, and he soaked them. All total, the bill was in the nine million range.

"He has to pay child support until the girls are eighteen or as long as they are still in college in addition to footing the bill for their college educations. We've been after that S.O.B. for so long, I called in sick to be at the court hearing. Watching Chris being nailed was one of the most satisfying things I have ever witnessed! Stan Mulclusky has been tracking that shit-head all over Europe for the last five years. Chris has been living like a king while his wife and kids were very close to living on welfare!

"The judge said Chris had one of two choices. Either pay the money or go to jail. If he could afford to live in Rio, Monte Carlo, Paris, and Milan, he could afford to settle what he owed to his abandoned family. The judge said Chris deserted his family and his responsibilities as if we didn't already know that! Chris was considered a flight risk because he hadn't paid spousal or child support for all those years. I really think the judge wanted to make an example out of him"

"I'm surprised he had that kind of money?"

"He doesn't," Tess said, shaking her head. "He came to the States because he wants a divorce. He needs to marry the rich bimbo he has been living with for several years. She looks to be about five months pregnant, and her straitlaced Greek, shipping magnate father is none too happy about it.

"The prick waltzed in, never said a word to his daughters and demanded Lauren sign the divorce papers. Lauren gathered the girls and told him she didn't want them in the room for the discussion. She called Stan and stalled Chris until the police could arrive.

"Chris was arrested on outstanding warrants, and Stan Mulclusky got a legal writ of some kind to prevent him from leaving the U.S. His passport was confiscated. I guess his fiancée thinks very highly of him because Daddy Big Bucks forked over the money. Can you imagine having that kind of money that you can just write a check for millions?

"When the check cleared the banks, and the money was safely in Lauren's account, the judge released Chris. Lauren signed the divorce papers, and Miss Daddy Big Bucks, Daddy, and Chris were on the next flight to Thessaloniki, Greece.

"Once he's beyond U.S. jurisdiction, Lauren won't ever see another penny from him. That's okay. Her accounting business is doing great, and now she has a killer bank account. The kicker is, if Chris gets behind in the support payments again, he won't be able to enter the U.S. without taking a chance of jeopardizing his freedom again. Personally, I'd like to see him in jail for a long time for how he treated my sister."

"So Lauren has seen the last of him."

"Absolutely, unless he's stupid enough to think he can sneak into the country," Tess crowed. "Lauren is beginning to realize the impact that kind of money is going to have on her life. My sister has matured a lot. Chris burned her so bad I didn't think she would ever be that trusting again. She cried for three straight days, but this time, it was tears of joy, not tears for the jerk."

"It's a shame, Chris doesn't see the big picture and what he's going to miss by abandoning his kids," Micah said.

"He's too self-centered to get it. Anyway, Lauren said, without my help, we would have never made it. She knew you guys wouldn't accept any repayment, but don't be surprised if she offers it. You have flatly refused every time we have offered. You get all snarly and upset when we raise the subject. Anyway, Lauren paid off my college loans. I didn't want her to do it, but she said she owed it to me. She didn't, but she paid them off anyway."

"I wouldn't say she didn't owe it to you," Micah disagreed. "She wouldn't have made it without your support and help. Until Chris abandoned Lauren and the kids, you were keeping your college loans to the bare minimum. A lot of that school debt was because most of your money was going to feed Lauren's kids and keeping the lights on."

"Family takes care of family," Tess said, laying her head on his shoulder.

"Yep, that's how it works," Micah agreed. He gave her a stinging smack on her butt.

"Ouch! What the..."

"Most of those tough times were unnecessary. I would have

helped more, so would my brothers and my family. You were killing yourself working multiple jobs and going to school. It still makes me angry. I'm glad that debt has been paid off. I have been frustrated for years that you wouldn't let me help more, or pay off those damn loans."

Tess closed her eyes, took a deep breath, and resisted the urge to rub her stinging buttock. "Listen, Bubba, I know you bought this building from Karina. If you rented this apartment, it would be worth about two thousand a month. Throw in the rent on the efficiency I lived in, and it would be more. Multiply that by five years, and I'm not stupid! I figure you have lost at a minimum a hundred and twenty thousand dollars in income from this apartment. There was no way we would have been able to afford to live here. We would have been living in a subsidized rent complex, and I might have had to quit school! We don't need to get into another argument over our not paying rent. We couldn't have paid as much as it's worth, but we could have managed a reasonable amount. My college debt may be paid, but our debt to you, and your family will last a lifetime."

"You don't owe me a damn thing, and it pisses me off when you say you do," Micah snapped.

"Did you come here to argue?" Tess demanded.

"No," he said. "I came to talk to you."

Tess gave another sigh, and she voiced her worst fear. "You regret what happened last week. You've had time to think, and you have been swamped with guilt and second thoughts."

"Second thoughts, yes. Regret and guilt, absolutely not." He turned and tilted her face and kissed her on the lips gently. "Here's a news flash. I've been over Carla for a long time. She was the one who wouldn't let it go, and if I tried to see someone else, she made both of our lives miserable. She's under a court-ordered restraining order to stay away from me, anyone I'm involved with, and my business associates. At some point, that ruling may affect her career. She can't sign on for any project if I'm involved with it. Still, she's the one who wouldn't stop harassing me!

"The judge said enough was enough. He would no longer tolerate her behavior. She's been warned a dozen or more times. He warned her and said if she wants to see the inside of a jail, he would be happy to accommodate her. I hope she got the message this time."

"I hope she lives up to her part of the agreements," Tess said. "You do realize she might be borderline, if not certifiably psychotic."

"I do, and so does the legal system. No one can be forced to take medication. Which is why I made sure she was offered a job, five thousand miles away. I'm sick of talking about Carla," Micah said. "I want to know what we are dealing with now!"

"With one kiss, my whole life was reawakened. It exploded with the possibilities of feeling and loving and living again. The sex was pretty darn explosive too. We have known each other for most of our lives, and your friendship means everything to me. I'm not sure where we stand. Can we remain best friends and be lovers? I know I can't give up one for the other. Can I have both in you?"

"Other than my sister, you and your family have always been there for me. You were the one person I could depend on," Tess said. "I knew you would do what was best for me, even if I disagreed with it. I think we can have both if you are ready to accept it."

"I miss having a partner," Micah said, pulling her into a close hug. "I miss having adult love in my life. I have definitely missed having passion and sex in my life."

"That's a typically male response. I think we have the sex part figured out," Tess teased.

Micah laughed. "Yeah, you almost put me in a sling last week. It had been a while for me."

"I'm all for giving you another workout. Only to help you build your stamina, of course," Tess offered.

"I'm willing," Micah agreed. "First, though, I have to know that we are doing this for the right reasons."

"Micah, can't we just make this easy and casual and see how it works out?" Tess asked with a sigh. "Can't we just hook-up and enjoy each other?"

He pulled away from her. "How long have you known me? I'm not a casual guy. I don't take having sex with a woman lightly. It means something to me. I don't like the expression—hook-up. Call me old-fashioned, but I want a relationship with a woman to mean something. Sex isn't casual for me, there has to be more."

"I hear the expression all the time," Tess admitted. "I have heard it so much, I've been desensitized by its use. You're right. The thing is I'm not ready to jump into a committed relationship based on one admittedly terrific day and night of fantastic sex."

"I'm not either," Micah agreed, and he looked serious. "For years, you've been telling me how sex in hospitals is rampant. I've heard the stories of everyone doing it everywhere; empty rooms, closets, even on the roof!"

"Working in a hospital is high-stress, or boredom while waiting for the next emergency," Tess interrupted. "Sometimes, people have sex to relieve stress."

"I don't have sex to relieve stress," Micah snapped. "I have sex with a woman because I care for her, and I want to make love to her. I need to know that whatever happens between us means something."

"I was the one telling you those stories of people being caught in the act," Tess said tartly. "I didn't say it was me doing it!"

"Good!" Micah growled. "Okay, are we at least committed

to each other exclusively until we decide what the next step will be?"

"Absolutely," Tess agreed angrily. "Don't forget I know how to cut off your wanker if I catch you messing around behind my back!"

Micah laughed at her words. "I'm a faithful kind of guy, remember? I just wanted to lay some ground rules."

"Okay, we have ground rules," Tess said sharply. "We've had several tip-toeing moments over the years that crossed the boundaries of best friends."

"Yeah, I know. I tried to keep all that separate because I didn't want to complicate things. I did, at one time, think I was in love with you. When it didn't work out, I buried the idea and moved on," Micah admitted.

Tess turned and looked at him in disbelief. "When?"

"It was at the end of my second year of college. I took Coyote to Arizona to spend time with our uncle. I met a girl while I was there. She was terrific, but I couldn't take it beyond a couple of kisses, and I have to admit I felt guilty about those. I thought of you all the time. By the time I returned to San Antonio, I was convinced I was in love with you."

Tess was staring at him, wide-eyed and doubtful. "Why didn't you tell me?"

"I was going to," he huffed. "We were sitting in Two Brothers waiting for a pizza, and Danny Monroe walked in. He slid into the booth and kissed you. He tried to suck out your tonsils, and asked me what I was doing with *his* girl."

"Oh my God!" Tess exclaimed, and she giggled. "I remember that idiot. I dated him for all of two months. He owns a mechanic's shop, is married and has four kids."

"Maybe, but you didn't deny being his girl. That made you off-limits," Micah said. "Two weeks later, I-35 was on another tour."

"I dumped that cheating Romeo after catching him with another girl," Tess recalled. "He was dating three girls at the same time, and we all knew each other! When we found out, we roasted his butt. I crossed off being a femme fatale from my list of goals. I concentrated all my efforts on school. If we are going to play true confession here, then I have to tell you that I have been in and out of love with you for the better part of a decade."

"Why didn't you tell me? Micah demanded.

Tess shrugged. "We've been passing ships. First, you were a local band on the music scene. Then, you were an international musical star, and I-35 singles were climbing the charts. I-35 got bigger and larger than life. Your path took you toward stardom, and mine took me in the direction of medical research and study. Carla had you in her clutches by the time you were twenty-two.

"I did decide to tell you once. You were in one of your split-ups with Carla. At least I thought you were, and I was determined to make you hear me. You had been living together for a while. When I finally connected with you, Carla was back, and we both know she hated my guts.

"I know you did things to help me, Micah, and I know you still deny it. I also know you did them under Carla's radar. God only knows what she would have accused you of if she had known. I figured I missed my chance, and it wasn't meant to be. I thought if I could hang in there, be a good friend—it would be enough."

"I have never taken you for granted," Micah said, kissing her on the temple and pulling her to him, so she was snuggled under his chin. "For a long time, you were my stability. You were the one person outside my family that I could depend on not to be star-struck or fan-giddy. You would nail me when my ego was being pampered too much. You would set me straight on being stupid or stubborn, sometimes on both at the same time. I have always been able to count on you to keep me grounded."

"It's been the same for me," Tess exclaimed. "How many times did you rescue me when I was a teenager? How many times did you pull my butt out of bad situations?"

"I set it on fire a few times, too," Micah chuckled. "I have realized since becoming an adult, that you being my *normal* compass hasn't been an easy job. It came with no benefits for you. I could snarl, and gripe and you would set me straight in a heartbeat. My professional world is full of fawning people who have hidden agendas. I might not have told you, but I have appreciated your no-nonsense, bullshit meter. Your ability to recognize the crap and find what is real has always amazed me."

"Why has it worked for you, but not necessarily for me?" Tess asked.

"For the same reason, I have been able to keep you grounded," Micah said. "When you are on the inside of the problem, you can't see it as clearly as you can from the outside.

"My bullshit meter wasn't working at all. Hence, I was in a relationship that was doomed from the beginning, but I was too dumb to see it."

"So, we are for real?" Tess asked and gave him a kiss that revved every atom in his body into high gear.

"Oh, yeah," Micah shifted, but he deliberately backed off. "Only there's one more thing we need to discuss."

"Whether we do it on the couch or the bed?" Tess teased.

"One more serious thing," Micah said, and repeated. "Very serious."

Tess leaned into him and waited. Micah's face looked uncomfortable, and she was delighted at his discomfort. "Well?"

"Birth control," Micah growled. "Tess we didn't... I didn't use any, not once. I never gave it a thought. I should have, I should have been responsible, and I wasn't. I do apologize. I wasn't the one who took on that responsibility. I was tested after we broke up—my doctor insisted. And, you should know that if you do come up pregnant, I'll..."

Tess burst into laughter, but at the embarrassed blush on his cheeks, she relented and interrupted him.

"There's nothing to worry about. I don't think you are the kind to sleep around, so I would venture to say you are safe too."

Micah frowned. "You know I don't sleep around, but I wasn't thinking of diseases. I was thinking more along the lines of pregnancy."

"I know," Tess admitted. "You are still safe."

"But... Oh, you're on the pill?"

"No, I can't get pregnant, Micah. Medically, the statistics against any possibility of my ever getting pregnant are astronomical."

"Why?" Micah gasped in surprise. He knew Tess loved children.

Tess rose from the couch, snatched the carryout boxes, and walked away from him. He picked up the remains of the dinner debris and followed. Tess had her back to him, tossing the carry-out boxes in the trash. When she turned, there were tears in her eyes. She waved him off as he came to her. "Sorry, I have known for a very long time, but every once in a while, it still gets to me."

"Why?" Micah repeated gently, guiding her over to the kitchen table, sitting down, and pulling her into his lap. "Talk to me, Tessa."

She was silent for a full minute before she met his eyes. She spoke with conviction. "I will have kids. I may not have them the way I would have preferred, but I will have kids. I haven't decided when I'm going to start the process. I had to finish my schooling first. At least, I don't have to worry about my biological clock ticking."

Micah stroked her cheek and wiped away an errant tear. "It's not a joke."

"No, there's nothing funny about it. It was the car accident I was in when I was ten-years-old. It was before we moved into your neighborhood. I'm sure I told you about it. I was hospitalized for several weeks. I was hurt really bad inside. That's not the clinical description, of course, but that's how I described it in my ten-year-old mind. I was too young at the time to think of the accident in medical terms or to worry about long-term complications. It was the hospitalization that made me want to be a doctor.

"The surgeons removed my spleen and my appendix while they had me open. That's standard procedure when a patient is already on the table, and open. They repaired minor damage to one of my kidneys. It must have been a mess in there. They either missed a direct hit to my left ovary or the injury was masked, and they didn't see it. As nature sometimes does, especially when the patient is on antibiotics, the ovary managed to die off on its own without infection or complications.

"Later, when I was in my teens, I was having debilitating cramping. The gynecologist went in microscopically. She discovered a dystrophic ovary and a partially closed fallopian tube to my remaining ovary. They cleared the tube, discovered endometriosis, and removed as much of it as they dared. The end result is that I have sporadic periods, usually only about three a year. I don't keel over in pain from them anymore, and I take meds for the endometriosis. The end result was I was told the possibility of my having children was off the charts—statistically impossible. My eggs might be viable, but I've been told my uterus wouldn't be able to sustain a pregnancy."

Micah pulled her into a long, rocking hug. "I'm so sorry, Tess. You did not deserve this."

## Chapter 6

Tess tucked into the hug. "I know it's unfair. That's my deal, Micah. It's something that you have to accept going in. I will have babies or older kids, they will be by surrogate or adoption, or maybe even foster kids. Somehow or someway, I will have children. Does being with a damaged woman scare you off?"

"Stop that," Micah ordered sternly. "You are not *damaged*. You are my Tess, and that is all you have ever needed to be— my Tess." He cradled her in his arms. Then he carried Tess to her bedroom. He wiped away the remaining tears on her face.

"What I am unsure about is getting into a relationship with you. With anyone else, it wouldn't be as scary because there wouldn't be so much at stake. I don't have a game plan here, Tess. If I wreck this relationship, our friendship will follow. I don't know if I can handle losing our friendship. You are one of very few people in this world that I can trust, and trust has become essential to me.

"You know me, and I don't jump in feet first with my eyes closed. I'm a cautious person, and this change between us has scared me. I am all in, or all out," Micah warned. "I'm not looking at you as a pretty plaything or breeding stock... Oh, crap, I cannot believe I said that! Why don't you shove my foot clear down my throat and out my ass! I'm an idiot!"

Tess rolled over in bed, and she howled with laughter. "I can't believe those words came from you! There's Texas redneck in you somewhere!" She sat up in bed, and her face sobered and looked pensive. "You may not have expressed yourself poetically, but I already know I am far more than my reproduction parts."

"I'm sorry! I'm a guy, and sometimes my mouth and my brain don't work in sync. Especially when I'm upset," Micah apologized. "Tess, you know what you are getting with this McKenna. You know I'm stubborn and strait-laced, and I walk a narrow line between what I believe is right and wrong. I stay on that line. I'm not a wild and crazy guy, never have been. Beyond my musical talents, the words that describe me are reliable, dependable, and responsible. It's who I am.

"You also know the lifestyle I expect to live. I have already tried going against what I knew in my heart was right for me. It didn't work. I believe in fidelity, I believe in being the head of my house, and if I deem it necessary, I believe in discipline. You know it because you have already been on the receiving end several times. My cards are face-up on the table. Tell me what road you're taking."

"We're okay, Micah," Tess said, pulling him to her and kissing him. "I've known for a long time that the McKenna family practices domestic discipline, and I have been the recipient of it. I already know you have a damnably hard hand. What goes on between two consenting adults is their business. You've busted my ass several times, and I didn't throw our friendship away. I didn't tell you to get lost because I value your friendship and love. I was the one who was standing on the sidelines, hoping someday you'd dump that bitch and see me! Not as a friend, but as a woman! Stop worrying. We're going to take this day-by-day and work out the kinks as we go. Now, when was the last time you played doctor?"

"Never, although I still think I might have a few tricks up my sleeve," Micah promised.

"I was on shift for sixteen hours. You had better get on with it before I fall asleep," Tess warned.

"You won't be thinking of sleep for a while," Micah promised as he slid his hands inside the loose sweat pants and peeled them down, revealing that she hadn't bothered with panties. He pulled off her sweatshirt, and her breasts were gloriously naked too. Micah kissed her deeply, thrusting his tongue into her mouth with a titillating beat as his fingers entered her and began pumping in a rhythm that matched.

"Oh," Tess gasped as his lips moved down, and he devoured her breasts. He trailed a slow torturous path downward until he was on her, sucking and teasing her clit. She writhed with wanting him inside her, and she grasped his cock, stroked it, and primed it, but Micah wasn't ready to give her what she wanted most.

Micah was in the mood to play. He teased Tess until she was seconds from an orgasm. He backed off, only to torment her again, and again, until he finally let her come. With his head between her legs, the only part of him she could reach was his hair, and she wound her fingers in what little was there, as her legs wrapped around his neck and shoulders. His tongue was playing a masterpiece in the pleasure he brought her, but she wanted more. She wanted him inside her, to feel the hardness and the heat of him.

Tess didn't know how he did it, but somehow, Micah was suddenly naked. Barely recovering from a massive orgasm, he was there. Micah hovered over her only long enough for her to wrap her legs over his forearms. He lifted her, and then he was inside, thrusting hard and powerfully. She was open to him, and he plunged clear to her core, over and over until her body seized again. As she shuddered, his fingers went to her clitoris. He wouldn't let the orgasm stop. It went on and on as he pumped and worked her. It became deliciously painful until her body gave a final jerk and relaxed. She was hot, wet, and exhausted. He tried to play with her, to incite another orgasm, but she knew it wouldn't happen. She was spent. She was, however, filled with a need to give as much to him as he had given to her.

Tess rolled to her knees, bent over him and took him in her mouth.

Micah closed his eyes as he felt his body reacting again. He was being awakened again, and he went to full arousal in seconds. At her sensual urgings, now she was in control, and he was pulsing with the searing need to come again. The wet slide of her tongue was almost more than his control could endure. With a sudden roll, he was on top. A hard thrust, and he was embedded in her. This was where he belonged. He thrust into her deeper and sent her spiraling into a whirlpool of desire. This time, there was no delay, and he came with a surge. They lay wet and exhausted, wrapped in each other bodies.

Micah wanted to say something, to tell Tess she was beautiful, magnificent, exciting... but when he raised his head, she nuzzled into his neck with closed eyes. He smiled and tucked himself around her. A long shift at the hospital, an emotional admission to him, and a long romp in bed had exhausted her. She had given her all and was sound asleep. He rubbed his thumb over the bluish circles of exhaustion under her eyes.

Tess deserved more than a casual romp of sex. She gave so much of herself to others. She needed someone who would love her, appreciate, and take care of her.

As he lay there beside her, Micah realized his newest venture would be convincing Tessa Foster that he could fit into her heart and her life on a full-time basis.

Micah leaned into the canvas with a tiny sable brush and tapped it into the wet paint. He stood back, smiled, and nodded. Even he admitted to himself that this painting was excellent. He could still nit-pick the tiniest of issues, but that was his nature. The portrait was one of his grandparents. He had borrowed his parents' large stack of photograph albums, supposedly to have them scanned to distribute to all the siblings. He had followed through, hiring someone to scan and label the photographs in the collections. He'd probably give them to his siblings for Christmas presents.

His real purpose had been to find photographs of his grandparents on his father's side. This painting was to be a gift to his father on his sixty-sixth birthday in a couple of weeks. It had taken a lot of research to decide on the background setting he wanted to use in this painting. This was the first time he'd painted from black and white photographs, taken on an old Eastman Kodak Brownie camera his father still had on a shelf in his office.

Micah had discovered translating gray tones into color an instinctual process. The painting was not of his grandparents as he remembered them, older, and failing in health. This painting was of his grandparents as he hoped his father would recognize them from his childhood, a couple in their mid-thirties.

He dropped his brush into a jar of cleaner and began to reorganize his workspace. He heard his sister's light footsteps walking across the unfinished part of the loft. He inhaled the aroma of his morning sustenance.

"Please tell me that is for me," he asked of his sister, eyeing the cup of coffee in her hand.

She grinned. "It is. It's not that wonderful concoction that you create in that scary machine. Still, I can handle a standard coffee pot." She stood looking at her brother's latest painting of a ranch couple. The woman was perched on a porch railing, leaning against a corner post, her body at an angle as she only had one hip resting on the railing. A man was standing beside her. She was watching him as he was raising a cup of coffee to his lips. He was looking at two boys wrestling in the yard with an amused smile on his face. His other arm was around her shoulders, his fingers tangled in her shoulder-length blonde hair, his thumb caressing the line of her jaw.

Macy took in every detail of the painting, and she shivered. She could feel the love the man and woman had for each other and their boys. It seemed to radiate from their eyes and the subtle body language. "They're so real, I feel like they're going to start talking at any moment. That's Grandma and Grandpa McKenna, isn't it?"

"Yes, do you remember them?"

She shook her head and smiled. "No. They died before we became part of the McKenna family."

"I forget that sometimes," Micah admitted.

Macy looked at the copies of the old photographs and studied the painting. "How did you interpret that, from these?"

Micah shrugged and grinned. "It's what I do. If I'm lucky, it works. If not, it goes in the trash."

"I have to get photographs of this one. It's truly amazing," Macy exclaimed.

"I'm thinking of giving it to Dad for his birthday."

"If you are going to give Dad the painting for his birthday, won't everyone discover that you are an artist? What happens to the *big* secret?"

"Not necessarily," Micah said, shrugging. "I've never signed a painting."

"Micah!" Macy scolded. "Why not?"

There was another shrug, but it didn't answer Macy's question. It also made Micah wonder why he hadn't.

"Someday, when you have the time, would you paint my birth parents for me?" Macy asked.

"I already have," Micah said, going over to a stack and pulling a canvas from it.

"Oh," Macy exclaimed, and she ran her fingers over their faces. "I was only ten when they died, but I still have my memories of them."

"It's yours," Micah said.

"Thank you," Macy whispered with tears on her lashes.

"What's on the agenda today, Sissy?" Micah asked as he came from the loft and headed for the coffee pot again.

"Breakfast on your deck, and watching the ducks on the lake. Relaxing, relaxing, and relaxing, until it's time to go to Mom's for dinner. I'm hoping this mid-week dinner won't be the big hoopla of her Sunday dinners. I was very grateful that the Sunday dinner was canceled."

"Dream on," Micah warned. "This will be the big push to talk you into returning to their house and staying there. When do your rehab appointments start?"

Macy smiled. "This coming Thursday, and after that, twice a week. I was hoping to get a few more days of peace before facing the folks again."

"You can't dodge the folks for that long. I'm surprised they haven't been calling every five minutes. We can't stay too late. Katie has school in the morning." He wiped his hands with hand cleaner and hung the towel neatly in place.

"Is Mom still demanding full family attendance every Sunday?" Macy asked.

"No, but old habits are hard to break. Katie and I usually go to church on Sunday dinner days. Part of the guardian agreement was that she be raised with religious teachings. Nick and Sally weren't particularly religious themselves. They did believe that children should be aware of the different faiths so they could make up their own minds as they developed. I've been giving her introductions into various faiths, a little of ours, and visiting other churches. Katie is only six. We go to church once, or twice a month, on our way to the family dinners. She can go to the Sunday school classes, while I attend the congregational sermon."

"You have managed to wean Mom's weekly dinners down to once or twice a month?"

"We go when I want to go," Micah admitted. "For a long time, I stopped going altogether. I got tired of listening to advice on things they didn't know the full details about and, frankly, it wasn't any of their business. Sometimes the family was almost as bad as the press.

"Most people saw Carla's crap for what it was, but there were reporters who were relentless. Her lies were proven lies, but once those accusations are leveled, there are people who will never change their minds. During the rough times, Coyote and Tess dug in here with me. Coyote is one hell of a good guy, and Tess is... well, Tess is a pit-bull. Both of them gave me hell when I needed it. Walking away from the relationship was necessary, but I don't usually quit on people. Then she tried to play dirty, and suddenly she was a victim. That really pissed me off. If there is one thing Carla isn't, it's a victim."

"I was fighting my way through those problems, and suddenly, I was a parent. I love kids, but I'd never been responsible for one. I floundered for a while. Mom even suggested that I give Katie to them to raise."

Micah raised his coffee cup and took a long swallow. "That wasn't going to happen. That little girl needed me as much as I needed her."

"Coyote called me a few times. I think he needed to use someone as a sounding board that wasn't so closely involved. I'm sure the folks weren't much help. Their answer is to head for their minister and look for God to provide an answer. I believe, Micah, don't think that I don't, but sometimes a good lawyer is a much better idea."

Micah snorted into his coffee. "Damn straight, Sissy! Stan came in real handy in finding the right representation when suing that stupid woman on a cell phone who killed Nick and Sally. She was texting on an Interstate at eighty miles per hour. Nick and Sally never stood a chance. All because she couldn't wait five eff'n minutes to pull over and return a text message.

"Believe it or not, her lawyers tried to reduce the charge to reckless endangerment. Rachel Worth had already been pulled over and ticketed three times for texting while driving. She knew what she was doing. She's serving a twelve-year sentence for vehicular manslaughter. She'll be paroled after serving five or six years. I haven't got to the point where I can feel much sympathy for her. Two innocents were killed because of her actions! Of course, she didn't kill them on purpose. But Nick and Sally lost their lives, and Katie lost both of her parents. There has to be accountability for her actions. That woman's attorney is still trying to have the sentence overruled, claiming it was just a *lack of good judgment* on her part. Damn straight, it was, and she killed two people because of it!

"I did get help from a grief counselor and Tess. It's handy when your best friend has completed an internship in psychiatry and knows the right people."

"Mom and Dad were concerned," Macy said.

"The folks need to learn when to interfere and when to mind their own business. Most of their kids are adults now, or almost there. We've been trying to teach them about boundaries for the last decade," Micah assured his sister. "If I make you one of my famous chocolate/caramel latte bribes, will you tell me what is going on between you and Mom? Katie won't wake up for another hour."

Macy considered the offer for a few seconds and nodded her head.

Micah whipped the coffees together and motioned for his sister to go outside on the deck.

"We spent a lot of time here at the lake when we were kids," Macy exclaimed. "I remember how we used to be covered with insect bites all summer, mosquitoes, ticks, and those awful chiggers. We still loved coming here."

"I don't think you miss the bugs," Micah said, grinning. "Do you miss anything about living in the States or Texas?"

Macy smiled. "The family and my friends but not much else. It was hard when I first moved to Paris, but I was determined to stick it out. I sort of miss the idea of Texas as home, but I have accepted that if I want to keep training and dancing with the best, that Europe is the place to be. I was very comfortable living in Paris. Now, I love living in London."

"You sound more European now than you do, Texan," Micah admitted appraising his sister. "You have a slight English accent, but it has an undefined European tone and cadence to it."

"I can't help it, I'm listening to accents every day," Macy exclaimed with a light laugh. "You should hear my friends. Accents are indicative of social class. We have dancers going to speech classes to change their accents."

"Do you like living in London more than Paris?"

"It's different, but London, in its own way, is just as beautiful Paris. Language hasn't been as big an issue, although there are a few very thick accents. Sometimes I need an interpreter. It figures. I finally became fluent in French, and I moved on," Macy complained, but she was smiling.

"London was interesting to visit, but I loved the countryside over there, especially the Lake District," Micah admitted. "If I hadn't had the lake here, I might have considered transplanting myself."

"The family would have had a fit if you had," Macy admitted. "As it was, they thought you were crazy when you permanently moved here with Katie."

Micah nodded. "I know, but living here suits me. The lake has become home. The townhouse always felt temporary, and it was. I was surprised to find out how many people expected me to hand off Katie to someone else to raise. My friends trusted me to raise her, not a nanny or a family member. I had to do the best I knew how to do, and if it wasn't good enough, learn to do it better. Parenting is hard, but I'm not stupid. The instant that little girl was placed in my arms, I knew she was mine."

"You scared everyone. It's not like you to be depressed," Macy said.

Micah shrugged. "I wasn't so much depressed, as I was pissed. My anger was justified. A woman I'd lived with for years betrayed me. Then because of a senseless act of stupidity, I lost two friends who were closer to me than some members of my family.

"I had a lot of support. I had the folks, Tess, good friends, and good lawyers. I didn't get platitudes from them. Most of their advice was down-to-earth honest. It was fight back, or rollover. The ball was in my court. I got a kick in the ass from Stan when I needed it. I decided Carla had bulldozed over me one too many times. She didn't expect me to fight back, but I did! I brought Katie here to the lake, and we learned how to become a family unit, just the two of us."

"What about everything you've put on hold?" Macy asked.

"I didn't put anything on hold. I've never stopped working," Micah disagreed. "I stopped being so public about what I was doing. I was never that fond of being in the limelight. I haven't missed it. I have written and sold a ton of songs and music in the last four years. I-35 still records. Last year's album equaled the sales of the previous album. It's true, we haven't toured very much, and when we did, we kept it to small clubs and weekend gigs. The schedule wasn't all about me. I doubt any of us would have had the time for a longer or a full-scale tour. We're not young bucks anymore, except for Coyote. We're adults with families and responsibilities.

"Coyote is still taking classes. Sully has been taking on major movie roles, and they are having babies one after another. I didn't become a recluse. I simply settled into doing what I do best. That's writing and producing music. I had to put the soundtrack business on hold for a little while, partly because of the legal entanglements. Once it was determined that Carla didn't have any investment in the music studio, I went back to running the business as usual but doing more of it remotely. Between dealing with false accusations and legal issues, and taking on Katie, I'll admit I was strung out for a few months.

"At the most, I lost six months, when I was trying to deal with Carla's crap in the beginning. My lawyers have spent the last four years fending off Carla, and her sleazy lawyers, and the courts. She started the battle. I won the war, and she's just about gone broke because of the stunts she's tried to pull!

"I like not being in the spotlight. I like being able to raise my daughter and not miss a single day of her life. I'm not a helicopter parent, although I am a bit strict. I haven't poisoned her, and I haven't turned her into a holy terror or a brat. Life is good on our end. Now, enough about me. Spill the beans!"

"What?" Macy exclaimed in mock indignation.

"I want to know what's going on with you. Spill it," Micah ordered. "Why are you here? I want to know why you returned to the States and immediately fled from the folks?"

Macy gave a sigh and took a slow drink of her coffee before speaking.

"Coming home was about getting Mom out of London," she said, exhaling a long breath. "When I called home to tell them I was having microscopic surgery on my knee, it was only to keep them in the loop. I have been repeatedly accused of not doing so. And it's true because I don't want them in my business. I live five-thousand miles away, and I've been making my own decisions for a long time. I had already made plans to stay with a friend who has an elevator to his apartment. I didn't expect Mom to call me from Heathrow two days later and tell me she was there to *take care* of me.

"Micah, you've seen where I live. It's a bed-sitter, a fourth-floor walkup. My little room has just enough space for a single bed, a wardrobe, a reading chair, and a lamp. It's a lovely little place, and I share the fourth floor, and a bathroom with four other girls, who are also dancers. I didn't have room for Mom to move in with me. I tried to tell her I had already made arrangements. As usual, she refused to believe I was capable of handling my own life.

"What was I supposed to do? She was already there! I went to the hospital to have my knee operated on. Several days later, we were bumping and falling over each other, and Mom was driving me starkers!"

"I'm sure she had good intentions," Micah interceded kindly. "Did you get into an argument or something?"

Macy took another swallow of her drink. "For the first couple of days, I was on medication, and I was sleeping a lot. While I was asleep, Mom decided that my place was too small, and she took it upon herself to start investigating flats with an estate agent. Micah, she found me another place to live. Not just to rent either, Mom expected me to purchase it. She told my landlady that I would be moving! Thank God, I talked to Mrs. Rothberry before she rented my place to someone else!

"Where I live is my business! I told Mom, flat out I wasn't moving. She got all whiny and started crying, telling me she only wanted what was best for me. Then, she drops her bomb-shell. Wouldn't it be just *divine* if I purchased a flat? Allison and I could share it. Or, her alternative plan was that I should join a stateside ballet company, and Allison and I could live together.

"I have to admit, I flipped out. I asked Mom if she had lost her mind because she was definitely delusional! I'm not giving up my position in one of the most prestigious ballet companies in the world. And, why in the hell did she think I wanted to live with and share space with a sister that I won't even speak to? I told her no in clearly spoken English that even she could not misinterpret as anything but a NO in capital letters!"

Micah was laughing, and Macy whacked him with a pillow.

"It's not funny! When I discovered her master plan, I made reservations on the next flight to San Antonio. I wanted her far away from London, and as fast as possible. If the Concorde was still flying, we would have been on it. I was so furious, if I hadn't had one leg out of commission, I would have put a boot in her butt and sent her flying across the Atlantic without an old plane!

"My buying a flat is a ridiculous idea. Purchasing a flat and living with Allison is an old *Twilight Zone* episode, which by the way are still playing on English television stations late at night! They consider the old show, 'campy'. Which is surprisingly accurate considering how I felt about the entire episode!"

Micah was still laughing. "I wish I had taped this, you should hear yourself. You sound so British!"

"Oh, that's not all, dear brother. We no sooner got on the plane, and Mom starts in on me about my settling the problems between Allison and myself. She didn't bother to ask me what happened between us. She just assumed I was at fault!"

"Uh, oh," Micah mumbled.

"Bugger, right," Macy agreed, looking off across the lake. "I was trapped on a plane, and she was determined that we were going to come to what she called an *understanding*. I had to fake being sick, so I could take a seat by the bathroom. It's none of her damn business. When we arrived in San Antonio, she and Dad started double-teaming me. It was either come here or catch the next flight to London. Coyote suggested I take up residence with him or come here.

"I have tried to be as polite as I can, but I don't belong here anymore. San Antonio is not my home anymore, and I won't tolerate Mom and Dad's heavy-handed parenting. I will not fall back into those old patterns. They are not dumping me into the role of Allison's keeper. Mom said that it was up to me to be the *bigger person*.

"What a load of dung! I did that for years, and I'm not having any part of it. I am tired of Allison's jealousy, and I am sick of being her whipping boy. If she wants to own up and apologize, I'll accept it, but I will not be her friend, and I will never be dumb enough to trust her again!"

"Allison is your sister, your twin sister," Micah said. "You can't write her off. I know she's difficult, we all do. Most families have a problem child, and she is ours. We older guys have decided that she needs a dose of reality. She is trying. She enrolled at the Austin campus in January. Maybe the fourth time is the charm."

Macy looked over at her brother and raised a single eyebrow. "Allison dropped her college classes within the first couple of weeks. She's been milking Dad for the cost of an apartment."

"What? Why wasn't I told?" Micah demanded.

"I don't think she has told anyone. At least not anyone who could put a stop to her scam," Macy said, shrugging. "The only reason I know is she mentioned it in a text. She did a contacts text message, and either she forgot I was on the list, or she did it deliberately. With Allison, anything is possible."

"If she is not in school, what is she doing?" Micah demanded.

Macy shrugged. "I'm not in Allison's circle of friends, big brother, and I don't want to be. It's not my problem."

"Coyote spends a good amount of his time in Austin. His classes are split between the two campuses. I'll drop a bug in his ear to check on her, do a little snooping," Micah said.

"Don't," Macy said almost automatically in defense of her twin. "Micah, let Allison live her life. We will be twenty-one in a couple of months. She needs to take responsibility for herself and her actions. It might help her to distance herself from the McKenna name. I am very proud of my big brothers, but you guys are a hard act to follow."

"That's Allison's problem," Micah said thoughtfully. "She's an average person drowning in a family of super-successful people. She has a classic case of *middle child* syndrome even if she isn't the middle child. She has felt like she wasn't good enough, and she'd rather quit than fail."

"You've been reading child psychology books," Macy said.

"I have a kid," Micah said in defense.

"The bigger problem is her attitude," Macy said. "She has never stuck with anything in her whole life. She starts something, and when she's not instantly good at it, she drops it. She's not willing to go the distance it takes to be successful. She is also never held accountable for her failures, and Mom backs that idea—on with the new, and hope it will be what will make Allison happy.

"Allison resents the success of the band, she resents my success, she even resents that we don't look alike. I didn't have anything to do with our genetics. It's not my fault I came out blonde, and she came out a brunette. The only thing she doesn't bear a grudge against is her trust fund. I will bet you dollars to donuts that she has blown most of it."

"I would take that bet, except I know she can only withdraw twenty-thousand dollars every six months. That condition is set in the trust until she reaches twenty-five. It can be extended at Dad's discretion, or he can shut down access to the trust altogether. I hope Allison finds her niche someday. I want her to be happy," Micah admitted.

"No one wants that more than I do. At the same time, I am not willing to sacrifice what I have worked for, to pander to Allison's ego, lack of ambition, and work ethic," Macy said. "Mom and Dad need to stop the money flow and wakeup. Allison needs to work or study at something. She needs to realize how privileged she is to have a supportive family and not take it for granted. Is it true that we only have limited access to our trusts?"

"Yeah, you gain more control as you reach certain milestones, eighteen, twenty-one, twenty-five," Micah admitted. "When we older kids, refused our trusts, Dad had the paperwork redone to split the money between you younger kids."

"I didn't know you three refused your trusts," Macy exclaimed. "That's not fair to you."

Micah shrugged. "There's only so much money a person needs, Sissy. I-35 has earned us more than we will ever be able to spend unless we become spendthrifts or stupid. We all live well. Plus, we have what we earn individually. Sully has his movies, I have my music studio, and we're all invested in McKenna Studio. All three of us still write and sell songs.

"Dad made sure that our finances were protected until we were old enough and smart to handle them ourselves. There are clauses in those trusts that he can take back control if he thinks the funds are being misused. Long before Dad became a music producer and part of our management team, he was a finance guru and a hard-ass about finances. He must have told you all this when he turned your trust over to you when you turned eighteen."

"I was on tour, and we never managed to connect," Macy said. "He sent me the paperwork, but since I had no intention of touching it, I never got around to reading it." She shrugged and made a face. "The paperwork is in a drawer somewhere. I have no intention of using it unless something goes really wrong with my ballet career, and I have to shift into another career or go to college. I have taken a few college courses, but it's hard to work them into my schedule."

Micah laughed and shook his head. "You're as bad as Sully when it comes to money. He makes it hand over fist, but Karina and his financial advisors make most of the business decisions."

"That clause also means I couldn't have used it to buy the flat in London that Mom wanted me to buy," Macy said.

"You underestimate, Mom. If she had managed to talk you into it, she would have made it happen."

## Chapter 7

Carole McKenna greeted Micah and Macy as if she hadn't seen them in months. It wasn't unusual because she always greeted her grown children that way. Sometimes it was months between visits. Her adult children all had busy careers.

"Are Lily and Noah here?" Katie asked.

"In the basement, honey," Carole said as the child took off at a run.

"Come in, come in," Carole effused. "Macy, how is your knee? Is it hurting? Have you been running a temperature?"

"I'm fine, Mom," Macy interrupted. "I've been following my doctor's directives. I'm doing exactly what I'm supposed to do." Macy glanced at her brother, and when their mother turned to remove something from the oven, she rolled her eyes and disappeared through the basement door.

When Carole turned around and realized her daughter was gone. She started firing off questions. "Micah, how is Macy? Is she okay? Has she talked to you at all? I'm worried about her."

"Mom, she has only been at my place a week," Micah exclaimed. "She doesn't seem overly concerned about the surgery. Macy knows what she is doing, and she wants to use this downtime to relax and visit old friends. She's earned it."

"I agree, but I wish she had stayed here. She needs to be looked after," Carole complained.

"Macy is used to being independent, Mom," Micah said, picking his words carefully. "I know where she is coming from, so you need to stop hovering and second-guessing her. If you don't, she's going to high-tail it back to London. I would like her to stick around for a little while, but she is an adult, and she will make her own decisions."

"Neither of the twins are what I would call adults," Carole denied.

"Mom, you can't lump them together. They live two separate lives, and have two different personalities," Micah warned. "Macy has been in professional dance companies for almost six years, and she has been living on her own since she went to France. She is a responsible young woman."

"They are not adults," Carole repeated.

"Now, you're being a hypocrite."

"Micah!"

"You and Dad were already married when you were her age. I moved out at twenty. Sully might not have technically moved out, but he was gone most of the time and definitely living a separate life long before he was twenty-one. Coyote left home at nineteen.

"Macy was only sixteen when she left home to study ballet. The twins are adults, and you need to face it," Micah reminded his mother.

"They're not acting like adults," Carole exclaimed. "Not with all this fussing and feuding going on. They should stop fighting—they're twins!"

"Once again, Mom, they are adults," Micah repeated firmly. "If they are having issues, it's between the two of them. Sticking your nose in Macy's business, trying to tell her what to do, and how to run her life, will send her packing. If you do that, I'm going to be upset with you."

Carole didn't respond except for a tightening of her lips in disapproval. He turned and made his way to the basement. As soon as he opened the door to the home music room, memories flooded his mind as pure pounding noise assaulted his hearing.

Noah, his younger brother, was pounding away on a full drum set in a wild rendition of an old Eagle song. The noise that assaulted his ears was professional level drumming, accompanied by Macy's barely competent piano skills, and his Katie pounding on a snare drum. Lily, his youngest sister, was watching them.

"Daddy!" Katie screamed and ran across the room to greet him. With a wild jump, she leaped into his arms.

Noah stopped drumming. Lily turned to her oldest brother and went over to hug him.

"Sounding good, Noah," Micah said.

Noah nodded, although he pretended teenage indifference.

"What about me, Daddy!" Katie demanded.

"Katikins, for a newbie drummer, you are terrifically loud," Micah told his daughter truthfully.

"Dinner's almost ready," a shout came from the top of the stairs in their father's low voice.

Noah jumped to his feet and bounded toward the stairs, followed quickly by the two younger girls.

"You would think they haven't eaten in a week," Micah said to Macy as he watched the mad dash.

"Noah's at that age when he inhales everything that falls within his path," Macy said, laughing. "We have a young man studying ballet about Noah's age. It's not safe to leave any food around him. He eats everything, and he's as skinny as a rail. How are they doing? I didn't spend a lot of time with them when I was here."

"Noah is doing great. Once he was given a set of drum-sticks, he set aside his ambitions to be a con man," Micah said. "He works off a lot of that excess energy drumming. He's already receiving pro-level offers.

"The last time I talked to Mom, she said that Lily is having some problems. She's calling Mom, Aunt Carole, and she's become sulky lately. Lily was claiming that she was going to be a dancer like her big sister, but lately, she's been refusing to even go to class. I guess she's changed her mind."

"I talk to Lily several times a month," Macy said frowning, and sounding distressed. "She told me she was taking entrance exams to go to a private school in the fall. She didn't tell me she dropped ballet."

"Kids her age change their minds all the time," Micah said. "Do you have any regrets about moving away from home?"

"Not a one. I made my choice a long time ago and would have made it earlier if anyone had ever bothered to ask me what I wanted. I've devoted my ambition to dance."

"You have turned into a wise little sister," Micah said, kissing the top of her head. "Let's go, Dad still doesn't like stragglers showing up to the dinner table."

Macy laughed. "Some things never change!"

Carole had outdone even her usually over-the-top Sunday dinners. She had prepared roast beef, fried chicken, and had all the traditional Southern side dishes she had been making for years. She kept an eagle eye on her family, taking note of Noah's plate piled high and her oldest son's less filled plate.

"Goodness, Macy, you aren't eating?" Carole exclaimed, noticing only vegetables on her plate.

Macy nodded. "I'm not very hungry."

"Take a helping of roast," Carole exclaimed, handing a platter of roast beef to her daughter. Macy set it on the table without taking any.

"Macy, you are as thin as a rail," Carole protested.

"I am exactly two pounds below my minimum weight for my dancing requirements," Macy said firmly. "I'll have to gain those pounds before I can return to dancing. Besides, I generally eat the same diet as a vegan."

Two of the three males stared in horror, their forks stopping midway en route to their mouths.

"Does that mean you don't eat meat?" Noah demanded in disbelief.

"Most of the time, no," Macy said, smiling. "It may be the same as heresy in Texas, but I rarely eat meat. I'm not part of a campaign or anything, it's a personal preference."

"It's utter nonsense," Daniel McKenna exclaimed. "You'll wilt away to nothing. It's not healthy. A body needs protein!"

Macy smiled. "Dad, for every book that heralds eating meat, there are two that expound the virtues of not eating it. It fits my lifestyle. I'm a dancer, and I am physically fit."

"I'll never believe it," Daniel exclaimed, pointing his fork at his daughter. "It's un-American!"

"Anti-Texan!" Noah agreed.

Macy grinned, but she didn't partake of the meat platters. She turned to the youngest member of the family. "Lily, how did you do on your tests?"

Lily's face beamed with a smile. "I aced them! I got my scores yesterday. Do you want to see them?" At her sister's nod of agreement, Lily bolted from the table and ran for the stairs.

"Honestly!" Carole exclaimed. "She knows better!"

"It's important to her," Macy reminded her mother.

A cell phone rang, and everyone looked around to see who was guilty of not turning off their phone during a family meal. It was considered rude by their father. All heads looked towards their paternal elder, as it was indeed, Daniel's phone.

"I'm sorry, Carole. I have to take this," Daniel exclaimed, rising from the table. "It's about Noah filling in while the drummer for the Stallions is in the hospital."

"Who gets to yell at him for not turning his phone off at the dinner table?" Noah mumbled to Micah.

"You've been asked to take over for Jason Allen?" Micah asked.

"Yeah, he's going to be in rehab with a broken neck for at least four months from plowing his car into a ditch. He has to wear one of those halo things that are screwed into your skull!" Noah answered. "Ritchie called Coyote wanting him to do it, but he passed. He said he's too busy to take on a part-time gig. Coyote called Dad to see if I could do it. Man, I would be stupid to pass on the opportunity, but Dad has all these rules!"

Micah nodded knowingly. "No drugs, no drinking, no smoking, no swearing around the kids," he quoted from memory.

"Yeah," Noah grumbled. "Geeze, it's rock and roll, not an amateur church show. It's not like these guys are dope heads or anything. Three of the guy's tour with their families."

"Good deal," Micah said, giving his youngest brother a high-five.

Lily came running into the dining room and handed an envelope to Macy. "These are my scores. I averaged ninety-eight percent on the tests. "I will be starting at Adams Academy in September."

"Good for you, kiddo," Micah exclaimed. "A McKenna in a prep school. That's newsworthy!"

"We haven't made the final decision," Carole said, giving Lily a stern look."

"Yes, we have," Lily countered. "I'm starting Adams Academy in September."

"What about your ballet classes?" Macy asked.

"Adams Academy will work a student's classes around what they call accomplished *artistic endeavors*," Lily said, stuffing her test results into the envelope. "If you are good enough at something, like piano or cello…"

"Or ballet," Macy interjected.

Lily shrugged. "Or ballet. They will work your school schedule around your artistic classes. They will even provide the transportation. Not that it matters. I'm dropping ballet to concentrate on academics."

"Why?" Macy asked, surprised. "I've seen you dance. You are very talented! I thought you loved dancing."

"I do love dancing, but Aunt Carole doesn't think I'm good enough, so why bother!" Lily said sulkily.

"Don't take that tone with me, young lady," Carole warned. "I am not forcing you to stop taking dance lessons."

"No, you are the one that won't let me study with Madam Bashlofski," Lily snapped back.

"That is enough, Lily," Carole exclaimed. "Take those papers to your room. We will discuss if you are going to the academy at a later time."

"What do you mean, if?" Lily demanded. "You promised, I could go! You gave me your word that if I made the admittance grades I could go!"

"I said no such thing!" Carole denied firmly. "I have had enough of your attitude!"

"I don't have an attitude!" Lily exclaimed. "What I have is a guardian that won't keep her word!"

"Lily, that is enough!" Carole snapped. "Go to your room!"

"Of course! You can lie and break your promises, but when I call you on it, I am the one that gets punished!" Lily shouted as she ran from the room.

Micah and Noah's heads had been following the verbal volley back forth, but wisely keeping their mouths shut.

Macy, on the other hand, had laid her fork down. "Why didn't you let her study with Madam Bashlofski?" she asked calmly.

"Because I didn't think she was ready for that kind of a program."

Macy's lips tightened with anger. "Of course, since you are the *expert*, you made that decision for her. A decision that could have a catastrophic impact on Lily's training for years if she chooses to be a dancer!"

"I don't have to be an expert to know what is right for her," Carole said tightly. "Lily has suffered a great deal for a child her age. She doesn't need the pressure of taking on training that intense."

"Lily is too young to remember very much before we were adopted. More likely, it's that what she wants differs from what you want for her," Macy snapped. "Madam Bashlofski only takes three new students a year. She only makes an offer to the best!"

Lily stomped into the room, holding her cell phone.

"I told you to go to your room," Carole exclaimed.

Lily pushed the button on her phone.

*"Mom, you promise?"*

*"Yes, I promise," Carole's voice repeated back.*

*"You swear," Lily's young voice asked. "You swear that if I pass the entrance exams and get accepted that I can go to Adams Academy, starting in September. Say it, Mom!" Lily's voice insisted.*

*"Say what?" Carole exclaimed.*

*"Say it, all of it," Lily insisted.*

*"Goodness, Lily," Carole's voice exclaimed. "I promise that if you pass the entrance exams with good grades that you can go to Adams in September. Is that what you want?"*

*"Yes," Lily insisted. "That's exactly what I want!"*

Carole got to her feet and faced her daughter in anger. "How dare you record me! Is this any way to treat your mother?"

"You're not my mother!" Lily shouted. "Technically, the only connection we have is that you think you're my warden! You won't let me go to a normal school, you won't let me study ballet. You promised I could go to Adams, but as usual, you are the liar!" Lily snatched the phone and ran from the room.

"This is why I don't want her taking on anything extra," Carole said wearily. "Lily has been behaving horribly lately. She won't even try to finish her home-schooling work. Her grades have dropped significantly. I don't know what has gotten into her, but she's becoming more and more difficult."

Macy pushed away from the table and shook her head in disbelief. "What's gotten into her? You're doing it again!"

"Doing what?" Carole exclaimed. She seemed to be confused.

"Trying to force your will over what she wants. Lily has gone to public schools all her life, but you suddenly pulled her from regular school for home-schooling last year. She was a straight-A student. She hates homeschooling, and she misses her friends. She has been in ballet since she was four-years-old, and when she gets an opportunity of a lifetime, you sabotaged her dreams!" Macy exploded. "First, it was me, and now it is Lily."

"I allowed you to go to Paris!" Carole exclaimed. "You were too young to leave home, and I won't let that happen again!"

"You didn't allow anything. Dad made the decision, and I had to almost kill myself to make my parents understand how important dance was to me!" Macy exclaimed, then she lowered her voice and spat the words of accusation in anger. "You turned down my offer from Madam Bashlofski when I was eleven. I could have had five years of world-class training by the time I got to Paris. But, no, what you wanted was more important than what I wanted. I lost out on five years of working with one of the premier ballet instructors in the world because of you!"

"She wouldn't take Allison," Carole snapped. "I wasn't

about to let that woman separate you girls, and I'm not going to let her interfere with Lily either!"

"Allison didn't have the talent or the work ethic to become a professional dancer!" Macy shouted. "The offer was for me! Not Allison. Why was I denied what I wanted because you didn't think I should ever do anything that didn't include her?"

"Because I thought it was best to keep you two together!" Carole explained. "You're twins, you should be close."

"For God's sake! We weren't born conjoined!" Macy yelled. "We don't have the same interests or talents. We never did, and we never will. I was the one that earned the right to study under Madam Bashlofski. I was the one that was denied my place in her classes. You favored Allison over me! I was the one you held back, and now you are doing the same thing with Lily!"

"Lily is a child, and as her parent, I will make the decisions for her. If she is still interested later, she can study with Madam Bashlofski when she is older!"

"That is a lie, and you know it. Madam only takes the best, and she only makes the offer once. If it's turned down, there is no second chance. She will find another student to take the slot. You ruined my chance to work with her, and now you have ruined Lily's chance. How could you?"

"Lily is too young, the same as you were to make that kind of decision. She will forget. She will get over it, and when the time is right, she will be able to make responsible decisions."

Macy threw her napkin on the table and got to her feet. "When someone shatters your dreams, you don't get over it! You don't forget it, and more importantly, you don't forgive it! I will not allow you to destroy my sister as you tried to destroy me!"

Carole shook her head. "You don't understand, and you never have. I was protecting you!"

"You were killing me!" Macy said in a deadly calm voice.

She turned to Micah, and tears were shimmering on her lashes. "I'm going to wait in the car."

The front door slammed with a solid thud, and Noah and Micah exchanged glances.

Carole excused herself, and with tears running down her face, she ran to the master bedroom.

"Daddy?" Katie's voice was small and scared.

Micah reached for his daughter and pulled her into his lap.

"No one is mad at you, honey," Micah reassured his daughter. "You're not used to hearing arguments, but sometimes they happen between grownups."

Daniel stuck his head from his den, called for Noah, and passed the phone to the boy as he jogged by. He looked around the empty table. "Where did everyone go?"

"Go get your things, Katikins," Micah said, giving his daughter a push towards the foyer.

"What happened to dinner?" Daniel demanded. "Where are your mother and the girls?"

"You missed a major dust-up, Dad," Micah said. "Mom left the room, crying. Lily went to her room, crying, and Macy went to my Land Rover, crying. They are all upset."

"What about?" Daniel demanded.

Micah shook his head. "Dad, you need to talk to Lily, and you need to have a long conversation with Mom. Those two have issues that need to be resolved before this situation gets worse."

"What about Macy?" Daniel asked.

"I'm no psychologist, but having spent time with one for the last couple of years, I would say her part in this is a lot of unresolved anger. There are some major underlying problems here that I didn't know about. Dig a little deeper, Dad, and find out what is going on. I'll catch you later."

"Hey, isn't anyone going to eat?" Noah asked, coming into the room and sitting at his place at the table.

"The women are mad at each other, and I'm taking off for higher ground," Micah admitted.

Micah gave his father a hug, his brother a high-five, and led his daughter from the house. Macy was curled in the passenger seat. She wasn't crying, but her face was tear-stained, and her eyes were still flashing with anger.

After getting Katie strapped into her safety seat, Micah got in and shook his head faintly. He nodded towards his daughter in the backseat when his sister looked like she was going to speak.

Once he was sure his daughter was safely occupied, he reached over, took his sister's hand, and gave it a squeeze. "She can still hear, even with the headphones on. We need to postpone any discussion until we get home," he said quietly

Macy nodded, but she looked out the side window, and Micah saw her wipe more tears away. A comfortable silence settled between the two siblings. It was only occasionally broken by a sweet, but slightly off-key voice singing along with her favorite cartoon movie.

Micah had Katie complete her homework when they arrived home. Macy unloaded the dishwasher behind them as schoolwork was done at the kitchen table. After he reviewed his daughter's homework, he sent her off to the family room to play.

## Chapter 8

When it was only the two of them, Micah gave his sister a look of inquiry. "Are we going to ignore the dead elephant in the middle of the room?" he asked.

She shook her head. "No, I'm not the quiet little mouse I used to be. I tend to speak my mind now."

"I'll say," Micah agreed. "That was pretty explosive stuff. I've never heard of Madam What's Her Name."

"No, you wouldn't have. Mom and Dad would have kept that episode of my life a secret. They wouldn't have wanted to spoil their perfect image as parents," Macy murmured bitterly.

When her brother gave her a look of disapproval, she returned it with one of frustration. "Madam Bashlofski was trained at the Vaganova Academy in St. Petersburg and was a prima ballerina for the Karinainsky Ballet Company. After she retired, she married a wealthy Texan and opened a school in San Antonio. Training with Madam is a *coup d'état* in the dancing world. Mom not allowing me to attend her school was a slap in the face to me, and to Madam Bashlofski. It was a setback that I had to work years to overcome."

"I'm sure Mom was only doing what she thought was best for you," Micah said as his sister began pacing.

"Was she?" Macy demanded. "Then tell me why Mom continually downplayed or dismissed my interests and talents in favor of Allison's?

"She had her own propaganda that she used to brainwash me for years. *Macy, you are more talented than your sister, we can't let her be discouraged and hurt. Macy, you will have your chance later, it's not going to hurt you do this for Allison, now. Macy give! Macy step back! Macy apologize!*

"The only time I was truly myself was when I was dancing. When I danced, I soared. When I began to excel in ballet, Allison decided to quit. Mom assumed I would stop too. She has favored Allison, ever since we came to live with your family," Macy walked over to the patio door and stared outward toward the lake. "And they wonder why I don't come home or visit?"

"They let you go to Paris for training."

"Do you know why?" Macy demanded.

"I thought it was because they believed in your talent," Micah said.

"If only it were that simple," Macy snorted. "Mom turned down my offer to train with Madam Bashlofski, and she acted like it was an insult, not an honor. She tried to get me to quit ballet altogether. Honest to God, she deliberately made me late for classes. When I was given a primary role, she sabotaged me every time by telling my teacher that she couldn't get me to extra practices.

"The letter with the scholarship offer for Paris Opéra Ballet School came in early January, and Mom intercepted it. She opened my mail! My mail! And, she hid it from me! You can't pretend that wasn't deliberate.

"I didn't know about it until the end of February. She sent me to her room to get something from the top drawer of her bureau. I guess she forgot she had hidden the letter there. If she had destroyed it, I would never have known!

"There it was. A placement offer in a summer program, and if I was as good as they believed I was, a full scholarship into the Paris Opéra Ballet School to start in September. I confronted her about it, and she said flat-out no. She wasn't going to allow her daughter to leave home and go live in Paris.

"Mom knew how important ballet was to me, but she didn't care. She did care about her never-ending crusade of supporting what Allison wanted to do! I begged her, and I called Dad and pleaded with him. Dad was involved with you guys at the time. He didn't know what was going on at home. He told me Mom knew best. Damn it to hell! It still makes me mad!"

"They let you go," Micah reminded his sister.

"Only because it was a doctor's recommendation! I had a breakdown, Micah," Macy said bluntly. "I shut down. I stopped caring, and I stopped eating. It didn't seem to matter what I wanted. I was being sabotaged by Mom and Allison. I wasn't in control of anything important to me. Mom and Dad were dealing with the careers of three superstar sons and a drama queen! I got lost. Dad has always had this blind faith that Mom is the perfect mother. I'm not saying Mom is a bad mother, but she screwed me over, and now she's messing with Lily. The facts speak for themselves.

"When Mom told me I had to quit ballet because I was hurting Allison, something snapped. She was making me stop something I lived for because she needed to take Allison to summer acting camp! I was fighting a battle I couldn't win, and I stopped trying. I couldn't control anything in my life, and I didn't see any reason to keep trying."

"Why don't I remember any of this?" Micah said. "Where was I?"

"You were working on your first soundtrack in Austin. You

were also flying on the weekends to wherever the next concert was scheduled. Micah, I'm not blaming you, or anyone else, except Mom. Your schedules were brutal in those days, and you were rarely home. There was too much going on in your lives for you to notice. I'm surprised you didn't have a breakdown yourself! You were so busy, you couldn't possibly have known what was going on at home!"

"That doesn't excuse me from not noticing that you were ill," Micah said. "You were thin, but you have always been thin. I don't remember anyone saying anything about you having an eating disorder."

"I didn't have an eating disorder," Macy denied. "If anything, I had a mental breakdown. I quit eating because it was the only thing in my life I could control. I understand this now, Micah. I didn't understand it when I was fifteen. It wasn't about starving myself, or my self-image. It was about a lack of control over my life."

"Control?"

Macy nodded. "From early March to May, I lost twenty percent of my body weight. I was screaming for help, although I never uttered a sound. I could go days without saying a word, and no one noticed. I disappeared in the hysterics of our homegrown drama queen and a mother that couldn't or wouldn't see me or what I needed.

"Mom could hear and see Allison loud and clear. I was invisible! It's like I never existed except as a support system for Allison, and I don't know why."

Micah hugged Macy to him. "You were so quiet, compared to Allison. I assumed you were going along with whatever she wanted because you wanted it too."

"No, I went along with the agenda because I was brainwashed and trained to give in to what she wanted," Macy said. "I did go along with it until I was told I had to give up ballet. Something broke inside me."

"I'm so sorry, Sissy. I wish you had said something!"

She shook her head. "No one paid enough attention to know. Sully and Dad flew home one weekend. It had something to do with contracts for him to do a movie or something. Sully saw it. He dragged me downstairs one day, lifted my loose sweatshirt, and showed Mom and Dad that every rib and vertebra was sticking out.

"The folks went into hysterics. They took me to a doctor, and I was checked into the hospital for tests. They thought I had cancer or something, but after several days of testing, the doctors sent me to a psychologist.

"Dr. Bailey got to the source of the problem in about thirty minutes. Mom went into total denial. Dad went into panic mode. He tried to take the blame, but Dad has blinders on when it comes to Mom. He thinks she's perfect, and believe me, she's not! I still blame Mom.

"She refused then, and she still refuses to believe, that she favors Allison over me. She quite literally drove me almost to the brink of no return. I weighed seventy-two pounds when I was checked into the hospital.

"After several sessions with the psychologist, Dr. Bailey told Dad that the best thing they could do was to let me go to Paris and gain my independence. He told them I needed distance from Mom and Allison, and the freedom to follow my dreams. Dr. Bailey saved my life. Dad made the decision to let me go to Paris. Mom was still squawking about my leaving Allison behind."

"I had no idea," Micah exclaimed, shaking his head. "I was so busy trying to prove myself and involved with the film score that I didn't realize you were sick. Dear God, Sissy, I'm sorry!"

"You aren't at fault," Macy said. "My love of ballet brought me to my senses. The first order of business at school was a weigh-in. I was told that I needed to gain weight. They gave the orders, and if I didn't gain weight, I wouldn't be allowed in the program. The school was and is very aware and proactive about eating disorders. I started eating everything in sight and discovered French pastries in the process. I started gaining weight, and I regained my health and strength within a few months."

"Have you had any side effects?" Micah demanded.

"Not that I know about. My choices have made me who and what I am. I love my life, Micah. I'm not stepping back into time. I won't tolerate Mom's warped perception of Allison being the charmed daughter that can do no wrong. I took a backseat to my sister for years. Now, for whatever reason, Lily has become her target."

"They let you go," Micah repeated.

"You don't get it," Macy exclaimed in frustration. "They were forced to let me go. You older boys formed a band when you were kids! Did Mom or Dad tell you that you were too young to record an album to sell it locally? Did they tell you that they didn't think you were good enough to make it?"

Micah shook his head. "No, never. They encouraged us."

"Exactly," Macy said, making her point. "I can't tell you how many times, Mom tried to *reason* with me; telling me, I didn't need to take ballet lessons anymore. She refused to let me train under Madam Bashlofski, and my offer came when I was eleven, the same age Lily is now. She denied an opportunity of a lifetime for me and didn't blink an eye while doing it. I wouldn't have had to leave home to get excellent training. Madam Bashlofski's school is in San Antonio, eighteen miles from our house!

"Mom's excuse that time was that Allison *needed* to take a special acrobatic class. Allison *needed* her attention. What about what I needed? Mom said she couldn't be in two places at one time. It was more important for my sister to enroll in an acrobatic workshop than for me to take ballet. A class that Allison dropped after four lessons because it was too *hard*! For Christ's sake, our parents are millionaires! Mom could have ordered chauffeured limos for both of us, but she didn't. She tried to squash my talent and ambitions in favor of Allison's meandering interests!

"Now, for whatever reason, Mom has decided that Lily is getting the stepsister treatment. My first instinct was to call the airline and go home."

Micah covered his sister's hand with his own and held it for a long moment. "Don't. Family problems can't be resolved with you in London. Stay at least until Dad's birthday. That's only six weeks away, and you have already set up a schedule for your physical therapy."

Macy closed her eyes and took a deep breath. "I've already considered my options and decided against leaving. I'm not a coward, and I am not going to let Mom do to Lily what she did to me! I need to spend some time with Lily and get to the truth about how she is being treated.

"I won't deal with Mom, but I will try to get it into Dad's thick head, that she isn't perfect! Something has gone very wrong here, very wrong. Lily was a straight-A student before she was pulled from her school. Why? And, you heard the tape! Why would Mom let Lily take the admission tests if she had no intention of letting her go? There's no logic to what is going on."

"Mom didn't say she couldn't go. She said she hadn't made up her mind yet," Micah said.

"I've heard that kind of double-talk before," Macy said. "Mom has no intention of letting Lily go to the academy."

"I think you need to have a meeting, and a calm discussion with the folks," Micah suggested. "No, yelling!"

"I'm not promising that," Macy said with a toss of her hair, but her eyes were troubled. "Could I have one of those lovely lattés you make? I'll make breakfast tomorrow."

Micah knew a change of subjects when he heard it. He

went to the coffee station in his kitchen and began to assemble what he needed to make the lattés. "Chocolate or caramel?"

"Both," Macy answered. "I'm greedy, I want both."

He smiled and got the machine going. "Good because you need to gain a few pounds." He reached into an upper cabinet, produced a box of chocolate-covered cookies, and motioned for his sister to go out on the deck.

"God! A month of eating like this, and I'll need an eating disorder to fit into my clothes," Macy moaned as she bit into a cookie.

Micah knocked debris off a glider and sat down, looking over the lake and enjoying the view for a few moments.

"I knew there were hard feelings between you and Allison. I didn't know about you and Mom. It explains why you've kept your distance, and don't want to come back to the States."

"There are other reasons, professional and private reasons," Macy said.

"None of this makes any sense to me," Micah said. "What you have described sounds deliberately spiteful, and that is not the person I know as my mother."

Macy shrugged. "You have your reality. I have mine. Why do you think I was gobsmacked when she called me from the airport with no warning? Even that had more to do with trying to manipulate me into helping Allison than it did with supporting me after surgery. The sad part was... when I discovered Mom's hidden agenda, I wasn't surprised."

Micah's cell phone rang, and he checked it. "Dad," he said to his sister.

"I am not ready or willing to talk to him or Mom," Macy said bluntly. "Dad will automatically fall back on his *Mom is always right* stance, and I won't stand for it. I need to send a few e-mails to my friends. May I use your computer?"

"Dad," Micah answered his phone. "I'll call you back in a minute," he said and disconnected.

"Use my office computer. The password is SoSheDances, no spaces."

"One of your favorite songs," Macy said. "Thanks."

Micah dialed his father back. He listened for a few minutes, but he disagreed with Daniel McKenna.

"I don't think you have the whole story, Dad. Have you talked to Lily?"

Micah listened and responded, "No, you have to get Lily to explain what is going on, and listen to her. Really listen to her. Make her play the recording for you. The recording is important. Once you do, you will understand why Lily is so angry. This is about Mom breaking a promise. It's also about Lily not getting a fair chance to fulfill her dreams."

Micah listened again before responding, "Macy is a different problem, and yes, she is angry and upset. No, I haven't heard from anyone. Coyote is an adult, he's not required to check in with me."

Again his father spoke before Micah replied, "Dad, this comes under the heading of you being the Head of your House. You and Mom have been a team for years, but sometimes you have to assess the situation and make a decision based on more than her opinion. What Lily wants and needs is important too. Think back six years? Macy was on a self-imposed death march because she was being denied a chance to follow her dreams. It's happening again."

Micah took the cookies and his empty cup into the kitchen. He hid the cookies since they were a sugar overload that he didn't want his daughter to consume and loaded a few dishes in the dishwasher.

Macy came into the kitchen.

"Did you find everything you needed?" Micah asked.

Macy smiled. "Far more. That is a sweet configuration. Do you launch missiles from here? Micah, if my being here is going to cause problems, I can stay with some friends of mine."

"Don't be silly," Micah said. "Maybe you didn't return to Texas voluntarily, but remember that you do have family here that loves you. Once you return to London, you may not get another break from your career for a while."

"That's true, too," Macy admitted.

"I talked to Dad. He wants to have a family meeting."

"Of course he does," Macy said, shaking her head dismissively. "He may not like what I have to say."

"I warned him," Micah admitted with a chuckle.

---

Micah considered his options, and he asked Macy, and Coyote if they would watch Katie for him overnight Friday and part of Saturday. He had been trying for three days to reach Tess, but her phone message said she was working. She wasn't supposed to be working. Her last official day at the hospital had been Wednesday the week before. She had promised that she would come to the lake. So far, she had continued to work, and she wasn't filling in with extra hours. She had been pulling long fourteen- and sixteen-hour shifts. Enough was enough.

He cruised the hospital parking lot, found her car, parked by it for a few minutes, and then he parked his Land Rover in the empty Head of Administration slot. As he walked by the security officer standing inside the main entrance, the young man stopped him.

"Sir, you can't park there."

"He's not here, is he?" Micah asked.

"No, sir, but you still can't park there, Mr. McKenna," the guard said.

Recognition had its perks. Micah glanced at the guard's

nametag. "The Head of Administration goes home on time every day, doesn't he, Jerome?"

"Usually, sir," the guard said.

"I'll only be here a short time," Micah promised. "A doctor I know is working here and hasn't been able to go home because she is overworked. She doesn't seem to be capable of saying no."

"I wouldn't know anything about that," the guard admitted.

"I do," Micah exclaimed. "I'll be right back. Emergency is that direction, right?"

The guard nodded.

"Jerome, you will watch over my vehicle, won't you? There has been increasing crime in this area lately."

"Yes, sir, Mr. McKenna," the guard nodded. He bent his head and whispered, "Will you sign an autograph for me? To prove to my wife that I met you!"

"On my way out, absolutely. We'll take a selfie together, and send it to her," Micah said with a smile. He passed through the double doors to another desk. "Excuse me, is Dr. Foster around here somewhere?"

"Yes, although she might have left," the nurse answered, and her eyes widened as she recognized him.

"She hasn't. Where would she be? Never mind there she is," Micah said, walking further into the restricted emergency area. Tess was talking to a male doctor and a nurse.

Tess was surprised to see Micah striding toward her. He had that 'don't mess with me' look she'd seen before, but not for a while. "What's wrong?" she demanded. "Who has been brought in?"

"No one, I'm here for you," Micah exclaimed. "Are you off duty?"

"Yes, I punched out, but why are you here?"

"I'm here because you have worked over a hundred hours

in the last six days. Enough is enough, Tess. You don't work here any longer," Micah said.

"We've been short-staffed," Tess said, noticing that every doctor, nurse, attendant, and patient were either watching or trying to listen.

"That shouldn't be *we*. You gave notice. You don't work here. Staff shortages are the Administrator's problem, not yours," Micah said firmly. "He is taking advantage of you. We are going home."

Tess pulled Micah aside. "Micah, don't make a scene. I work with these people."

"I don't give a damn about these people," Micah said in an equally hushed voice. "Have you looked in a mirror lately? Your eyes are blood-shot, you have bags under them, and you are as white as a sheet. You are walking exhaustion. You told me the worst was over, and you would be able to rest, but you are not doing it. You are letting the hospital staff take advantage of you, and I won't have it."

"I'm on my way out."

"Yes, you are," Micah repeated. "With me, now!"

"Micah!"

"Tess!" Micah snapped with a steel tone to his voice she hadn't heard in a long time. "Don't argue. You won't win."

"We are going to talk about this!" Tess threatened.

"Fine! But it will be after you have had twelve hours of sleep!"

"All right!" Tess exclaimed. "I have to get my purse!"

"I'll be waiting, and I am driving," Micah said with a glint in his eye. "You are too tired to be driving. I've already disabled your car."

Tess stopped in her tracks and glared at him. "I can call security."

"Go ahead, Jerome Latimore is watching over my Land

Rover," Micah said mildly. "I have to stop and have my picture taken with him on the way out. His wife is a fan."

Tess slammed into the locker room, opened her locker, and grabbed her purse.

Belinda McGuire, a young night nurse, came in behind her, followed by two more nurses. "Do you know him?"

"Yes, I know the idiot," Tess snapped.

"You know Micah McKenna?" one of the other nurses asked again. "What about Sully or Coyote?"

Tess closed her eyes. "Yes, I know them. I've known them since we were children!" She ignored the women and left the locker room. The man himself had followed her and was leaning against the wall.

"Ready?" she demanded.

"When you are M'lady," he said with a grin, pushing away from the wall. He offered his hand to her.

Tess was furious, but she was also aware that every woman in the department was watching her with envy. Micah was such a damnably charming man, and he didn't have to say a single word. It was his confidence and the gentleness in his eyes. She took his hand, but she refused to look at anyone as he escorted her from the hospital.

## Chapter 9

Micah opened his eyes to two things that were delightfully different from his normal. It was daylight, and he was snuggled into Tess's breasts. She was still asleep, and she was gloriously naked.

As she stirred, she stretched lazily like a cat before she jerked awake. Her eyes flew open, and she jumped.

"Easy, there," Micah exclaimed.

Tess curled into him. "Sorry, I'm used to racing against the clock. What time is it?"

"It's only six a.m. Go back to sleep."

She shook her head. "I'm used to catching sleep in short naps rather than long stretches."

"How do you do it?" Micah asked. "I have worked long hours before, but not the kind of hours you put in regularly. How can it be safe? Doctors treating patients when they're so tired they are walking zombies?"

"We run on adrenaline, and there are overlapping shifts. One doctor is fresh while another is winding down. We can usually find downtime and catch a nap here and there. We cover for each other, run our diagnoses against each other. It's standard procedure. Hopefully, that is now in my past. I haven't really decided what I'm going to do next."

"I'm hungry. Let's go for something to eat."

"We can eat the leftovers from last night," Tess said.

Micah shook his head. "I like my three meals separate and defined as breakfast, lunch, and supper. Reheated manicotti is not my idea of breakfast." He shuddered.

"Doctors and nurses get in the habit of eating whatever is available and edible. Cold pizza for breakfast, donuts for dinner."

"We're going to have to set new rules."

"Really?" Tess exclaimed incredulously.

"Yes. Regular hours, regular eating, regular loving. You need a good breakfast. Why don't we go to Shorely's? They have fantastic pancakes."

"Ha! Who has been out of the loop? Shorely's closed last year," Tess said dryly.

Micah looked stunned. "No, kidding?"

"You don't visit the Riverwalk area very much," she reminded him.

"No, I come by and check on Farinelli's Restaurant and the apartments above it, once in a while."

"You don't want to become a recluse, Micah. It's not healthy," Tess warned.

He shook his head. "I haven't, and don't try to psycho-analyze me. I had a bad relationship, and I lost two of my best friends and gained a daughter. Contrary to the tabloids' reports, I'm not hiding out. I haven't had a break-down. I've been busy. Try using your psychobabble on yourself and figure out why you are afraid of taking time off!"

Tess jolted into a sitting position, and the covers fell from her body. She gave him a shove with her hand. "Psychobabble! It's not my specialty, but don't insult my profession! You have to admit you've taken the break-up with Carla a lot harder than most men. Most people just move on!"

"It's hard to move on when you're dealing with a crazy person who is trying to destroy you!"

Tess studied him for a few minutes. "You've never told me what happened. I never asked before, because it wasn't any of my business. I think it is now. What have you been hiding?"

Micah faced her. "This goes no further than you, ever. The Carla I was living with, the woman I was trying to build a future with, wasn't who I thought she was. I wanted marriage, permanence, and, eventually, children. She didn't, and her excuses had worn thin. Even before I had my 'wake-up stupid' moment, we were on shaky ground, very shaky ground. The constant break-ups and reconciliations were a clear sign that she didn't want anything permanent. I was too dumb to see it.

"We had a meeting scheduled with a client in New York City, and I came down with a killer head cold and an ear infection. She went to the meeting, and I stayed home and went to the doctor. Generally, I respect people's privacy, but she called me for financial stats she'd left behind. I was looking for the paperwork, and I didn't find it where she told me she'd put it. We shared an office at the townhouse. I couldn't find it in my files, and I went into Carla's. They weren't locked or hidden. I wasn't intentionally invading her privacy. I discovered a file that indicated that Carla had had an abortion."

"She didn't tell you?" Tess asked.

He shook his head. "When the shock wore off, I kept searching, both at the home office and in her work office. Over the years we were together, she had at least three abortions. She never told me. I also found an alter ego Facebook page. During our break-ups, and even while we were together, she'd was involved with other men."

"Bitch!" Tess exclaimed.

"I've never actually called her that, but I've thought it a

million times. I thought I was in a monogamous relationship. Obviously, I wasn't. I'm not the kind of man who wants anything to do with an *open relationship*. The more I investigated, the more I discovered. I called Stan, and he hired a detective. In less than twenty-four hours, I was sent photographs. She'd used the business trip to be with another man. Someone I knew and had worked with on several projects.

"When Carla came back, her belongings were in a rented Pod outside. I'd heard all the screaming, the yelling, and all the excuses before. Of course, everything was *my fault*. The terminations were the final straw.

"For her, it was her body, her choice, her right. Fine, but those babies were also a part of me. At least, I think they were. You don't live with someone, have a relationship with someone, and not even discuss it!"

"Bitch! How could she?" Tess repeated.

"That's what I kept asking," Micah said.

"Now, it makes sense," Tess said.

"I don't take relationships lightly," Micah said. "Please remember it."

"I know, and I will. If we ever run into Carla again, I may have to deck her," Tess rose from the bed fully naked and headed for the bathroom.

Micah followed her but stood outside the door to give her a few moments of privacy. He stepped inside when she turned on the shower and was waiting for the water to warm. "It hasn't been easy. My first instinct was to give Carla what she wanted and be done with it. But the deeper we dug into things, the more I realized how much I'd been duped. That's when I decided to fight fire with fire.

"When she started fighting dirty, Stan Mulclusky waded into the trenches with me. He never liked her, and he was more than capable of dealing with her and preserving my reputation. I'll have you know, I have been advised many times by friends on how I *should* have handled the situation. Some of their solutions were brutal.

"I was trying to take the higher ground, but she made that impossible. There's nothing Stan likes better than to take on a good fight."

Tess turned to him with a grin. "Oh, I know that for sure, and while a good mud-slinging competition isn't necessarily the way to go, you had the dirt on her!"

Micah nodded and stepped into the shower behind her. "I was trying to be a decent guy and not totally destroy her. Stan kept telling me to forget it, and go in for the kill. Metaphorically speaking, of course." He lowered his head and captured her lips.

Breakfast was pop-tarts and cold cereal without milk eaten straight from the box. Still, it was worth it for the time spent together learning how to satisfy other appetites. They spent the morning and most of the afternoon in Tess's bed. Tess took naps in between long sessions of sex.

When Tess stretched and yawned and opened her eyes, she realized that for the first time in months, she wasn't fatigued.

"Wow, how long have I been asleep this time?"

"Five hours, this time," Micah said, looking over from where he was sitting in a chair with his ever-present music notebook in hand. "You look better. There's color in your face, and it's not gray! The shadows under your eyes are lighter, too."

"That's a result of the orgasms you are giving me every time I do wake up," Tess admitted with a smile.

He returned her smile and tossed his notebook on the floor. "Come here."

Tess walked over to him, still naked, uninhibited, and beautiful. He pulled her into his lap.

"Now, I want you to tell me what the heck has been going on this past week," Micah demanded. "You said your contract was over. You said you were coming to the lake, and you didn't. Instead, you have been working yourself to death!"

"I'm used to hard work. I've been pulling these crazy schedules for years. You weren't around to harass me about it," Tess said, laying her head on his shoulder.

"That doesn't answer my question."

Tess shrugged. "We've been swamped!"

"It's not *we*, Tess. You don't officially work for the hospital anymore. Now, what's going on?"

She shook her head and closed her eyes.

Micah knew Tess. He raised his hand and smacked her hard on the bare ass.

"Micah!" she straightened and tried to remove herself from his grip. "I can't believe you did that!"

Another spank landed precisely in the same stinging spot and another and another. Tess was trying to get off his lap, but he had a tight grip on her.

"Micah!"

"I want to know what is going on," Micah demanded. "If I have to ask again, you're going over my knee!"

"I'm not a kid!" Tess exclaimed, jumping to her feet.

"Neither am I," Micah said. "Talk to me!"

Tess took three steps in one direction, reversed herself, and paced angrily across the floor. "Micah McKenna, I will not..."

"Enough," Micah warned. "You know me, Tess. I spanked you for the first time when you were about twelve! I haven't changed. Yeah, I have given you a few playful spanks during sex, and you liked it, but there's a difference between play and for real. You are pushing for the real thing, and that was a teaser. Now, tell me what is going on."

Tess sat on the bed, jumped to her feet, and pulled on a white tee shirt and bikini panties. "I've been working toward my goal of specialization of cardiothoracic surgery for eleven years. Working in the ER has paid for a lot of that training."

"I know, you're one of the smartest people I have ever known," Micah said. "That's taking into account that I have a card-carrying Mensa genius as a younger brother."

When she didn't say anything further, Micah moved to sit on the bed, and she sat beside him.

"I was rejected by Dr. Dennison's program."

"So?" Micah asked. "You said you didn't particularly want to work with her anyway."

"That's not the point!" Tess exclaimed.

"What is the point, Tess?"

"I've never been rejected before," Tess mumbled.

Micah smiled.

Tess bounced to her feet and pointed a finger at him. "This is not funny!"

"No, it's not," Micah agreed. "Tessa, everyone gets rejected at some time in their life."

"I haven't!"

"Then, you've been very lucky," Micah exclaimed. "I wish I could say the same. Tess…"

"You've been a golden boy since you were sixteen! What have you ever been rejected from?" Tess demanded angrily.

"Lots of things," Micah admitted. "Songs that I wanted to publish and people told me they were crap. Jobs I wanted, and they wouldn't even consider me because of my music career or because of preconceived ideas about who and what I am."

Tess sat beside him again. "What if I don't make the grade, and I don't get any offers?"

"Stop it," Micah said, pulling her into his lap. "So, you didn't get a job offer. Once! You explained the program to me, and you also said you didn't think it would be a good fit! Why are you throwing yourself into a blind panic? You haven't even had your first interview with that Dr. Snowman guy at the Naval Hospital. If I know you and I do, you have at least a half dozen applications in for fellowships and job possibilities. True?"

Tess nodded. "It's not Snowman. It's Dr. Kirby Frost at the National Naval Hospital. He is one of the best in his field."

"Honey, so are you. You have the credentials. You stayed at the Dell Seton because of Lauren, and your nieces. You needed to be here for them. Tess, one rejection shouldn't have thrown you off-kilter like this. You have an overload of skills. They wouldn't be trying to hang onto you so desperately at the hospital if you didn't. You run an ER department, and that's not easy. You also have credentials there for the surgical department."

"Hospital departments are territorial. They rarely let me operate," Tess complained. "I know I am good at running an ER, but that's not what I wanted to specialize in. ER has paid the bills. I need to get accepted into a program or fellowship that is my preferred specialty."

"You will if that's what you want," Micah said. "You've also said you might change directions. Use this break to think about what you want to do. No one says that a goal you made at sixteen has to be the end-all goal for your life. You can change your mind and go in another direction if that's what you want."

"My head tells me the same thing, but then I go into a panic, and think, what if I don't get another offer? What if I have to return to the ER?"

"Would that be so horrible? You save lives every day! Tess, you are physically and mentally exhausted. You have been going full blast all these years with no downtime, no vacations, and no way to get away from the stress.

"You're coming to the lake as you promised. You are going to sleep late, eat decently, and relax enough to be able to focus on what you really want and go after it. You didn't want the Dennison Program, so it's no loss. How many other medical practices or fellowships have you found that you are really interested in?"

Tess sprawled back on the bed. "Three positions are local, and I'd kind of like the idea of staying local. Lauren is based here, and so are you. There are five other positions and fellowships scattered over the country. I'll be doing some traveling this summer."

Micah grinned and pulled her over to him, and with a quick move, she was yanked over his lap.

"Don't you dare!" Tess threatened.

Micah whacked her across the bottom hard.

"Micah!" Tess squealed.

"We need to work on getting you de-stressed. I believe in D/D, Tess. One of the tenets is maintenance spankings. Maintenance spankings don't require a reason, they can be given *just because* the dominant partner believes you need one. The intention isn't to punish or discipline."

"I'm a feminist, damn it!"

Micah whacked her hard across the bottom and continued to smack her as he spoke. "All the more reason for you to understand. As a woman, you get to decide if you want to live a D/D lifestyle or not. You don't mind being spanked erotically.

*Smack!* "We've already tried it, and you were fine with it. You object to the idea of being spanked because you've been taught that would make you a weaker person, a submissive. I don't ever expect you to be submissive except in the privacy of our sex lives or our relationship with D/D. Maintenance spankings are neither erotic nor disciplinary, although I don't have a problem with any kind of a spanking.

*Smack!* "Maintenance spankings are cathartic. They act as attitude adjustments and stress relievers. At the moment, you need both.

*Smack!* "Women need to cry! You need to uncork all that stress and let it go. Even strong women need to cry."

Tess was listening between whacks, and she knew that other than getting into a full-out, scratch his eyes out fight, there was no way she was going to stop Micah. With every sentence, he accentuated his explanation with a hard whack.

"If we're going to be involved, it doesn't pay to piss me off. My practicing D/D is my way of showing my partner that I care what they do or don't do.

"I am spanking you. Not from anger, but because it's important as my partner that you understand that I need you to be the best person you can be. Right now, you are too stressed to make good decisions. You can tell me later if a sore bottom works as a de-stresser."

---

It was mid-afternoon before they left Tess's apartment and made their way to a favorite delicatessen. Micah had already called home twice, Katie was going fishing, and they were planning on taking one of the sailboats out. Of course, he had to remind his siblings to use life vests, even though he knew it was unnecessary.

Stocked with sandwiches, chips, and soda, from a favorite delicatessen, Micah drove to a community ballpark outside the city limits.

"It has been years since I had the time to watch a game of softball," Tess exclaimed when they parked.

"It's been a while for me, too," Micah admitted. "We used to watch Coyote play all the time."

"He was good."

"Still is, when he can find the time," Micah said. "He's not in a league, but he gets into pick-up games once in a while. He should have more time now that he's finally finished with college."

"You make it sound like he's been in college forever," Tess protested.

"He's been taking college courses since he was twelve," Micah complained.

"He has multiple degrees in tough subjects!" Tess exclaimed in defense. "Mathematics, physics, chemistry. What he's accomplished academically is phenomenal, Micah. Coyote is a genius!"

"I've known that since he was four years old. It doesn't change the fact that he's been going forever," Micah complained. "He's got all these degrees, and I don't think he's decided what he wants to do with them. He's never lost his interest in music."

There were a few seconds of silence as they both contemplated the idea.

Tess broke the moment. "I have wondered what is he going to do with a Ph.D. in Physics? What's he studying now?"

Micah shrugged. "You know, I don't think he's ever told me. He so smart, he blows me away, but he's also very private. Hey, come on and grab a seat. The game is starting!"

It amazed Tess that Micah could see the brilliance and potential in all his family and friends, but he never recognized it in himself. His statements about his younger brother were based on the pride he felt for Coyote.

Micah had an ego. H knew his worth as a musician, a songwriter, and a director of musical scores. He had earned his self-worth with the respect of his peers, hard work, and a lot of natural talent. Awards and accolades and the income he had earned didn't seem to matter much to him. It was his talents, his family, and his friends that were important to him.

They found seats on the bleachers, and Tess sat gingerly as she had been doing all day. She smiled to herself. She really wanted to rub her bottom, but she wouldn't. A reminder, Micah called it, of his earlier spanking. If anyone ever discovered that Tess Foster allowed herself to be spanked, they'd send her for a psychiatric evaluation. She had, though, because it was Micah who had spanked her. It hadn't been the first time, and it probably wouldn't be the last.

She'd always known the McKenna family practiced domestic discipline. She'd experienced spankings from Micah before. They had been the disciplinary kind, although he was only a few years older than her. The first when she'd been caught smoking and had accidentally started a fire in a backyard shed. There had been several more as a teenager. As an adult, a professional, and a feminist, she wasn't sure what was going on between them. Still, Micah had battered her poor bottom until it was bright red and sore.

She wasn't sure his explanation wasn't a bunch of mumbo-jumbo to use as an excuse to wallop her, but she had felt a lot better after a good cry. The cry, of course, was because he wouldn't stop whacking on her butt until she had been bawling her eyes out. Afterward, he had held her and rocked her. Eventually, they'd made love again, The making love session was without any erotic spanking. She was already tender!

A few people recognized Micah in the crowd. He ignored them or gave a slight wave and smile when someone shouted his name. He kept his attention on the game and Tess. The Alamo Freedom Fighters lost to the Tornadoes 7 to 19, a sad fate since both Micah and Tess were fans of the Fighters. As they exited the stands, he disposed of their trash into a can and wiped his hands on his jeans.

"There are back-to-back games. The next one starts in about thirty minutes. Are you interested in sticking around? Your nose is pink, so maybe you shouldn't be in the sun much longer." Micah said, touching his finger to the tip of Tess's nose lightly.

"I'm fried," Tess agreed. "Maybe I can get around to some outdoor activities while I am off. It has been a long time since I have jogged or exercised outside. If I did work out, it was in the rehab room in the hospital."

"The rehab facility is in the basement. It's below ground level," Micah said as they walked to the parking lot. "You are coming to the lake with me, aren't you?"

Tess tilted her head to give him a questioning look. "Are you ready for a live-in guest?"

Micah laughed. "Absolutely. Well… maybe not. I have a six-year-old in the house. More important, I have a full house right now, and no extra bed space."

"I told you to finish those bedrooms when you built the house!"

"I know. You told me, the architect told me, Dad told me, Coyote begged me, but there was a reason I didn't finish the rooms upstairs. I wanted Coyote to get on with his life. I didn't want to give him a room he could call his own."

"So, where do you plan on housing me?" Tess teased. "I've been an ER doctor for the last three years, I can sleep almost anywhere. Do you have a spare closet?"

Micah grinned at her. "I would like to hang you in my closet to keep you close by… but Macy is using my bedroom because of her knee surgery. I'm sleeping on the daybed in one of those unfinished rooms. Still, there are plenty of places to choose from. You can stay at Sully's house, or at the main lodge. Sully's would be closer. It's been renovated, and they rarely have time to use it."

"I lived in a one-room efficiency for most of the last five years. I only need enough space for me and my computer. Your mom and dad's place is spectacular, and so is Sully's." Tess mused. "I'll look around when I get there and decide. I have some things to get finished before I can come."

Micah shook his head. "I'm giving you three days. After

that, I'm hauling your ass out there. I'm giving you fair warning too. Your ass is going to be a lot sorer if you don't keep your word this time."

"I have work to complete."

"You can complete it at the lake. I paid a fortune to get a satellite system out here. There is nothing you do here that you can't do there."

"I suppose," Tess said. "I will still need to stay in contact with the hospital, but I promise I won't go in unless it's necessary. I'd like to lock into a job before the first of the year."

"What happened to rest and sleep?" Micah asked.

Tess laughed. "I'll get that done in between looking for a job, updating the website, writing a couple papers for medical journals, and finding the time to have lots of sex with a bossy, over-testosteroned guy."

"Good," Micah teased. "Invite him out. We have a lot in common."

# Chapter 10

Micah closed his book and turned off the light by his favorite reading chair. It was quiet. Macy had gone to bed earlier, and Katie had been asleep for hours. It was after midnight, and he knew he needed to be in bed, but he had too much on his mind.

Someone had tripped the security alarm on the main gate earlier, and Micah had a pretty good idea who did it. She'd been smart enough to stay out of camera range. The family members all had remotes, but there was a code box with a simple six-digit code. Very few people were given the manual digits needed to get in. Someone had tried to breach the parameter, failed, and by default, locked the system. The security company had called. That meant he'd had to reset the security codes.

Tess was due at the lake in the morning, so he'd called her with the new code. In the morning, he'd send an e-mail to everyone who had a remote. He'd been over to his parents' house earlier. It had been the original lodge when the property had been a recreational vacation retreat. He checked it over, made sure all the doors and windows were secure. Other than needing a good dusting, it was in order. It was the same at Sully's place.

Micah went about the house shutting off lights and checking the doors. Over the years, they'd had a few problems with drifters, trying to take up residence in the old cabins. He took security seriously. He and his brothers had all experienced problems with what they called *the crazies*. Fans who went overboard in their quest to get their attention.

He looked through the side door window and froze. There were lights on in Sully's house. He could barely see his brother's house because of the thick woodland and brush, but the lights were definitely on. He pulled his cell phone and listened as his brothers' cell went straight to voicemail. Sully was supposed to be through with filming the scenes in the Northwest. He was supposed to be in New Zealand.

Micah backtracked quietly to his bedroom. He touched his sister lightly on the shoulder. "Sissy!"

"What?" Macy was instantly awake.

"There are lights on in Sully's house. He's not answering his phone, so I have no way of knowing if it's him or a drifter has broken in. I'm going over to check it out. If it's him, I'll kick his butt for not warning me that he was coming, and I'll call you with the all-clear. If it's not, I'll call the police and get back here ASAP. I have already checked all the doors and windows. I'll activate security once I'm outside. I want you to go into Katie's room. If the intruder alarms go off, grab her and get into the closet. She knows where the button is to activate a hidden panel to a panic room, If you activate the system, the security company will automatically call the police."

"Shouldn't you call the police?" Macy whispered.

"It would take thirty minutes for them to get here, and I don't know who is over there. I'll take a baseball bat and binoculars. I should be able to get close enough to see who is inside."

Micah gave her the code to activate the panic system. "We've never had to use it, but I had it installed just in case. Go! Set your phone to vibrate, and don't wake Katie unless it's necessary."

"Be careful," Macy whispered, grabbing her cell phone off the charger and following him to the door.

Micah nodded, and he slipped outside and into the woods. He got to within twenty feet of Sully's house, and he knew instantly by the music playing who was there. Just to make sure, Micah used the binoculars until his brother came into view. He called Macy and gave her the all-clear. He apologized for scaring her and disturbing her sleep. He told her he would see her in the morning, along with his battered and bloodied brother.

Pocketing his phone, Micah walked around the house, deliberately making a lot of noise. He pounded on the door with the end of the bat.

"Who's there?"

"Your pissed off brother, you idiot!" Micah snarled.

Coyote opened the door and studied Micah standing on the threshold with a baseball bat and a scowl on his face. "I was trying to slip in without bothering you," he said, opening the door.

"I was about to crash for the night. I was checking the locks when I saw the lights. I thought there was a squatter, or someone breaking in over here. Don't scare the shit out of me like that! Call me!" Micah growled. He saw a duffle bag, two guitar cases, and several boxes marked *books* in the living room. "Have you come for a visit, or are you moving in?"

Coyote walked off toward the kitchen. "Coffee?"

"Sure, when have I ever refused coffee," Micah agreed. "What's going on?"

"My lease was over on the student efficiency in Austin,"

Coyote said. "I called Sully, he's okay with my staying here for a while."

"That doesn't explain why you're here, not that's it's any of my business."

Coyote shrugged. "I would have stayed with you, but you're full at the moment. I need a break, and I have some things to finish, so I'm going to be bunking here for a while. The lease for the apartment in San Antonio is over too. I'm going to stick everything in a storage unit until I make some decisions," Coyote said. "I also want to borrow your truck. I've got some friends who will help me move Saturday morning."

"How come I didn't know about this?" Micah asked.

Coyote took his coffee into the living room and sprawled in a chair. Micah followed him, perched on the arm of the couch, and waited. Coyote took his time, as was his habit, before speaking. "I'm telling you now. I'm an adult, big brother, and I have some life-changing decisions to make. I want to make them and not be unduly influenced by anyone else."

Micah leaned forward and took a long hard look at his younger brother. He knew that look. He had seen it every morning in the mirror for months on end when his life had imploded. Something was going on, and Coyote wasn't ready to talk about it yet.

"I hear you. If I can help with anything, just tell me what."

Coyote nodded and seemed to steady himself. "Thanks. I'm done with school. Finally, I think. Maybe not."

"That's decisive," Micah said, laughing.

Coyote laughed. "Wasn't it? Truthfully, I don't have a clue what I'm doing right now."

"It's not like you're homeless, or without a career," Micah said.

Coyote laughed. "No. My petty problems don't compare on any scale with those of most people."

"Okay," Micah said. "It's after midnight, and you need to

get some sleep. I need to get some sleep. Just remember if you need anything, I'm here for you."

Coyote looked around at the A-frame house that had been expanded and renovated. "I'm not suffering."

Micah grinned. "I'll see you in the morning for breakfast. There's nothing to eat here, unless you brought it with you. I know because I cleaned out the refrigerator after Sully was here the last time. He brought in a bunch of guys for a couple days of fishing. There was stuff in the frig that had turned green and was growing hair. I should have worn a hazmat suit. It was scary crap!"

"You always were a wuss," Coyote said.

"Shit head," Micah snarled, but he was grinning as he slammed the door behind him and went home.

---

Micah was trying to get Katie to decide what she wanted for breakfast when Coyote strolled in.

Katie screamed and leaped into her uncle's arms. He twirled her around, blew a raspberry on her cheek, and kissed her before dropping her into her chair. "What's for breakfast, Shortie?"

"Pancakes!" Katie yelled.

Micah shook his head. "No. I'm not sending you to school on a sugar overload. Oatmeal, yogurt, or fruit on cereal and toast?"

"Oatmeal and toast," Katie decided. "Can I have peanut butter on my toast?"

"May I, and yes, that sounds doable," Micah agreed. He opened a frozen container of oatmeal and slid it into the microwave, and shoved several slices of bread into the toaster. Coyote, do you want the same, or do you want to rummage?"

"I'll rummage," Coyote grumbled as he headed for the kitchen cabinets. "Do you have coffee?"

"When have I ever *not* had coffee?" Micah demanded.

"Point taken," Coyote said.

"Tell him to make you one of his unbelievable lattes," Macy suggested coming into the kitchen.

Coyote set a large jar of peanut butter on the table and twisted the lid off for Katie. He hugged his sister. "You doing okay, Sis? Dufus hasn't poisoned you yet, has he?"

"I'm doing fine. I'm resting and spending some time with old friends, and some of my favorite people."

"I'm one of Aunt Macy's favorite people," Katie said, looking up from smearing peanut butter on her toast.

"You're on the top of my list too, Punkin," Coyote said.

Macy went to the cupboard and removed a box of raisin bran cereal. "Grab two bowls. This and toast are as good as it gets around here for breakfast."

"Is there any real milk? Not that substitute crap he had last time I was here," Coyote asked.

"Whole milk, not even two-percent," Macy teased. "I had him buy it on the way home yesterday."

"Hey, who was after me about eating healthy?" Micah demanded as he turned around with a latte in his hand. He pulled it back. "Give me any grief, and I'll keep this."

Macy narrowed her eyes. "If there's chocolate in there, I can take you."

Both men burst into laughter as Micah handed over the latte, and Coyote rubbed the top of his sister's head as if she was still six years old. Coyote went straight to the coffee pot for the real stuff. He wanted it black and potent with caffeine. He poured himself a large mug and topped off Micah's cup as he walked by.

The front door opened, and Tess walked in. She was quick enough to stop Katie from leaving her chair and kissed her on the top of the head. She whispered something in Katie's ear, and the child giggled and returned to eating her breakfast.

"Is this a private meeting?"

"No meeting, and there's breakfast if you want to scrounge," Micah answered.

"I figured on that," Tess said, and she produced a box of donuts from behind her back. She set them on the kitchen island. "I came prepared."

"Yeah!" Katie clapped.

"No," Micah said sternly. "After school, maybe, but not before school."

Tess made a face as Coyote snagged a chocolate-covered donut from the box. "Sorry, but the boss has spoken. I'll squirrel a couple of them away for an after-school snack." She looked over at Micah. "You are so strict!"

"Don't start," Micah warned. "I'm the one that will get the phone calls if she is hyper and can't settle down."

"That's why I stopped in here, first," Coyote said, ignoring Micah's warning and breaking off a piece of donut and popping it into Katie's mouth. "I'm heading to my place in San Antonio, so I thought I would drop Katikins off at school and save you the trip."

"Thanks."

"By the way, the next time you change the gate code, warn me so I can reprogram my remote. I almost plowed into the gate last night. It took me three tries to figure out which code you were using this time on the box. If I'd missed on the last try, I would have had to call the security company," Coyote complained.

"Sorry, I wasn't expecting anyone but Tess today," Micah said. "*Someone* did try to get in earlier yesterday and locked down the system. I reset the code, but I forgot to send a text message to the family about the remotes."

Coyote rolled his eyes and pulled out his cell. With very fast thumbs, he sent a message. "It's done!" he said. He draped his arm over his sister's shoulder. "Sissy, how would you like to go to a Spurs practice this afternoon?"

"I thought their practices were closed to the public," Macy said.

"They are unless you can wrangle passes to get in, and I happen to have two. Plus, I have tickets for tonight's game, courtesy of my favorite professor, who is a season ticket holder. He can't go, and he didn't want to waste the tickets.

"I'm going over to my place to start packing, and before you ask, no. You're not going to help. I know what I'm going to keep and what I'm going to toss. You'd just slow me down.

"I called a friend of mine who works in the main office at the university. There is a lecture this morning, part of an eight-part series on poets of the eighteenth century. Today's lecture is Elizabeth Barrett Browning and the Poets of Romance. I know how you love that girly stuff. Anyway, she said she could get you in on a guest pass if you want to attend. It's from ten to two. Otherwise, you will have to find something to do for four hours before we go to the Sports Center."

"I would love it," Macy exclaimed. "She's one of my favorites! But…" She looked over at Micah.

"Hey, don't turn down girly poems for me," Micah said. "Or basketball, with all those tall guys in shorts." His eyes went to Coyote, who was stepping out to the deck to answer a call.

"Why don't you make a day and a night of it. The beds will still be in the apartment. Instead of driving back here tonight, stay overnight at his place, and he can drop you off for rehab in the morning. If he's still busy packing or moving his stuff, I'll drive in to get you later."

"Rats," Macy exclaimed. "I forgot about the appointment."

"I can take her to rehab and bring her back," Coyote said, returning into the kitchen. "The guys are going to be there tomorrow around eight. Between us, we have two pick-ups, and I'm not storing that much. A lot of what's in there will be put by the dumpster. An hour, maybe two, and we'll be gone, and so will most of the furniture. The pickers are fast in that neighborhood."

"It sounds like a plan to me," Macy said. "I'll be glad when I get the okay to drive again. Having to depend on someone to drive me is the pits."

"Aw, it's just like old times," Coyote said.

"Well, that's today and part of tomorrow planned," Macy exclaimed. "I'll go get dressed and pack an overnight bag. Thanks, Coyote!"

"Don't take too long!" Micah yelled after his sister. "Katie has to leave in eight minutes!"

"Come on, honey, finish with your breakfast," Micah said to his daughter. "You have to brush your teeth and get your bookbag and your jacket."

"Excuse me," Tess said, ambling across the living area toward the powder room.

The phone rang, and Micah was talking to someone while Macy carried her bag out and set it by the front door. Katie came running with a jacket thrown over her head. She was wearing different colored sneakers than the ones she had been wearing when she went into her bedroom. Coyote tied his niece's shoes while Macy helped her with her jacket. They were at the door when Micah stopped them with a "Hold it!"

The three of them stopped, turned, and looked at him.

"Katie. Hannah's mom is on the phone. It's Hannah's birthday tomorrow, and Mrs. Woodlawn wants to know if you would like to go to Six Flags with them as their guest for the weekend. That way, Hannah will have someone her age to be with instead of hanging around with just her mom all day," Micah said.

"Can I, Daddy? Please, please, please!" Katie exclaimed.

"Yes," Micah said into the phone. "Of course she wants to go. Okay, I'll send a note and call the school so you can take her from school today. Call me when you get back, and I'll come to get her." He spoke for another minute and disconnected the call.

"Katie, are you sure you want to go? You will go home with Mrs. Woodlawn today after school and spend the night in a hotel at Arlington, spend Saturday at the park. You'll have to stay another night in the hotel before coming back. I'll come to get you, Sunday when you get back. Are you okay with that?"

"Daddy, I'm a big girl now. I like playing with Hannah and we get to go to Six Flags!" Katie was so excited, she was bouncing.

"Okay, but remember if you call, I'll come to get you," Micah promised.

"I'm a big girl, and it's Six Flags!"

"Okay," Micah agreed, and he looked at Macy and Coyote. 'Now it's time to panic. We have three minutes to get a bag packed for her and get her off to school on time." He took off, with Coyote, and Macy on his heels. He grabbed a small roll-away Disney Frozen suitcase and tossed it on the bed. "Four of everything, just in case, socks, panties, two pairs of jeans, two pairs of shorts, four tee shirts, one set of jammies, and an extra pair of sneakers. Grab that little bag in the closet. It's already packed with her toothpaste and stuff for her overnighters at Mom's." As Micah reeled off his mental list, Macy, and Coyote quickly located the items while Katie was following them around offering her advice.

"Not that shirt, the pink one to go with the pink jeans! No, not those sneakers, I need the pink ones!" Katie complained

There was a scramble as Macy took over the clothing selections following Katie's advice.

Micah tucked her favorite sleeping bear in the suitcase and

zipped it shut. In less than two minutes, his daughter was ready for an overnighter.

Coyote grabbed the small bag as Micah picked up his daughter and carried her on his hip. He set her down, hugged her, and reminded her to behave. Tucking some money into a side pocket of the suitcase, he told Katie to give it to Mrs. Woodlawn to spend at the amusement park. He handed his brother a quickly scribbled note to turn into the school office.

Micah waved them off and went into the house, closed the door, and leaned against it for a few seconds with his eyes closed.

"Where did everyone go?" Tess asked, joining him.

Micah poured two mugs of coffee and took a donut from the box.

"Gone," Micah said, dramatically. "I have peace at last. Macy has gone off with Coyote for a day of Elizabeth Barrett Browning poetry and goggling basketball players. Katie is going to Six Flags with a friend. It's just you and me."

"Isn't that a good thing?" Tess asked.

"Oh, yeah. That's a really good thing," Micah said, leaning over and giving her a kiss. He wasn't expecting anyone to return until late tomorrow afternoon. He smiled, thinking of the possibilities, and he frowned as he automatically answered his cell phone.

"What's the gate code?" Carla Mancuso demanded.

"None of your business," Micah said.

"I need to talk to you."

"No dice, and if you breach the parameter of my property, you'll be violating the restraining order. I'm not playing your games anymore. The judge has already warned you. If you violate the order again, you're going to spend some time in jail."

Micah pulled the phone from his ear, but Tess could hear the obscenities being screamed.

"I'm recording these calls, and I will turn them over to the police," Micah promised.

"She's still pestering you!" Tess exclaimed. "She's nuts!"

Micah chuckled. "Is that your professional opinion?"

"Sometimes I have to call it like it is," Tess admitted.

"I've stopped thinking about her, or I'm trying to," Micah said. "The only woman I'm thinking about now is you. We have until tomorrow afternoon, how would you like to spend the time? You'll have to stay in the lodge, Coyote has claimed Sully's place. He's already moved from the efficiency he rented in Austin, and he's moving out of the apartment in San Antonio. Something is going on, but he's not talking."

"The lodge won't be a hardship," Tess said. She got to her feet, walked around the kitchen table, and straddled him. We can go over there later. My stuff is in the car."

"Sounds good to me," Micah agreed. He shoved his chair away from the table and stood, as Tess wrapped her legs around him. "Our first stop is my bedroom. Crap, crap, crap!"

"What?" Tess asked, dropping her feet to the floor.

"I forgot, Macy is using my room," he said.

"We have plenty of time," she said, laughing. "Let's go to the lodge."

---

Tess looked around the room she'd decided to use. It was spacious, and like everything connected to the McKennas, it was substantial. Intended as live-in space for a manager, the room was next to the kitchen.

Micah had gone to his house to get some basics for the kitchen. If she knew him, and she did, his kitchen which they had left behind with the breakfast clutter would be spotlessly cleaned before he returned. Tess would have to make a run to the grocery store. She had already decided to use the breakfast nook as her workstation. She'd been to the lake properties many times, although she'd never stayed at the lodge before. She didn't want to spread out and take over while she was there. It was the vacation home of the senior McKennas.

The next few months of her life were going to be different. She had papers to write, and interviews to schedule. She had a good reputation, and she'd worked long and hard for it. Now she was dealing with Micah too. Their love life was spectacular, but she wasn't sure how he was going to fit in with her workloads. He had his problems, and somehow if they decided their relationship should go to the next phase, they would have to merge their lives together. She hadn't considered doing that with any of the men she'd dated over the years. They hadn't been Micah. He'd been her cornerstone since she'd been a teenager, and one of his traits was that when he wanted something, he worked hard to get it.

Tess was unpacking her suitcases and boxes when she heard Micah in the kitchen, storing things away. She peeked around the door to make sure it was him, and slipped into a tiny scrap of black lace, before sauntering into the kitchen.

The look on his face was one of delight, and Tess didn't have any doubt about what she'd be doing for the next several hours.

# Chapter 11

Today's painting subject was a wizened old man sitting on a bench, whittling a toy, beside a little boy. The boy wasn't watching what the man was doing with the stick of wood, he was looking at the man's face with adoring eyes. All that was complete on the canvas was the faces.

Tess lent her hand to help Macy lower herself to the low beanbag without hurting her knee, and handed her a cup of coffee. The entire McKenna family seemed to be addicted to coffee. She started walking around the studio studying paintings that she hadn't seen before.

"Feeling better?" Micah asked his sister, referring to the previous day when Macy had returned from the physical therapy session exhausted.

"Yes, I am," Macy answered. "Why do you do the faces first?"

"Because they are the most important part. If I don't get the eyes, nose, and mouth right, trying to complete the picture would be a waste of time."

"Who are they?"

"I don't know. This picture was taken at the fairgrounds last year over by the duck pond. Punkin was feeding the ducks, and I saw these two sitting on a park bench. I asked if I could take their picture."

"If you don't know them, what difference does it make if you can't get a nose or a mouth perfect? Who would know the difference?" Tess asked.

Micah shrugged. "I would. That's part of the challenge."

"I'd like to send some of the photographs I took of your paintings to my boyfriend," Macy said.

Micah spun around to face his sister. "Boyfriend?" he echoed. "This is the first I've heard about a boyfriend. Dish it out, Sissy."

"Don't let him intimidate you," Tess said from where she stood, looking at a painting.

Macy rolled her eyes. "I don't mind. Micah knows how to keep his mouth shut." She turned to her brother. "His name is Maxwell Barrington-Smythe."

"That's a mouthful," Micah groused, looking over his shoulder. "That sounds very upper-crust British."

"His family is upper-crust British, but they are also very nice people," Macy agreed. "His father is a solicitor, and he has a position on the Queen's staff. Something to do with economics, I think. His father is a bit stuffy, but his mother is wonderfully down to earth. Max is a partner in the Parker-Barrington Galleries."

"Why does that sound familiar?" Tess said joining Macy, and sitting on the floor. "Oh, yeah, the P & B Gallery in New York City. I went there when I took a special training class in the Big Apple. Classy stuff!"

"London, Paris, New York, and soon to be in Los Angeles," Macy said, nodding.

Micah turned around again. "How old is this dude? This

jet-setting, high society, rich guy who's dating my twenty-year-old sister?"

"Don't be mean!" Tess warned.

"Max is twenty-seven," Macy said.

"Twenty-seven," Micah growled, and he tossed his brush into a jar. "That's way too old for you."

"Do you want to hear me out, or not?" Macy warned. "I might remind you, big brother that you are only five years older than Max, and you are also wealthy and have been for a decade. You were also living with a woman at twenty-one."

He opened his mouth to protest and snapped it shut. His sister was right. He didn't have a leg to stand on with his argument. "How long have you known this guy?"

"Three and a half years," Macy admitted.

"Three years! And, this is the first I've heard about this guy?"

Macy shrugged. "Max is my business, and like you, I have learned that sharing the details of my private life with the family isn't the best idea. If Dad knew about Max, he would have already had a private eye investigating his background, would have demanded a meeting, and interrogated him ruthlessly. I live in London. That's five-thousand miles away. I don't need Mom and Dad sticking their noses in my business."

Micah nodded his head in agreement. "Yes, he would have, but he's only trying to protect you."

"I don't need or want that kind of protection," Macy said simply. "My significant other is one of the good guys. Contrary to some people's opinions, I am very capable of running my life, without interference."

"If you're not going to paint, can we take this downstairs?" Tess suggested. "You guys live on coffee, but I need a diet soda fix."

"Sure," Micah agreed, draping a cover over his painting,

and tossing a few brushes into a jar. "Give me a few minutes to clean and put everything away."

Tess stretched in the lounge chair on the deck, with her cold drink. Micah and Macy came out and sat on the glider. "You'd better start talking before he starts grilling you," she warned Macy.

Macy did as she was handed one of her special lattes. "Maxwell and I met at a gala charity event in Paris. It was a three-part evening. There was a ritzy dinner, tickets to the ballet, and a tour of an up-and-coming art gallery. The tickets were outrageously expensive, but it was the kind of thing that wealthy, and high society people flock to, and the event sold out in hours.

"I didn't go to the dinner, but I was the principal lead in the production of Swan Lake, and the principal dancers were invited to attend the gallery tour.

"Max's mother asked to be introduced to me, and she introduced me to her entire family. Max's mother is Irena Tarrington. She was a Demi-soloist—or Second soloist—for the London Ballet for fourteen years. That's a long run, and she's almost a legend in the dancing world. She's a wonderful lady, and she's still involved with the London Ballet, although only in a fundraising and publicity role."

"Is this guy the reason you moved to London?" Micah asked.

Macy nodded. "He was part of the reason, but I was offered a contract with the London Ballet based on my skills as a dancer. My position is Demi-soloist, and for my age, that's an excellent position."

"Okay, I'm getting the picture," Micah commented. "But what kind of a guy is this Barrington-Smythe, who was dating my seventeen-year-old schoolgirl sister when he was twenty-four years old? There's a name for guys like that."

Macy grinned. "I knew you would pick up on that. We only

had three dates before I turned eighteen, and I didn't tell Max I was seventeen, so it wasn't his fault. He asked me out, and I accepted. He was very upset with me when he found out, but it was too late. We were already a couple."

"You're in love with him," Tessa said softly. "I can hear it in your voice."

Macy smiled. "Yes, I am."

"Do I need to ask this guy about his intentions?" Micah asked.

"No," Macy exclaimed solemnly. "His intentions have already been made very clear to me, thank you very much."

"And what are they?" he asked.

"None of your business," Tess exclaimed.

Macy pulled a necklace chain from her shirt and drew it over her head. She handed it to her brother. Attached to the chain was a classically styled engagement ring. A huge diamond was set in platinum.

"You're engaged?" Tess exclaimed.

"Not officially," Macy denied. "Max has asked, and I've agreed to marry him. We've known we would get married, from our first date on. We decided not to make a public announcement until after my twenty-first birthday. That way, while there may be some objections, I'll be a legal adult, and no one can stop me.

"We haven't told very many people. I've told you and Coyote. Coyote doesn't tell secrets, and neither do you. I'm trusting you not to tell anyone, without my permission until we are ready to break the news. That won't be until after my birthday, and I'll be back in London before then."

"Wow," Tess exclaimed, looking at the ring and passing it back to Macy. "What's this going to do to your career?"

"Nothing, for a while," Macy said. "Trust me, when I say, we have discussed all the ramifications of getting married in exhaustive detail. Max is willing to follow me wherever my career takes me for a while. Most ballet companies are in major cities. Max says he'll either open new locations for the business or spend his time seeking new artists. He knows my career is limited to however long my agility holds out. Most dancers' careers are over by the time they are in their thirties. I won't wait that long. We want a family. I won't sacrifice my desire to have a husband and children to extend my career in dance. I love ballet, but I know there is life beyond dancing."

"Wow," Micah said. "My little sister is a grown-up, and you really sound like you have your head on straight."

"Just because I'm your little sister doesn't mean I'm an air-head!" Macy exclaimed. "I've told you my secret, big brother. Now, are you going to let me show my boyfriend your work, or not?"

When Macy returned inside the house, claiming she had to take more photographs, Micah offered his hand to Tess. "Let's go for a walk."

"I'd forgotten how beautiful and peaceful it is here," Tess said as they walked around the lake toward the lodge. "I'm going to have to go to the grocery store today."

"Later," Micah said. "I have to pick up Katie this after-noon. We can stop at the store on the way back. I don't get much alone time, so we have to take advantage of it when we can. Do you have a problem with that?"

"Not me," Tess said, pulling him to stop and kissing him. "I'm taking the first break I've had in years. The first part of my agenda is to have sex as much as possible. I'm making up for years of abstinence. I'll worry about the rest of my agenda later."

"I like the way you think," Micah said with a smile.

Hours later, Tess slid from the bed and headed to the bathroom. They'd spent most of the morning hours in a long marathon of sex. It was still hard to believe she was with Micah. He was a magnificent lover.

The petty part of her sent an *'up-yours'* finger to Carla. She'd disliked and grown to despise his past partner with a venomous passion.

Tess turned on the shower and wasn't surprised when Micah stepped in behind her. He kissed her deeply, turned her around, and bent her over. His hand slid between her legs, and she steadied herself with her hands against the tiles. He plunged deep into her. She gasped at the ferocity of his taking her, but damn she was enjoying it.

He repeatedly plunged upward into her. When she couldn't help a sob that broke from her throat, suddenly, he withdrew, turned her around, and lifted her to straddle him. She hooked her legs around his hips as he anchored her against the slippery tiles. Thrusting hard into her, he greedily took what she offered.

Tess opened her mouth, but Micah covered her lips with his and muffled an orgasmic scream as she came in a flood of sensations. He wouldn't release her mouth, though, as he continued to plunder her with his tongue and his engorged penis. Driving her to another orgasm, Micah pounded and pounded until he finally let himself come. He released her slowly, laying his forehead against her shoulder, and slowly, carefully, lowered her to her feet while steadying her balance.

They showered, continuing to allow their hands to touch and feel. They kissed and laughed, too spent, to manage anything else. Finally, they dried each other off, still lingering, touching, and enjoying. It was the most fantastic shower sex, Tess had ever experienced, and she'd thought what they had done before had been awe-inspiring.

Micah carried her to the bed, and his conquest of her body

continued. His possession was absolute. He gave her his heart and soul. Tess knew the love she felt for him was real.

The phone calls started around noon. One after another, and they persisted. Micah had to check each incoming call. He was expecting a call from Mrs. Woodlawn, the mother of the birthday girl. After the tenth ignored phone call from Carla, he called Stan Mulclusky, his attorney.

"I'm sorry," Micah said to Tess. "I don't know how she got my number again."

"This has been going on since you gave her the boot?" Tess asked.

"Off, and on," Micah said, nodding his head. "She might be off her meds again."

"Did you ask for a court-ordered mental evaluation?"

"We did," Micah said. "She's definitely emotionally unstable and neurotic, but it's not illegal."

"Harassing someone when there is already a restraining order in place, is breaking the law," Tess said. "And, heads up, the word neurotic is no longer used in a psychiatric diagnosis."

"I'm not a psychiatrist. I'm the target of her visceral hatred," Micah said. "According to her, I am responsible for everything that has gone wrong in her life for the last decade.

"Stan will take it from here, but that means I have to go by the phone store and get my number changed again. So far, they've been accommodating, but this must be sixth or seventh time. I'm out of patience dealing with Carla, and Stan's been after me to counter sue her."

"Why don't you?" Tess asked.

"We are in an age of enlightenment," Micah said wearily. The sympathy is always for the person with a disorder regardless of how they are behaving. We're supposed to be tolerant and forgiving. I usually am, but after four years of this crap, I'm over it. Public and legal opinion rarely sides with the victim no matter how much trouble they cause a person. In most cases, they have to be charged with a serious crime, or they have to start shooting before the legal system realizes they are destroying another person's life."

Micah returned to his house, and Tess went with him. He listened to several messages left on his phone. Something had triggered Carla to start harassing him again. Micah was alternating between his office, and talking to Stan on the phone. He didn't feel comfortable leaving Tess alone.

"What's going on?" Macy asked, looking from Tess to her brother. "Have I worn out my welcome?"

Micah looked shocked. "No! Honey, never think that—I want you to stick around until you absolutely have to go back."

"Something is going on."

Micah crossed the room and hugged his sister. "Very true, but it has nothing to do with you. Carla is on the rampage again. This, too, will pass. She's been warned too many times. Stan says she will either abide by the court's rulings or she's going to spend some time in jail."

"I thought she was going to move to England?"

"She hasn't left the States, and she's running out of options," Tessa said.

"It's time to consider playing hardball," Macy suggested.

"I agree," Micah agreed. "But, so far, that hasn't been very successful. All her lawyers have to do is stand up and quote a few doctor's diagnoses. She promises to go back on her meds, and she's let off with a warning. I don't want her turning her attention on someone else."

"Who?" Macy said, but she turned, looked at Tessa, and smiled. "Tess?"

Tess nodded. "We've decided to give it a try."

"Yes!" Macy exclaimed, beaming, and fisting her hands in the air. "I've always thought your friendship was special. This is wonderful! This is another secret, isn't it?"

"For now," Micah admitted. "You are not the only one who doesn't like interference in their love life.

Macy hugged Tessa, and then Micah. "I'm so happy for you!"

"Did you send the photos to your boyfriend?" Micah asked.

Macy nodded. "Sometimes he's as bad as you about reading his personal e-mails. He checks his business line every ten minutes. He's arguing with Jamie about who gets to take the next trip to Los Angeles. The LA gallery is Jamie's project, but Max wants to come to see me while I'm over here, and I miss him. If he makes the trip on company business, he will write off the entire trip as a business expense."

"Tightwad?" Tess queried.

"English thrifty," Macy countered with a smile. "Why should they pay for an extra trip to the States, if someone from the business has to make the trip anyway."

Micah's phone rang again, but he didn't pick-up the call.

"I called Dad," Macy said suddenly.

Micah looked to his sister. "Give it to me."

"He wants to have a big family meeting this weekend to discuss what he calls *the family issues*. The problems are between me, Mom, and Lily. I told him, this doesn't have anything to do with Allison. This is strictly about Mom making promises to Lily and purposely sabotaging her training prospects in ballet. I also told him the rest of the family, as in *the boys*, aren't involved, and I don't want you involved."

"What did he say to that?"

"He did his usual soft-shoe, about the family making decisions together. I told him that I considered that statement bullshit. That he had abdicated the responsibility of the daughters in our family to Mom a long time ago. I told him I didn't appreciate how Mom treated me, always favoring Allison over me. I told him if he wants a meeting, I will be there. But it will be on my terms, me, Mom, him, and Lily. No one else is involved. I also told him I'll do whatever I have to do to make sure Lily is allowed to follow her dreams. I will not allow Mom to crush her spirit, or her dreams!"

"How did that go down? Micah asked.

"I think he probably fell out of his chair in shock. He said he would call me back," Macy said. "Micah, I've had time to think about this, and I am not backing down. I didn't have anyone in my corner when I was dealing with Mom." She held a finger up when he opened his mouth to protest.

"You would have been, had you known, but you didn't. I know what Mom is doing to Lily. I lived it. I am not going to let her do the same thing to Lily. I will fight for my little sister."

Tess gave Macy two thumbs up and smiled. "Sissy's got her mad on!"

Macy blushed. "Yes, I do! Although I will admit, Dad caught the brunt of my being pissed about something entirely different."

"Trouble with the boyfriend?" Micah asked.

"No," Macy intoned, sounding impatient. "No, the trouble is with my credit card company."

Her brother's eyebrows scrunched, and he frowned. "Are you overextended?"

"No. My wallet was stolen about a year ago. I was traveling with the company at the time, and I didn't notice it was gone right away. When we are on tour, our hotels and meals are provided. We don't have a lot of free time to shop. I didn't check my purse for a couple of days, and when I did, my wallet was missing. I called Max and had him go over to my place and get my credit card and banking records. By the time I reported my credit card was stolen, over thirty-eight thousand dollars had been charged to it."

"Why didn't you tell us?" Micah demanded.

"I'm a big girl, Micah. I can handle my problems. The bank I use has protections against identity fraud. Because I am an international traveler, I call them ahead of time to tell them where I'm going to be."

"I did learn a few lessons from Dad. I was protected, but it takes months to get that kind of thing straightened out," Macy said, sounding frustrated. "It's a nerve-racking process. Max had one of his brothers acting as my solicitor to try to resolve the issues. I changed banks, and I had to have my credit cards replaced. Whoever stole my wallet is a brazen shite. They have re-opened new credit cards in my name, and spent ridiculous amounts of money."

"I saw a show on TV about identify theft," Micah said thoughtfully. "It's one of the most difficult crimes to both catch and prosecute."

"Tell me about it," Macy said sarcastically. "The person who is targeting me is constantly traveling. For the last six-months they have been focusing on cities in the States–New York, Miami, New Orleans. Oh, and casinos are a favorite, Las Vegas and Reno were big hits. I haven't been to half of those cities, and the only time I was in Las Vegas was when I-35 was on tour. I think I was about thirteen at the time."

"Isn't there a way to safeguard yourself from that?" Tess asked.

"Yes, but they don't work, when someone is determined," Macy explained. "On a lot of credit cards, you can get instant credit in five minutes or less, and a new credit card is on its way to you in the mail."

"I can call Stan and see if he knows anyone who specializes in this kind of crime," Micah offered.

"The bank has a whole department dedicated to consumer fraud," Macy said. "Unfortunately, the thief seems to be one step ahead of them all the time. The phone call was to verify the information on a new card, which I had to tell them was fraudulent. I didn't request a new card. They have issued a card to someone with a New York City address and charges are coming in on it. I'd already alerted my bank that I was in the States and that any charges outside of Texas wouldn't be me."

"They can't hold you responsible, can they?" Tess asked.

"No, because I have a record of notifying them where I will be all the time. It's a royal pain in the butt. I've had to block myself from using my credit card as much as possible. It's good for my personal finances but lousy for my credit rating."

## Chapter 12

Coyote let himself into Micah's house and looked around. He didn't hear his niece or see his brother or sister around. He jumped when he heard someone swearing. He knew the two legs he saw sticking out from under the kitchen sink didn't belong to his brother. Although the jeans and the size were correct, there were too many clues that indicated the man under the sink was not his brother.

Micah did many things, and he did most of them well. He could swear with the best of the guys at times, but the words coming from under the sink were not ones he would use around his daughter. Also, plumbing and the type of music blaring from an old boom box on the floor would be listed high on his brother's 'I don't like' list. Coyote glanced toward the loft, but before he got to the stairs, he heard his brother at the piano. He was playing with one hand and writing lyrics with the other.

"Hey!" Coyote shouted over the clanging on the pipes.

Micah didn't answer or notice him until Coyote touched his brother on the shoulder. Micah jolted with surprise.

"How can you concentrate with all that going on?" Coyote

asked loudly as a string of swear words were heard over the loud beats coming from the radio.

Micah pointed toward the deck. Once outside, he spoke. "I have a six-year-old. I could tune out a nuclear blast. I'm attuned to two things. When I hear her cry of pain, or when it gets quiet. When she's hurt, I try to fix it. When it gets quiet, that generally means she's into something that is against the rules." He jerked his head toward the kitchen.

"The garbage disposal stopped working last night. George is the father of one of the kids in Katie's class. He doesn't mind picking up odd jobs in the evenings and weekends. He's loud, but he's good."

"Where is everyone?" Coyote asked.

"Macy is at a rehab appointment. Tess is with Punkin. They are walking around the lake, gathering leaves for an art project," Micah answered. "George's language is beyond color-ful. He says he doesn't swear around his daughter, but I'm not sure I believe him. About every third word is a swear word, and I don't want Punkin to hear it. What happened last night? I saw you leaving well after midnight."

"I spent part of the night in the Dell Seton Emergency. This morning we were at the police station while a friend of mine was filing complaints with the police. She has two black eyes, a broken nose, and a broken arm."

"Who?" Micah demanded.

"You don't know her. She was in one of my study groups," Coyote said. "She wasn't admitted to the hospital. This isn't the first time her husband has done this to her. I think she called me because, by sheer size, I would be intimidating to him. She knows I'm safe. She's got two little boys, four and seven.

"She filed charges, but get this... two hours after her husband was arrested, he was arraigned and released on bail on his own recognizance. He's a cop, with the Austin Police

Department. This is the fourth time she's been to the police claiming abuse. She spent more time in the emergency room than he did in jail. I called a friend, a woman I know who's a pastor of a small church. Leah took her home with her until we can get her into a safe situation."

"Give me her information, and I'll call Stan," Micah said.

Coyote grinned. "I was hoping you'd offer his services. He'll take the case from you and fight harder for her."

"He took Lauren's husband to the cleaners, and we owe him for that. He stayed on Chris' butt for five years, and no one deserved it more than that louse. Tess and Lauren think Stan is a knight in shining armor."

"That's not how I would describe him, but he knows how to get the job done," Coyote agreed.

Micah was watching his brother. "He does. There's something else, spill it."

Coyote nodded. "My friend, Karen Marks, needs a safe place to hide out. The women's shelters are full. The last time she tried to leave her husband and went to a shelter, her husband attempted to take the kids from her. He almost succeeded even though he was being charged with assault."

"How is that possible?" Micah demanded.

"Anything is possible with the right connections," Coyote said. "She needs distance and security. I thought maybe she could use Aunt Lydia's apartment over Farinelli's. It's empty, the security is good, and it's the right price."

"Free," Micah said with a wry grin.

Coyote shrugged. "Karen needs help, and Sully is somewhere out in the boonies. He's either not answering his phone, or he's in a non-service area. I figured if I cleared it with you, he'd be okay with it too. If we sic Stan on Karen's husband, maybe, the jerk will steer clear of her. If she goes to social services for help, he will find her in a couple of phone calls. We need to keep her whereabouts off the grid, so her husband won't find her. School is officially over next week, so she can work under an assumed identity until the assault charges go to court. Meanwhile, Stan can get a restraining order and do some snooping. Stan needs to find out how her husband has been allowed to get away with this crap and remain on the force."

"What does she do?"

"She works in accounting at the college administration office," Coyote said. "That's how she's been able to pay for classes at the university. If you work for the college, there's a huge discount. I thought maybe she could work at Farinelli's temporarily in the kitchen, where she won't be seen."

"She might be a better match for Lauren's CPA firm. She could work online from home. I think most of Lauren's employees work from home," Micah said. "If she doesn't have a computer, we can front one for her."

"So, you're on board?" Coyote asked. "We won't have a problem with Karen living there unless her husband causes it, I promise."

"The apartment is empty, and Aunt Lydia's furniture is still there. The utilities are still on. If you vouch for her, that's good enough for me."

"Thanks," Coyote exclaimed. "How are things going here with Macy?"

"Other than the major explosion between her and Mom, things are going smooth."

"I heard about it, but I'm steering clear," Coyote admitted.

"Wise move, Bubba," Micah agreed. "But if you have any spare time while you're in Austin, check on Allison. She's gone AWOL."

Tess found herself tossing and turning in bed. The lodge was vast, empty, and silent. She was used to sleeping in small rooms, with bright fluorescent lighting, and a ton of noise. Maybe she was slept out. She and Micah were managing to carve out time for each other. They weren't using it for sleeping, but the sex was titillating and exhausting. It helped to have Macy around to babysit.

Tess looked through the window. She could see lights on the second floor of Micah's house in the distance. She glanced at the clock on the bedside table. It was three in the morning, and there was no emergency, but Micah was awake and most likely at his easel. She got dressed to go join him. She stopped at the coffee pot, filled two mugs, grabbed a cold soda for herself, and headed for the loft.

In the loft, Micah was painting an almost life-size portrait. It was of Katie sitting in a Ferris wheel seat. The expression on her face was a combination of fear and absolute delight. The male figure seated beside her wasn't finished, but she could tell from the sketch it was Coyote.

"Do you finish a new painting every day?" Tess asked, handing Micah a mug. She looked around. "I thought Macy was watching you in the mornings?"

"She had a rehab session yesterday afternoon. She comes home from them tired and hurting. She usually sleeps late the next morning," Micah said. "Sometimes I can finish a painting in a couple of hours, sometimes it takes a couple of days, and sometimes I have more than one going at the same time," Micah answered with a shrug. "I'm not one of those painters that takes months to finish one painting. I see it as a challenge. Can I do it? I might take some classes someday if I could ever find the time. Who knows, I might discover I'm doing everything wrong. Wouldn't that be a bummer?"

Tess laughed. "They don't look wrong to me. In fact, I found a couple of portraits of myself tucked over in a corner. When did I become a subject?"

Micah tossed several brushes into a jar of cleaner. He walked over to her and took her into his arms. "I painted one of you partially nude, but I had to hide it. When I started the painting, it wasn't my intention, but then the face morphed into yours. I guess, you were on my mind. I wasn't working from memory or first-hand knowledge then. I may have to paint a new portrait, this time based on reality."

"Will I have to pose for it?" Tess asked.

"No, I can do it from memory," Micah promised. "Why don't you come with me? I moved the daybed into the unfinished side of the loft. It's empty over there except for the bed."

Hours later, Tess stretched on the narrow bed and preened. "Who would have thought it? Micah McKenna, the quiet workaholic, is a sex machine!"

Micah's phone rang, and he looked at it, read the message, and flushed. "We've been caught. It's Macy. She wants to know if it's safe to come up."

Tess laughed and got to her feet. "Tell her to give us five minutes to get dressed."

"Man! Caught by my little sister," Micah said, sending a message and pulling on his jeans. "I feel like a teenager caught in the act!"

"Macy's had the same boyfriend for over three years. If you don't think she's having sex, you've got your head stuck in the sand. Grow up, because she has. I'm going back to the lodge. I have a paper to start, and I have to make some interview appointments. I might even take a nap."

"I'll see you later," Micah promised with a kiss.

Micah might have been a little embarrassed, but when Tess walked into the kitchen. Macy gave her a high five.

"Take good care of him," Macy said seriously. "He deserves it."

"Don't I know it," Tess agreed as she stepped onto the patio. There would be no nap in her immediate future. She was buzzed. She stepped into the morning dawn, stretched, and began to jog to the lodge.

"Max was impressed with the photographs I sent him," Macy said, dragging the pink beanbag chair across the floor.

Micah looked over his shoulder at her. "You look pale this morning."

Macy shrugged. "I'm a wuss when it comes to pain. I guess I've been lucky so far. I haven't had very many of the muscle strains and sprains that come with the job. I'm going to love this painting when it's finished. I get first dibs on it if you're giving it away. Coyote has several of your paintings in his apartment. He's moved them into storage by now. What's with him lately? He tends to be quiet, but he's gone practically mute."

"I don't know," Micah admitted. "Little brother keeps his personal business close until he's ready to spill it. Like someone else I know."

"You know more than most," Macy said. "Please, keep it quiet! Did you know there's a name for the type of detail you get in your paintings?"

Micah laughed. "Really?"

"Really," Macy said. "It's called hyperrealism. It's as close as a human can get to a photograph, and you did know it. You're a terrible liar!"

"I'm a realist," Micah said, not bothering to deny her accusation. "So, it makes sense. "I appreciate art, I just don't understand a lot of it. I prefer stuff I can understand. If someone has to explain the nuance of a painting to me, I wouldn't be prone to buying it. I like local art exhibits at fairgrounds and high schools."

Macy giggled. "Max would cringe if he heard you say that! He does understand all the interpretations of art. Are you going to let him see your paintings in person?"

Micah turned around with his brush in hand. "If it gets

him here so I can meet him, absolutely. I have several issues. Can he keep his mouth shut? And will he give me an honest opinion based on what I paint and not who I am? Oh, and will he do so without any expectations of my allowing him to sell my stuff? I'm not sure I'm ready for that."

Macy gave a little jump of delight. "Yes, yes, and yes. If you want, I won't even tell him who you are until he meets you in person. I didn't identify the painter as my brother. I told him it was an artist I'd come across."

Micah grinned. "I like it. I still won't be sure I'm getting an honest critique. The guy is after my sister."

"The guy already has your sister," Macy said. "You are your worst critic, in everything you do, from songs and music tracks, to painting," Macy said. "Now, get back to work. I'll sit here, watch, and not interrupt you again."

Several hours later, the results so far were beautiful. Because of the interruptions, this canvas was going to take several sessions. In the painting, Coyote sat beside his niece, looking down at her with his face displaying laughter, affection, and pride. Macy went downstairs and returned with her camera while Micah was scraping and cleaning his painting board. She also took pictures of him performing his ritual of cleaning his brushes and workspace and was careful not to get his face in the frame.

"Daddy!"

"Recreation time is over," Micah said, giving one last swipe to his painting area and glancing at the clock.

Macy looked over at the wall clock. "How long did it take you to paint that, so far?" she asked.

Micah looked over at the clock and shrugged. "About four hours, I guess. It's one of the benefits of insomnia. Now my real day starts. You missed three calls yesterday while you were at rehab. The folks are calling here because you're not answering your cell. Dad is about to pull out the big guns to settle the dust-up."

"He can try, but I'm beyond being told to apologize and keep my opinions to myself," Macy warned.

---

Annoyed and slightly pissed off, Micah unplugged the house phone. He muted the sound on his cell and decided to let the voice mail take the messages for a while. All hell was breaking loose over at the McKenna homestead, and his parents were trying to drag him into the middle of it. Fine! If he was going to be in the middle of the mess, he would solve the damn problem.

"Daddy, I am done with my addition," Katie said from the kitchen table where she completed most of her homework.

Micah looked over to a schedule that he kept posted on the refrigerator by habit. He didn't need reminders most of the time, but if he got distracted, sometimes he forgot the most basic day-to-day functions. Forgetting to eat a meal at his age wasn't that important but forgetting to fix a meal for his daughter when she was younger, had made him feel like scum.

"Do you want lunch first, or a reading period first?" he asked his daughter.

"I'll read first," Katie said, sliding off her chair. "I like the new book about Laura and Mary. Aunt Macy says there are more books by the same lady."

"Yes, there are," Micah said, smiling. "They are the favorites of a lot of little girls. I'll order you the whole set. There was a TV series based on the books, too. Maybe we can find it on one of the cable stations. You run along and get your book and have some quiet time, and I'll check your homework and fix some lunch."

Katie ran off to her room as Macy came into the kitchen.

She sat in the chair that her niece had vacated. Micah pushed the papers in front of her. "You check these. You owe me!" he growled. "If they're wrong, don't mark them, use a flag. She has to turn in those worksheets."

Macy selected a little packet of red flags from a pencil box and started adding the problems. "Did I hear something about lunch?"

Micah bared his teeth at his sister. "I have been on the phone all morning. Why aren't you dealing with this hornet's nest? You're the one who stirred the pot!"

Macy calmly placed a flag on an incorrect answer. "You're mixing metaphors. I'm only part of the problem. Besides, you know as well as I do how this family works. Everyone has to voice their two-cents worth. I'm avoiding the endless whining. I told Dad I'm not ready to talk to Mom. Not apologize, as he seems to think I should be doing… but talk. Lily said Mom has confiscated her phone. She thinks Mom deleted the recording."

Micah shook his head. "Lily is threatening to run away. She says she wants to live full-time at Adams Academy, which is also a boarding school. She said she would go to boarding school to get away from Mom. I don't think Mom and Dad are going to let that happen. And even if Mom did destroy the tape, we all heard it."

Macy shrugged. "Welcome to my world of dealing with Carole McKenna. Dad is not happy with me because I refuse to cow to his demands of going home to hash all this out. I need to do some research. Mom has blown Lily's chance to study under Madam Bashlofski. Maybe I can find another advanced program that would accept Lily. If I'm lucky, it might be like my school in Paris, where it's associated with a highly academic school."

"Is she that good?" Micah asked.

"She's exceptional," Macy admitted. "It was a stab in the heart to realize Mom had destroyed Lily's chance to work with

Madam Bashlofski. Don't shake your head at me because you don't want to believe Mom is an obstructionist. Mom is, and it's unfair. Not letting Lily study is the equivalent of Dad breaking your fingers to keep you from playing musical instruments!"

"I get it," Micah said, looking for deli meats in the refrigerator to make sandwiches for lunch. "I'm just not happy about it." He stopped suddenly and turned around and looked at his sister.

"What?" Macy demanded.

"I'm turning into my father," Micah said in a shocked voice.

Macy looked down to the homework she was checking to keep from laughing. When her brother turned back to the refrigerator, she rolled her eyes. She was tempted to respond, but she clamped her mouth shut. Micah was almost a clone of Daniel McKenna. Hardworking, and intensely loyal, her brother was the embodiment of all the decent values Daniel had instilled in his sons. It had been those same characteristics that had drawn her to Maxwell Barrington.

---

Micah dropped his daughter off at school. She would be going to another birthday party and a sleepover. It was her third in as many weeks, and he'd added two more to her calendar before school was out for the summer. It should have been a good time for him to spend with Tess. Except, she had driven to Dallas for an interview at a private medical practice.

He dropped Macy off at the rehabilitation center. She was scheduled for a session with a therapist. When that was over, she had to have a series of scans taken to determine how her knee was healing. She came prepared with her iPad and several magazines. Micah told his sister he had some business to attend but promised to be at the medical center within thirty minutes after she called him. He drove across San Antonio to meet his father at a favorite café for a late breakfast.

This was a clandestine meeting to try to ward off a clash of the titans. The McKenna family was tighter than most, but all families grow and change. The McKenna family was top-heavy with strong, opinionated personalities, and there were occasional arguments and clashes within the hierarchy.

Both his mother and father had resisted their children becoming adults, moving out, and having goals that didn't require their parents' input. Some of that resistance might have been because they formed the band when they were so young. They had needed their parents to help in driving them to shows.

Everyone assumed when I-35 music had hit the charts, they had been instant hits. It wasn't so, Micah and Sully had begun performing at local gigs as children. With the support of their parents, they had performed at every venue that would accept them. Coyote had joined them in their quest when he was only eight-years-old.

Because McKenna was also a family business, the dynamics of the family had layers that were intertwined and complicated. The three natural-born children were closely tied to McKenna Productions, Inc., which was run by their father, Daniel. Their music was still produced under the McKenna label.

Of the four younger children, the three girls were not musically talented. Noah, the youngest brother, was the exception. He was becoming exceptionally good on the drums. Daniel was overseeing the launch of Noah's career as he had his older sons.

Daniel was still heavily involved in his older son's musical interests, especially in the production and marketing of their music. It was something every one of his sons appreciated and valued. They recognized that without their father's skills their independent success would have been buried under the powerful mega-corporations that ran the music industries.

This meeting was not about business, it was about family. Micah loved and respected his father, but he had clashed with his dad over the years on many different issues. He had been too busy in his teenage years to find time to rebel, but later as a young man and ready to spread his wings, they had locked horns many times.

He needed to talk with his father about two of his sisters and his mother. The third sister at the moment was only a peripheral worry.

Micah spent the next ninety minutes having a serious discussion. In the end, Daniel admitted that in his quest to protect and direct his son's careers, he had unconsciously slighted his daughters. His father agreed he would discuss the matter of Lily's dance training and schooling with her and listen to what she had to say without Carole being present.

Carole had been the one who had instigated the changes that Lily resented. She'd been a popular student at her school, with a straight-A average. Lily had been given no valid reasons why her mother had decided to homeschool her or why she wouldn't allow her to study with Madam Bashlofski.

Daniel admitted privately to his oldest son that he was concerned about his wife's health lately. He thought she might have some kind of mental issue. She had become snappish, bitter, and outspoken on matters that weren't really that important. He had already suggested she make an appointment with a physician.

Micah agreed, and he told his father of Macy's accusations, and the harm Carole's decisions had caused in her career. They couldn't undo what had happened six years earlier. Unless Carole had some valid reasons for her actions, he doubted Macy was going to easily forgive or forget.

When the meeting was over, the two men, father, and son hugged and went their separate ways. Each had an objective to accomplish. Neither would speak of, or mention their private meeting to either mother or sisters. There were some things best kept between men.

Micah got into his Land Rover and rummaged in the glove compartment to find a small bottle of anti-acids. After swallowing several, he sat behind the wheel a few minutes and let the air-conditioner do its job. Closing his eyes, Micah leaned against the headrest. He hated conflict… minor, major, whatever. He smiled grimly and shook his head. He wouldn't allow his daughter to use the word hate. As he had explained to Katie, hatred was an evil emotion. Even so, the word fit, and he couldn't think of a substitute that would describe how he was feeling.

He wondered if it was a rite of passage to discover your parents weren't perfect. Realistically, he knew no one was perfect. Everyone had flaws, and God knew he had his share. As parents, though, his folks had come close to perfection. Even if they were experiencing a rough patch, he knew they were exceptional.

His cell phone rang, and it was Macy. She explained she would be at least another hour because there had been an emergency in the office. The medical crisis had delayed all the appointments, and the doctors were behind schedule.

Micah unconsciously started nodding as his sister spoke. The delay would give him time to visit another person, provided she would see him.

---

Driving into the parking lot, Micah called Macy. She said it would be another fifteen or twenty minutes. He pulled a music notebook from the glove compartment, but he didn't write anything down.

Micah was settled in his life and routines. It had taken a while, but he had found a balance between work and parenting. His daughter had been his top priority for several years. Now there was Tess to consider. She was an old friend and a new lover. Tess hadn't had an easy life, although he and his family had tried to help when they could. Everyone considered him so upright and strait-laced, but he had a devious side when needed. He'd needed it to steer money into scholarships and grants that couldn't be traced to him. Stan had been helpful in those endeavors.

Micah thought of Tess, and he smiled. He hadn't given much thought to a love interest in the past couple of years. It was there now. Maybe it had been there all along, but he hadn't recognized it for what it was. Most adults needed that kind of relationship and commitment. It just so happened he was also the faithful kind. Until his life with Carla had imploded, he'd never looked or even considered being with another woman.

Music had always been his mistress. He lived and breathed music, wrote it, played it, performed it. Music was an integral part of his being. It was what he was put on earth to do besides being a father and husband. Any other interests had to share time with the people he loved. He had been fortunate his family had traveled with him, supported him, and took care of him and his brothers during those early days.

He and Tess were just beginning, and they needed time to explore where they were going. One thing Micah did know was his talents had been bred into him. They were vital to him, and they had served him, his brothers, and his family well. His life was enriched by his talents, but what he did didn't compare to Tess's brilliance, her skills, and compassion for human life.

What he did enriched human life. Tess saved lives. Her

herculean efforts had already cost her more than a decade of study, research, and practice. She might be embarking on several more years of specialized training. Whatever decisions Tess made, he was already committed to supporting her decision. He knew to establish a long-term relationship with her would require that he become the support system to her as she had been to him. It was a role reversal he could handle. Tess was worth it.

He had kept a low profile for the last couple of years. He'd taken care of his daughter and managed to stay on higher ground when Carla had tried to drag him into a mud pit. Even the judge had commented on his composure after all the legal shenanigans she tried to pull.

He was able to paint now because he had spent the majority of the last couple of years in one place with a stable routine. The hours he spent painting had become less important to him than spending time with Tess. Time management was about compartmentalizing what was important. He had also noticed the insomnia wasn't kicking in every night. When Tess was beside him, he slept soundly.

## Chapter 13

**M**icah drove Macy to her second rehab session for the week, dropped her off, and took the interstate to his parents' home. With Katie on his heels, he knocked and surprised his mother with a visit.

"Micah, Punkin!" Carole exclaimed, giving them each a big hug. "Where's Macy?"

"Daddy took her to the doctor to fix her knee," Katie supplied.

"How long will she be?" Carole asked.

"She doesn't know from session to session," Micah said. "She'll call when she's finished."

"Are you hungry, do you want something to eat?" Carole asked. "Coffee? I can make some fresh."

"Coffee sounds good. Punkin, why don't you go find Lily?" Micah asked.

Katie ran off, and Micah sat at the kitchen table. "Mom, I came by to ask a favor."

"You know you can ask anything, honey," Carole said, smiling.

"I have to go on a business trip for a couple of days. Macy

is going to watch Katie for me. I'd like to take Lily to the lake so she can spend some time with her sister and help keep track of my whirling dervish."

Carole filled a coffee cup and set it in front of her son. "Why don't you leave Katie here?"

"Because you and Macy aren't exactly getting along right now. Lily needs to spend some time with her big sister. She hasn't so far because of this rift between you two. I don't know if your meeting Saturday evening is going to settle anything or not."

Carole sat across the table from her son, but she looked down into her coffee cup. "I don't think I want Lily spending a lot of time around Macy right now."

Micah couldn't believe what he'd just heard. "Excuse me?"

"You heard me," Carole stated flatly. "I don't think Macy is the kind of influence I want around Lily. We're having problems with Lily right now. She's being willful, stubborn, and talking back. I don't think allowing Lily to spend time with Macy is the right thing for her right now."

Micah pushed his coffee cup away. "Macy is her sister, her birth sister."

"Macy is too independent. She has deliberately set herself apart from the family. I'm not going to allow Lily to go in the same direction. Look at how she's treating Allison. Macy refuses to even speak to her twin sister. Now she's attacking me over how I'm raising Lily," Carole exclaimed.

"Okay," Micah said gently. "Macy being independent is true, but since when has that been a crime. She's been living on her own for six years. She lives on another continent and has been building a successful career in a disciplined art form. That's not deliberately distancing herself from the family. It's following her dream of being a dancer. The chances of her making it to her level were astronomical, but she's done it.

That's a good influence on Lily, seeing someone working hard toward a goal.

"As far as the feud with Allison goes, you heard one side of the story and assumed Allison's version was the gospel truth. I'm not telling you anything you don't know already, but Allison is a liar. She has lied to all of us older guys, conning money from us, and whatever else she thinks she's entitled to have. We weren't brought up with that attitude, and I don't know why you let her get away with it. You and Dad need to cut off the money flow and make her buckle down to reality before it's too late.

"That's not true," Carole said, shaking her head.

"It is true," Micah said firmly. "Allison is entitled, and immature, and if you can't see it, the rest of us can. We have all stopped the *borrowing* that never gets paid back. We've also learned that at least half of what she says is a lie.

"Macy is not attacking you. She is supporting her little sister because, apparently, she went through something similar when she received her offer to attend an elite ballet school. I heard the tape, and I was there and heard the yelling going on about you, not allowing Lily to study with Madam Bashlofski. It didn't make sense when you prevented Macy from attending an elite school, and it doesn't make sense now. Removing Lily from public school when she was a top student doesn't make sense either. Her school is ranked as one of the best in the city. You haven't removed Noah from his high school."

Carole jumped to her feet. "I told you, I'm not going to allow Lily to go the same way as Macy," Carole snapped. "I will not let that happen."

"Then you're going to lose her, Mom," Micah said sadly. "You can't pull the plug on someone's dreams. It's wrong. Even if the person doesn't have the talent to reach those goals, they have the right to try."

"Micah," Carole exclaimed reproachfully.

"I mean it," Micah said. "I'm going to find Punkin. We need to leave."

"Leave her here," Carole exclaimed. "You can swing by and get her later."

Micah shook his head. "No, I don't think so. If you think Macy is a bad influence, I can't, and I won't agree with you. I want my daughter to grow up believing any dream she wants to go after will be worth the effort. I want her to be independent and know she has to work hard for her goals, or they're not worth having."

"I'm not killing their dreams. I want them to understand a woman should think of her family first, not a career," Carole exclaimed.

"If a woman wants a family and places motherhood ahead of a career, no one should fault her choice. If she wants both a career and a family, all power to her. No one stood in your way, Mom," Micah said. "You and Dad were a successful duo in the music scene. The decision to quit a singing career and become a stay-at-home mother was your choice. You helped us older boys when we were kids and started a band. You supported us. You haven't tried to stop Noah from showcasing his talents. I don't understand the double standard. Why don't you think the girls should pursue their dreams?"

"That's not what this is about," Carole denied.

"From my viewpoint, it is," Micah said. "Never mind the favor. I'll see if I can snag Coyote to help watch Punkin, or I'll reschedule."

"Honey," Carole said, following her son. "You're misunderstanding. You'll understand when your daughter gets older and wants to be independent. You'll need to protect her."

"I intend to protect my daughter, but there's a difference between protecting her and denying her something she needs to complete herself. It would be different if we couldn't afford it, but that's not the case.

"I want Katie to strive for independence. You didn't smother us, boys, Mom. Why are you trying to stop the girls from doing what they want and need to do to be happy? You tried to do it with Macy, and now you're doing the same to Lily."

"You don't understand," Carole snapped.

"No, I don't!" Micah snapped. He instantly realized what he'd done and apologized. "I'm sorry, Mom, I didn't mean to yell at you. I don't understand, and I don't agree with what you're doing. I'm going to get Katie and visit with Lily for a few minutes. We're leaving. I sincerely hope you change your mind set before you go so far as to permanently damage your relationship with Lily. She has a right to a decent education, and whatever she wants to set as a goal." He kissed his mother on the cheek and left the kitchen. He hated seeing the hurt look on her face.

Micah connected with Coyote on his cell after he pulled into the parking lot of the rehabilitation center and asked if he would be able to help look after his daughter.

Coyote grumbled, more from habit than necessity. But, since he'd kept his brother's truck for a lot longer than he needed, he owed him.

"I am cleared for take-off," Macy exclaimed as she climbed into the Land Rover.

"What does that mean?" Micah asked.

"Driving! I can either rent a vehicle or borrow one of yours, so you don't have to drive me to these torture sessions."

"Good deal. We'll have a driving lesson around the lake this afternoon."

"You can't drive over twenty miles per hour on the lake road," Macy protested.

Micah grinned, and she punched him in the shoulder.

When his phone rang, Micah answered the Bluetooth connection and barked, "Ring me in about twenty minutes."

Twenty minutes later, he pulled into a convenience/gas station and stopped at the gas pumps. He unhooked Katie from her safety seat. He fished into his pocket for his wallet and handed his sister some bills. "Will you tell Loraine, that's the woman at the register, to give me forty dollars in gas, on pump five, and buy some fresh milk, bread, eggs and anything else you think we might need."

Macy nodded and guided Katie inside, realizing her brother wanted his conversation to be private.

Micah stuck the gas pump nozzle into the gas tank and answered his cell on the first ring. "What's up?"

"It's legal to talk on the phone when you're in a vehicle, as long as it's not handheld," Coyote growled.

"No privacy, Punkin and Macy are with me," Micah said.

"Yeah, okay," Coyote agreed. "Allison finally made contact. She says she's fine, she's an adult, and I should quit bugging her. Yes, she quit school three weeks into the semester, but what's the big deal? She's decided to travel around a bit. She's traveling with a friend she wouldn't identify, and I should stop pestering her. She doesn't need her big brothers shadowing her every move. Oh, but, could I deposit some money in her checking account. She's running a bit short this month!"

"Same old, same old," Micah said. "At least she's okay. Did you make the deposit?"

"No!" Coyote answered. "So, what do we do?"

"We dump it on Dad," Micah answered. "Technically, she's right."

"Dad isn't going to see it that way," Coyote said.

"Then it's for to him to decide what to do about it. If he wants to track Allison down, he'll do it. For all we know, she might be checking in every day with the folks. They might know all about her quitting school and her traveling agenda."

"Do you really believe that?"

"No," Micah admitted. "But short of hiring a private

detective to hunt her down, there's nothing we can do about it. It's none of our business."

"I got the call, so I'll talk to Dad," Coyote said. "I'll set the alarm for early Thursday morning, that's when Tess is due back, right?"

"Right, her flight arrives at ten, and tomorrow is the last day of school for Punkin. Sometime this weekend, Macy needs some driving practice. She needs to practice in the Mini Cooper and the Land Rover. I'm taking the truck."

"Yeah, yeah, any other chores you need to pawn off on me?" Coyote grumbled.

"I'll have a list ready, numbered by priority, and color-coded with little checkboxes," Micah promised, and he disconnected the call with a grin.

"You look happier now than you did a few minutes ago," Macy said. She set a bag of groceries in the backseat and helped Katie get strapped into her car seat.

"Coyote was checking in. He's going to be your housemate from Thursday evening until Sunday afternoon."

Macy cocked an eyebrow. "Tess is due back. Is this business or pleasure?"

Micah grinned, but he didn't feel a single twinge to his conscience. "Both. I have a meeting with my studio guys about the new soundtrack project, and we need some private time."

"Are you going to be around for the big showdown Saturday evening?"

"You said it was your show, and it didn't involve us guys," Micah said, but he leaned over and pulled an envelope from the glove compartment. "This might help."

They were on the highway before Macy raised her eyes from the letter. There were tears in her eyes. "How did you do this? Madam Bashlofski never gives a student a second offer if the first is turned down. Never!"

"It was easy. I begged, pleaded, and promised Madam

front row seats at your next lead performance. Complete with airfare and 5-star hotel accommodations—regardless of where the performance takes place."

"Micah, that's bribery," Macy exclaimed. "And it's going to cost you a bloody fortune!"

"Sissy!" Micah said sternly, and he lowered his voice. "No swearing in front of my kid, even the British version. Besides, sometimes it's nice to be able to toss a bit of incentive around to make people happy. If Lily gets the training she wants, it will be worth it.

"P.S. kid. Madam Bashlofski is your fairy godmother. One of your teachers filmed you dancing, and contacted Madam. She was the one who contacted the Paris Opéra Ballet School about your talent. It was her recommendation that sealed the deal. She's why you received your offer to train there. She's been keeping an eye on your career."

"Oh my God!" Macy exclaimed. "I've always wondered. I've never met her, and I owe my career to her!"

"She might have put in a good word for you, but you're the one who has put in the work," Micah said. "I made a lunch appointment for you next week with her."

---

"If you need to, you can call Mrs. Mayers to watch over Katie while you're with Macy in the vehicles. At least until she gets used to driving on the right side of the road again."

"Micah, go away. You've made your lists. You have your cell, and nothing is going to happen. Between the two of us, we can handle a six-year-old for seventy-two hours," Coyote complained.

Micah kissed his daughter again and got into his vehicle, waving as he drove off.

"Man, sometimes he's a pain in the butt!" Coyote exclaimed.

"He's overprotective," Macy agreed.

Coyote frowned down at his niece, who looked happy enough. "Okay, Punkin, no wild parties. Don't binge on more than two Disney movies before bedtime, and don't forget to brush your teeth! If you do, the whole world is going to explode... so don't. Got it?"

"Got it!" Katie said, giggling.

---

Micah stood at the bottom of the escalator. He was waiting for Tess. He'd seen a few cell phones aimed in his direction. There was no such thing as privacy these days. Finally, there she was at the top of the escalator and gliding toward him. She was smiling broadly.

"That smile tells me your interview went well," Micah said, taking her suitcase.

"This smile is for you, "Tess said. "The interviews did go well. I was warned that there are five other candidates in the running. There will be a second interview, and maybe a third. Dr. Frost has two fellowships open."

"You'll get it," Micah said.

Tess smiled. "I can hope, but I'm not going to stop looking at other possibilities."

Micah waited until they were in the truck before he leaned over and kissed her. "I've missed you."

"I've missed you, too," she whispered.

Micah drove from the airport parking lot and headed north.

Tess gave Micah the run-down of her interviews, not only with Dr. Frost but with several of his associates at the Naval facility. She had never been to Washington, D. C. before. A walking tour of the National Mall had been one of the high-lights of the trip. She'd walked from the Lincoln Memorial to the U.S. Capitol. She'd toured the Lincoln Memorial, and had walked the length of the Vietnam Memorial, and several other sites in the heat and humidity of summer.

"I'd love to take in all the sights and the museums, but I didn't have time this trip," she exclaimed. "Have you been there?"

"Several times, but in the surrounding states where they have bigger venues. That was in our younger days. We were there for a winter concert the year we won our first Grammy. We went to a few of the bigger monuments, but it had to be after dark. Mobs of crazed fans were a problem then. Causing a disturbance in that area would have been disrespectful. We shook hands with the President, but it was one of those, get in line and keep moving deals. He probably didn't have a clue about who we were."

"I'd forgotten about that," Tess said.

"I'm like you," Micah said. "I like to play tourist when I'm in a new city."

Tess's head turned as Micah drove past their exit. "Where are you going?"

"Austin," Micah said. "I've cleared the next three days for us. Except for a few hours here and there, when I have to get some things done. I've booked a suite at the Diskill Hotel for three nights.

"Micah!" Tess exclaimed. "I would have flown into Austin if I had known. You could have warned me. All I have is jeans and business suits."

"Then, we'll go shopping," Micah said. "Or we'll stay in, and use room service. I love my family, Tess, but lately, I'm beginning to feel boxed in. I wanted to surprise you, and I want some private time with you that I don't have to share with anyone else." He turned to her. "Unless you'd rather go home to the lake."

"No! You can't make an offer like that and try to rescind it! I've never been past the lounge at the Diskill Hotel. Thank you!" Tess exclaimed. "I'm very sure in that part of town, I'll be able to find a dress shop and everything I need."

## Chapter 14

They checked into the historic Diskill Hotel and went to their suite. Clothing wasn't a concern for the next several hours, as they never got past the bed. When their mini-marathon of sex was over, both of them left the high-end hotel dressed in jeans, and they weren't the only ones in casual dress.

Less than six blocks away, Tess found a boutique that supplied everything she needed except for shoes. The only issue they had was when Micah used his credit card and paid the bill.

"I'll pay you back," Tess said as they left the shop.

"This is on me," Micah said firmly. "You didn't know I was going to spring this on you, and it's my treat. Don't give me a hard time. Say thank you, like a good little girl."

"Thank you!" Tess said. "If I hadn't already checked the sad state of my checking account, I wouldn't accept. But, I did, so I will. Now, let's go over to that shoe store! I'll warn you ahead of time, Mr. Deep Pockets. I love pretty shoes, and I rarely get to wear them. We, doctors, tend to go more for comfort than fashion."

With the shopping done, Micah said he had several errands he needed to run. Tess had the option of staying at the hotel and using some of the amenities or going with him. She chose to go with him.

"This is your townhouse?" Tess asked as Micah pulled in front of a Federal-style brick townhouse in an exclusive neighborhood.

"It is," Micah said. "I need to check on a few things."

Tess followed Micah. He frowned at the front door lock. It had scratches on it, but the door opened to his code. The townhouse was an open concept layout. From the living room, you could see the dining room and the kitchen. Everything was state-of-the-art, sleek, and modern in style. It was beautiful, but not what Tess had expected. The inside felt cold, white, gray, and blue. Hospital colors, she thought, sterile colors.

Micah was walking around, opening appliances, and checking in closets. From what she could see, the interior was empty and devoid of all personality.

"What did you do with all the furniture?" Tess asked.

"What Carla didn't take, I sent to an auction house," Micah said. "I was premature in making that decision. Now, I've been told I should hire a staging company to make the place look lived in and appealing to the buyers. I've watched a few of those Do-It-Yourself stations on TV. This seems to be what is popular now. I told the renovator to do what they thought was best for selling it. Checking in with my real estate agent is the next stop. I was just checking to make sure Carla didn't get in and leave any surprises behind."

"Has she done that before?" Tess asked.

He nodded. "She trashed it. What she didn't know was I'd already had cameras installed. She smashed the marble countertops and sinks, broke cabinets, poured gasoline on the hardwood floors.

"That's when the mental evaluation was court-ordered.

Before all this crap started, we negotiated a settlement. It wasn't something we had to do. We were trying to get her to back off peacefully. It was a substantial settlement. After she accepted it, she changed her mind, and decided she wanted everything.

"She did over a hundred and fifty thousand dollars in damages to the townhouse, and she was ordered to pay every cent it cost to fix it.

"What saved me from what she considered justifiable retaliation were those cohabitation contracts. Carla insisted on signing them every year like clockwork. They protected her income and investments from me. What she didn't realize was they were also protecting me from her. Settlement investigators determined that over eighty percent of her expenses during the time we lived together were paid by me. I didn't have a problem with that when we were living together. When we split, she wanted more than half of what I was worth. She had zero invested in the townhouse or the business. I figure between her crazy episodes where she's had to repair what she tried to destroy, and her attorney fees, most of the settlement has been spent and legally it should have been returned.

"Stan sent someone to the airport a couple of days ago to make sure she got on a plane going to London. After the last episode of her phone harassment, and locking down the security at the lake, she was arrested, again. If you didn't know already, there are cameras at the entrances, and all over the lake property. She was caught on camera. The judge finally had enough too. He fined her a thousand dollars for a violation of the restraining order and warned her the next time there would be jail time. He also suggested she get counseling when she reached her destination."

"She should be on meds," Tess said.

"I lived with her off and on for six years before there was any hint of what was going on. Others could see it, but I sure couldn't. When I called her on what she'd been doing, that's when she flipped out. Which makes me either an idiot or a patsy."

"No," Tess said, going to him and giving him a hug. "That makes you a man who got involved with someone very young, and you kept trying to make it work. The two of you had different agendas. You are a tolerant man until you can't give any more, and you draw a line. If it had been anyone but Carla, they would have moved on. She had gotten her way for so long she believed she was entitled to it. You thought differently, and that's when she went nuts."

Micah laughed. "I expect to hear that kind of opinion from Coyote, not you."

Tess smiled. "I call it like I see it. I'm not speaking in a professional capacity at the moment. By the way, I very much prefer your house on the lake."

"So, do I," he agreed, looking around. "This looks like a five-star hotel suite. I've stayed in more than my share of them, and this place is impersonal."

He signed the final papers with the realtor, and the townhouse was officially on the market. The real estate company would deal with changing the locks and hiring a staging company. The townhouse would remain under security surveillance until it sold. An open house would be scheduled as soon as possible.

The next stop was on the outskirts of Austin, in an industrial complex. This was a newer area of the city. The building wasn't what Tess had expected for the music studio. She was surprised to see a parking lot full of vehicles. She had been under the impression Micah had closed the studio. When she said so, he looked at her with surprise.

"I wasn't going to close the studio and put people out of work because of her crap! She didn't own any part of the business. Carla might have continued to work here after we opened, and she was pulling a damn good paycheck, but McScout did not belong to her. She was eventually court-ordered to stay off the premises. She knew every person who works here would have called the police on her. I didn't realize how much she was disliked until things started falling apart. She hadn't made any friends, that's for sure. When the employees realized I wasn't going to defend her any longer, boy, did I get an earful!"

There were multiple large open areas. There was a lot of electronic equipment, and she didn't have a clue as to how it was used. The offices were sectored off with half-walls, and glass partitions. People smiled and waved as Micah strolled across the complex.

A man who looked vaguely familiar came from his office and offered his hand. "Good to see you, Micah. Did you hear from the Sterling brothers?"

"I did, and that's why I'm here. I wanted to hear your opinion on the project. First, though, this is Tessa Foster, a friend of mine. Tess, this is Bryon Norfork. He's the head guy in charge of keeping this place afloat."

Bryon laughed. "Sure, I am." He turned to Tess. "Don't believe it. Micah is as involved now, as he was when he was running a soundboard, he just does most things remotely. Are you a performer?"

"No," Tess said. "I'm a physician. Aren't you a country-western performer?"

"Was," Bryon said, cheerfully. "I still stick my toes in the water, now and again. When my wife had quadruplets, and I already had three squirts at home, my touring days were over. I was lucky enough to hook-up with this guy!"

"Tess, I need a few minutes with Bryon to discuss the Sterling project. Christina Lance is in a recording session, would you like to sit in on it?"

"Are you kidding?"

"No," Micah said seriously. He motioned at a young woman at a desk, and she joined them. "Kylie Franklin, this is Tessa Foster. Could you take her into the sound studio, where Christina is recording? I'll come to the studio when we're done."

"No problem," Kylie said. "This way."

Tess followed the young woman to a small entry space. She was handed an oversized set of earphones. "You're allowed in because the boss said so, but don't make any noise, and don't get in the sightline of Christina Lance. She's fairly new to the business, and she gets distracted easily," Kylie instructed. "The guys are cool about visitors, but please don't disturb them with questions. I'm expecting an important call, so I have to go. Someone will tell you when the recording session takes a break."

Tess was taken into a studio recording area, where there was a large window looking into a room where a teenage girl stood in front of a microphone. Tess stood where she was told to stand, and she watched and listened as the recording artist sang the same song many times. Sometimes the performer stopped and asked to restart again. At other times, one of the technicians would stop the music and ask the recording artist to start over. This process was repeated multiple times.

When Tess noticed heads turning, she looked around and saw Micah step in.

Christina Lance stopped singing and exclaimed, "Micah!"

The technicians stopped what they were doing and turned to face him. There was a chorus of "Hey, Boss. Good to see you! How's it going!" remarks.

"How is she doing?" Micah asked a man who was operating the large soundboard.

"She great as long as her jerk of a manager isn't around," the man said. "If we can keep him out of here, she's great to work with. When he's around, he micromanages everything she does and undermines her confidence. Christina needs to dump him and take on more creative control."

"We're talking with her parents, but don't spread that around," Micah said.

The door between the recording room and the control room flew open, and the young woman ran across the room and hugged Micah. "Where have you been? I haven't seen you in weeks!"

"I've been busy," Micah said, untangling himself. "How is the recording going?"

"Jerry, says it's going good," Christina exclaimed, and she backed off as Micah pulled Tess over to his side.

"Tess, this is Christina Lance, one of our newest artists. These guys are Jerry Wyhammer, Troy Seinfield, and Skip Johnson." He looked around at the technicians and his newly signed artist. "This is Doctor Tessa Foster. Is there anything I should know about? Anything I can fix?"

The men shook their heads, and the young woman was biting on her lower lip, and giving Tess a jealous look, as Micah's arm was around her waist.

"We could use a new cappuccino machine," a young man introduced as Skip said.

"It's not the machine," Troy argued with a grin. "I've shown you a dozen times how it works, and you still can't do it right! Stick with the soda machine, kid!"

"Maybe one that isn't so complicated," the young man said, ducking his head sheepishly.

"I'll look into it," Micah said, smiling with amusement. "We have to be going."

"See ya, Boss," the men said, putting on their earphones. The man at the soundboard pointed Christina Lance to the recording room. With a pout, she returned but not before she cast a look of jealousy toward Tess.

"What?" Micah asked when Tess had turned her head to look at him.

"Why is the company called McScout? Why not McKenna?"

"Because when I did an online search on McKenna, there were dozens of companies with the same name, including our family studio. After several frustrating weeks of trying to come up with a unique name, unsuccessfully, I typed in McScout, and bingo, there were no hits. Scout is my middle name. There are businesses named McScot, and Scout, but not McScout."

"It's not what I expected," Tess said.

"What did you expect?" Micah asked.

"I remember when the studio was just an idea. We went down to that horrible little place that needed a lot of work. It was on 6th Street, music row."

"True, and we were there for a couple of years. When we had that last big flood, every building on the street flooded. Dozens of businesses were destroyed, ours included. It was either rebuild or relocate. I decided music row, while it's quirky and trendy, is not in the best part of the city. That part of town is becoming more run-down every year. We were renting the building, and the owner wasn't willing to renovate it to our specifications, so I went looking elsewhere. We're on the outskirts of the city limits now. The buildings are new, and the area is more secure because most of them are used for industrial purposes."

"Is the studio just the one floor?" Tess asked.

"No, it's the entire building," Micah said. "I purchased it before the interior was completed, and had it built to the specifications I needed for the studio."

"That explains a lot," Tess said. "The townhouse, the studio–Carla, was living high, and she wanted to continue her reign, even though she wasn't footing the bill for it."

"That sums it up," Micah agreed.

"Christina Lance has a crush on you," Tess said.

"She's still a kid, seventeen when she signed on, she might be eighteen by now," Micah protested. "I deal with her parents, and she's lucky because they are terrific people."

"She is young," Tess agreed. "I had a crush on you when I was still a teenager. Be careful, and don't squash her. She's at that vulnerable age."

"I've been trying to ignore it," Micah said. He stopped at a red light and swung his head in her direction. "My business is done. Do you want to go shopping or do something else?"

Tess took a deep breath. "I want to return to that beautiful hotel room and jump your bones repeatedly. At least until it's time to get dressed and have dinner in that fancy restaurant downstairs."

Micah grinned as the car behind him honked. "That sounds like the perfect way to spend the rest of the afternoon!"

Lying on the hotel bed, Micah paged through a magazine and waited. A block from the hotel, when he had stopped for a traffic light, Tess had jumped from the vehicle and said she'd meet him in the room. She was striding away and disappeared into a shop before he could stop her. The name on the shop she ducked into was *Unmentionables*, but still, Micah was waiting. He didn't see much purpose in sexy underwear. He wanted Tess naked and under him, over him; he didn't care as long as he was inside her.

Damn! He was waiting, and since all he could think of was Tess, he was becoming more uncomfortable. Ever since they had reunited, he'd been walking around fully aroused most of the time. It had only been a couple of hours, since they'd made love, but he was in bad shape again.

He thought of her and all they'd done together. They were very inventive in the different ways they'd had sex. Neither of them was shy. Damn, his cock was aching. He flipped on the TV, but baseball or tennis wasn't a substitute for being buried deep inside Tess. Frustrated, he pulled off his clothes and walked into the massive shower

Tess was walking toward the hotel. What had she been thinking? Micah didn't need sexy lingerie. He liked her best naked. She could feel the crotch of her panties dampening as she walked. He didn't need to touch her. Just thinking about him set her off.

She tossed the lingerie bag onto a chair and went into the bedroom of the suite. She felt disappointed when Micah wasn't there until she heard the shower. She walked into the bathroom, ignoring everything except the naked man standing in the huge walk-in. She stepped in fully dressed and went into his arms. His mouth covered hers while his hands slid to her waist, unsnapped her jeans, and yanked them down.

Tess tugged off her boots, ripped off her socks, her jeans, and she was pulled upright, as Micah's hands were trying to unbutton her blouse, unsnapping her bra and tossing them outside of the shower. His hands covered her breasts while his lips covered her mouth.

Tess felt his erection against her belly, and she leaned into him.

He kissed her throat, gripped her ass, and pulled her into him. He lifted her to her tiptoes, but she wasn't tall enough.

She moaned in anticipation. Micah turned her around, guided her from the shower, and into a room, connected to the bathroom. It contained only a massage table. He lifted her to the table, positioned her just so, spread her legs, and thrust his engorged cock into her. He wasn't gentle. He was taking her hard and deep, the way she liked it.

When she came, Tess was sure it was the best three minutes of her life. How he was controlling her orgasm, she didn't know, but God, he was good at it. Until she'd had Micah, her orgasms had been hard to come by. Now she had them regularly, and the journey to get to that point was pure perfection.

Then it was Micah's turn. He pulled her off the table, and he lay on it. Surprisingly, he was still large and hard. "Ride me, Tess!"

Tess didn't have to be asked twice. She climbed on the table, straddled him, and rode him like a bucking bronco. She rode him until he came deep inside her again.

When they finally rolled off the table, they looked at each other, and both of them knew there was more to come.

"Tess," Micah's voice was raw and gritty.

"Yes!"

Micah turned her on her belly, bent her over the padded table. He took a buttock in each hand, pulled them apart, and inserted himself.

"Oh!" Tess exclaimed, and he pushed into her deeper.

"Oh!" she breathed when he began to rock, and buried himself to the hilt and pounded into her. If he was rough, she didn't care. The sensations he was creating inside her were worth it. If she was sore later, it was still worth it.

Micah wore her out. He was a machine that couldn't be shut off. When he did come again, she felt it. Body temperature within body temperature, she wasn't supposed to feel it, but she did. She was convinced of it, and his semen warmed her inside. He buried his face in her back for a few moments before he turned her around. He kissed her deeply, and she could still feel his erection hard against her. She looked down, and she couldn't believe it. He was hard and erect.

"You're Supersex Man," Tess exclaimed. "You're not taking anything, are you?"

"Nope, this is all me, and it has become a permanent condition when I'm around you," Micah admitted.

"I feel like I won the lottery," she laughed. "And I didn't even have to buy a ticket!"

Tess didn't get to wear her new dress or her new shoes. They called room service, and a fantastic meal was delivered.

She never bothered to wear her new lingerie either. Beyond pulling on the hotel complimentary robes after they showered, neither of them had worn anything. They did take a break for dinner. They did settle in, and watched a movie neither of them had seen, although it had been available for years.

Unspoken between them, they knew. She and Micah were simply resting their bodies. They would be having sex again as soon as they were ready for it.

They talked of this and that, his career, hers. They even spoke about Carole McKenna. Micah described what he considered unreasonable behavior. Tess couldn't and wouldn't make a diagnosis, but she did recommend several specialists who worked with older women. She also recommended a counselor or psychologist.

Micah forwarded the doctor's names to his father in a phone message. He deliberately turned off his phone and set it aside.

When Micah leaned in to kiss Tess, she felt a flutter inside. His breath fanned her cheek and neck as he went rock hard again. Strong musician hands stroked her breasts. The bathrobe was tossed aside, and she was pulled into his lap, so she could feel his erection.

"I know," Tess panted.

With a groan, Micah kissed her and carried her to the bed. She was to be his buffet, as he kissed her breasts, suckled them, and moved downward. He moved around her on his hands and knees, kissing, touching, stroking. When he reached her center, he took her with his mouth, his tongue was as wicked as a serpent.

Tess's body gave a physical jolt as he teased her with his tongue, circling, sucking.

"Micah!"

Her need was almost his undoing, but he would control himself. Micah would also control her. He licked her, slow and hot before inserting his fingers into her, pumping in her. She moaned and opened for him further.

"I know, sweetheart, I know," Micah soothed, but he wasn't ready to give her what she wanted. Not yet. He turned her over, stretched her arms straight out, and positioned her with her chest on the mattress and her bottom held high by bent knees. He stroked her bottom with his hands, slid his cock against her but not in her, and stroked several times.

Then he backed off and spanked her bottom, rubbed it, and smacked her again. He'd spank her, not too hard, but enough to feel the burn, and he fondled her. Then it was two smacks, and he stroked, fondled, or inserted his fingers to see if she was ready.

This pattern went on and on. Tess wasn't crying, but her bottom was stinging, and she was panting, pleading with him to take her.

Finally, Micah turned her over and slid into her with one long thrust. "God, do you know how good this feels?" he moaned.

"Yes! Please don't stop!" Tess gasped.

Micah had no intention of stopping. He thrust harder, and Tess's legs tightened around his waist, and climbed higher, nearly to his shoulders.

He smiled when he saw her half-opened eyes watch him sliding in and out of her, and she moaned with the pleasure. He withdrew only to pound into her harder and faster. When she came, it was a struggle not to release. He wanted so badly to come, but he wanted her complete submission and satisfaction first.

Micah pounded into her, and when Tess felt her muscles tightening around him, she held on. She shuddered, moaned, and finally stopped quivering inside with the last of the orgasm.

He gave Tess time to pull her mind and body together, and

then he began to thrust again. Micah wanted more for her, from her. It was almost painful when he started the rhythm again, but not a hurting kind of pain. This was a feeling Tess wanted to experience again and again. He worked her to that peak again, and when she came this time, he let himself go too. They fell together, exhausted, but they both knew this was going to be a weekend of total conquest.

---

Macy turned into the lake compound and slowed her speed considerably. This was her first time driving to her rehabilitation appointment and back. She was capable of making the trip, and she did, but she was exhausted.

Her knee was healing, but she had been warned not to expect to return to work for four weeks beyond her eight-week medical sabbatical. As Macy entered the house, she asked her brother if she could use his computer to send a copy of the medical reports to the ballet company physician.

"I keep telling you to use my computer as your own, Sissy," was Micah's reply. He gave his sister a concerned look. "You look tired."

"I'm tired after every session. My knee is healing on schedule," Macy said. She smiled and asserted a little more effort into pretending not to be exhausted.

"We got in late last night, and you left early this morning," Micah said. "Will you tell me what happened at your meeting with the parental titans?"

Macy pointed to the latte machine, and he opened the cabinet that held all the ingredients. She settled on a kitchen barstool.

"The meeting went very smoothly. I'd already talked to Lily and told her to keep her temper under control. I think the folks must have decided everything ahead of time. Dad said Lily would be registering at Adams Academy in mid-August. He told her they would prefer she didn't board there, but the option could be discussed during the Christmas break. By then, she'll have spent some time there, and made some new friends. Dad said, if she still isn't happy living at home, they would consider it.

"When I produced the letter from Madam Bashlofski, Lily screamed with excitement. I didn't tell her how you got Madam to change her mind, so I inadvertently took credit for it. Mom didn't look pleased about it. Dad said he would make the transportation arrangements for Lily to attend the classes. He also told Lily he expected better grades from the academy than she'd been receiving from the homeschooling assignments.

"Lily was a little cheeky. She said if she hadn't been so far ahead in her schoolwork, she wouldn't have received the top grades on the entrance exams. Dad must have been in contact with someone at Adams Academy because he agreed. Two weeks before school starts, Little Sis will be taking another series of tests to see if she should jump a grade.

"Dad also suggested Lily should come out to the lake and spend some time with me. We can spend some fun time together, and I can give Lily the inside track on what it takes to become a professional dancer."

"The meeting went over a lot better than you expected," Micah exclaimed.

"Didn't it?' Macy asked, accepting the latte. She crooked a finger at her brother, and when he lowered his head, she kissed him on the cheek. "I know you were involved somehow. Dad had already set the agenda. I don't know what you said to him, but thank you. I also know Mom has been making doctor appointments. They tried to deemphasize that our mother might need some help or medication. I don't think it was something they wanted Lily to know about. They waited until she left the room before mentioning it."

"There were no discussions about your problems with Allison?"

Macy shook her head. "Mom tried to raise the subject, but Dad shut her down. He said he had some things to settle with Allison himself. My twin is MIA. Lily didn't know what that meant, and Dad told her Allison had quit school again. She wasn't answering her phone, and they didn't know where she was living at the moment. Dad masks his emotions, but he's hot under the collar about it. He said before he concerned himself with our tiff, he had some things that had to be discussed and straightened out with Allison. I hope I'm a continent away when that happens.

"Coyote told me later she stuck Dad with five months' worth of overdue rent, and who knows how much tuition money was lost when she quit. Dad has locked down her trust and her allowance. The money flow has stopped, and she's got some explaining to do. Do you think she might be taking drugs?" Macy asked.

"I hope not, but at the same time, I wouldn't be surprised," Micah said. "She's been making some awful decisions for the last couple of years. If she follows the same pattern she's had for years, Allison will come home, whining that she needs help. They'll take her in, and she'll be good for a couple of months. She'll get bored, and she'll suck the folks for a place to live and a vehicle."

"When are they going to see the real Allison?" Macy asked.

"No parent wants to admit their kid is out of control. Hopefully, it will be this time."

## Chapter 15

Tess stretched on the lounge chair, watching as six little girls, ran around chasing each other, screaming and giggling.

"You'd better be listening," Lauren said in a loud warning voice from her place on another lounge chair. "If one toe goes into the water without permission, it's naptime for everyone!"

Tess smiled as she watched the little girls chasing after a butterfly. "I don't know how you do it!"

"Lots of practice," Lauren said. "How are you enjoying your break?"

"It's easy to get used to not working around the clock," Tess admitted. "I was called in once for a seven-car collision on the interstate. It was a busy evening, but I came home, and I didn't have to listen to another pitch by Dr. Pickerton about rejoining the team."

"Home?" Lauren questioned.

"It was a slip of the tongue," Tess said, shrugging.

"How serious are you and Micah?" Lauren asked.

"Does it bother you?" Tess asked.

"Why would it?" Lauren asked. "I haven't dated Micah since I was a junior in high school."

"That's good because he's mine now," Tess warned.

"You've had a thing for him since you were about sixteen or seventeen," Lauren said. "Do you have any idea where you might be going? Micah is well established in Austin and San Antonio."

"We're still at the beginning stages of our relationship," Tess said.

"Do you love him?"

"I think I do, and it scares me to death," Tess said honestly. "The real, long-term kind of love. Neither of us has made a commitment, but he's not the flighty type."

"Neither are you," Lauren said. "I think he's perfect for you."

Tess shook her head slightly. "That's what scares me. He has a high-profile lifestyle, and I have a high-stress lifestyle."

"You have to start living a real life at some point. You've been hiding your private life behind the excuse of '*Doctor—I don't have time,*' for far too long."

"My job has been making life and death decisions," Tess reminded her sister.

"For other people," Lauren said. "You're at your best in high-stress situations at the hospital. It's been in the man and woman areas where both of us have failed. I failed in my marriage to Chris, but I got my daughters from it, so that made it worth it. He's still an asshole. He was a deadbeat as a husband, and he's worse as a father. He wouldn't gain anything by re-entering his daughters' lives, therefore, it isn't worth his effort. You, dear sister, haven't given anyone a fair chance. One mistake and you shut them down, and bury yourself in work."

"With our parents' marital records, both of us are sort of soured on men," Tess admitted.

"I'm dating Stan Mulclusky," Lauren said.

Tess turned to her sister. "Really?"

Lauren nodded. "We've spent a lot of time together over the last several years. He's been fighting my battles for a long time. Over the last year, our relationship began to change. Because he was still representing me, it wasn't a good idea to let it be known. The girls love him, and it's reciprocated."

"Is it serious?"

Lauren nodded again, but her eyes were on the shoreline. "Katie! Back away from the lake, and bring the girls over into the grassy area!" She turned to her sister and smiled, although her eyes were still on the children. "I know my marriage to Chris was a Class A catastrophe. I was a fool to allow myself to be bullied and used. I accept that while I was at fault too, Chris was... is, and will probably be an asshole of a human being all his life. Stan isn't. He's been there backing me and giving me encouragement when I needed it. The girls are a lot, but I want more than children in my life. Stan is a good man, and I miss having love in my life."

"Then go for it," Tess said. "I'm happy for you!"

"Good," Lauren said. "I wanted your approval. It means a lot because you have been there for us too. Before the kids start school in the fall, we're going to have a simple, quiet ceremony."

---

Tess lowered her iPad as Micah walked onto the patio. He sat beside her and kissed her. "Did you have a good day with Lauren?"

"It was terrific. Are you done with business for the day?"

"Yeah, we passed on the project. The Sterling brothers weren't happy with our decision, but it was a unanimous vote. It wasn't a good fit for the studio. The Sterling brothers have a history of changing scripts at the last minute and deliberately adding scenes which would change the rating, and that's not how we work.

"Everyone who works for McScout Productions has a reputation for being honest and forthright. We don't play games with people after the contracts have already been signed. We'll go so far as an R rating, depending on the content, but we won't do NC-17. All of the senior staff agrees that we want to keep the content viewable to our children. As parents, we don't want to be involved in projects that would at any time embarrass our families."

"Do you have to pass on a lot of opportunities?" Tess asked.

Micah shrugged. "Not so many that it makes a difference in our bottom line. The studio has a solid reputation. How was your day with Lauren and the girls?"

"It was a rare day. She stays busy, that's for sure. Did you know she was dating Stan Mulclusky?"

"No, I didn't, but I think they make a good match," Micah said thoughtfully. "Thanks for keeping an eye on Katie today. Everyone had somewhere they had to be."

"She loves playing with the girls," Tess said.

"She's worn out," Micah agreed. "I sent her to her room for a little quiet time, and when it got too quiet, I checked on her. She's taking a nap, which doesn't happen too often these days. She stopped taking naps about a year ago. Macy is here, and she can keep an eye on her. She took Lily over to Madam Bashlofski's ballet school this morning. Lily will be taking two classes a week starting next week."

"How is your mother handling these decisions?"

"Not well, but in this particular case, she was overruled. I don't think that has happened very often in the last decade. She has double standards going, boys versus girls, and Allison versus Macy. She has several doctors' appointments scheduled, one with a psychologist. Hopefully, all this will settle down, and the mother I remember will be back."

"She'll still be the mother Macy remembers too. That double standard is a bitch to overcome. Macy has seen a counselor over the way she was treated," Tess said.

"I know," Micah said. "For a twenty-year-old, she's got her head on straight. I'm not sure I was that confident when I was twenty."

"You were," Tess said. "I remember it clearly, and so does my backside."

"You're due for a little maintenance," Micah said with a gleam in his eyes.

"I got plenty when we were in Austin," Tess assured him. "You have a butt fetish."

"I don't deny it," Micah said, pulling her into his lap and caressing her nicely rounded bottom. "Can you set your book aside for a little while? Macy will watch over Katie until one of us comes home. Coyote went to the store for some fresh steaks. He wants to grill tonight."

"Definitely," Tess agreed, as her lips met his.

Micah spent a few hours with his lady, and they walked to his house, hand-in-hand. Coyote's Jeep wasn't back. He found his daughter and his sister in his office.

Macy was talking to someone on a live feed, so he motioned for his daughter to come with him, so his sister could have some privacy.

Tess had her head in the refrigerator, and she reappeared with several jars of condiments. "If you have potatoes, we can make potato salad."

"We have a big bag of potatoes," Katie said, going to the pantry, and Tess followed her.

Macy came into the kitchen with a wide smile. "I was talking to Max."

Micah made a face. "Do I need a drink first?"

"The strongest thing you drink is coffee! Admittedly very strong coffee," Macy chided, but her eyes were sparkling with excitement.

Micah sat at the kitchen counter. "Okay, give it to me!"

Macy was almost dancing. "These are direct quotes. 'Beautiful, remarkable, talented. If the paintings are half as good as the photographs, I'm interested. Who is the artist? Where can I view his work? Do you know him? May I contact his agent? I would like to see his work in person.' Max does not get this enthused about a new artist very often."

Micah looked upward at the loft area and then to his sister. "I'm not sure I'm ready for this."

Macy looked disappointed. "Max is usually much more reserved. He wouldn't take the time to see your work if he didn't think you were exceptional. He's coming over to the States to finalize some contracts for the LA Gallery. After he's finished there, he's going to fly into San Antonio."

"Are you ready to let everyone in on your secret?" Micah asked.

"No! This is about Max Barrington-Smythe, Art Connoisseur, wanting to meet a talented artist," Macy said seriously.

"Uh-huh," Micah snorted. "You get to keep your secrets, but I don't."

"I'll get a promise of silence from him before we let him see anything. You don't have to let Max represent you. I'm not trying to force you into anything."

Micah closed his eyes for a moment. "Sissy, I'm not sure I want to be represented. My learning to paint was about healing myself."

Micah went for a walk to clear his head. He did want to know if what he painted was good. As simple as that was, it was strictly for his ego. Showing interest in having his work viewed might have been a mistake. He'd learned a long time ago, egos could become self-consuming. The bottom line was he didn't think he had time to launch a side career in art. Getting involved with Tess had cut into his painting time, and he hadn't given it much thought. Spending time with Tess was far more important than anything he could paint on canvas.

***

Coyote came in carrying two grocery sacks. Tess and Macy were in the kitchen preparing something, and he looked over Tess's shoulder on the way to the refrigerator. "Great, I love potato salad! Where's Big Bro?"

"Daddy's upstairs," Katie said. "We're going to make brownies!"

"Would one of you dump this stuff in the frig for me. I need to see Micah about something," Coyote said, as he jogged across the room. Tess began to unload the groceries.

Micah was standing in front of the painting of his grand-parents.

"Wow," Coyote said.

"Do you remember them?" Micah asked.

Coyote nodded. "Some, but not like this. This is awesome. It's like our history coming to life."

"I'm going to give it to Dad on his birthday," Micah said.

"That's cool. You're going to make the old man cry, and he hates to cry in public. Can you make a print from this? I'd like a copy of it, and I know Sully would too."

"I don't know. I think a reproduction is called a Giclée print, but I don't know how that process is done. I'll have to do some research, or just paint it a couple of times."

"Good deal," Coyote agreed and pointed to the painting of him and Katie on the Ferris wheel. "That one is mine."

Micah took a deep breath of exasperation. "No, that one is mine. Every time I paint something for myself, you snag it."

"I'm your secret keeper," Coyote said, grinning. "Besides,

you can repaint it. Does this mean you're going to let your secret out?"

"I haven't decided," Micah admitted. "I have several weeks until Dad's birthday."

Coyote waited. He knew his brother, almost as well as he knew himself. He waited.

Micah stood staring at the painting, and he looked around the room, surveying the stacks. "Macy thinks it's weird I've never signed a painting. What's your take on it?"

Coyote looked at the lifelike portrait of himself and his niece. He looked around at the paintings. "I think you've painted your way out of depression and grief from losing Nick and Sally. The breakup with Carla was part of it, but it wasn't the main event. If she had moved on, as any decent person would expect, you might have reacted differently.

"You're an optimist, brother. You love life, and that's what comes out in your painting. When you started painting, it was a crutch. Now, it has become part of your creative DNA. When you're ready, you'll sign."

The brothers returned to the kitchen and asked if there was anything they could do to help. After receiving a negative from the women, they migrated over to the piano. They still had a couple of hours before it would be time to start grilling.

Micah asked his brother to give him an opinion on a song he was writing. Sitting side-by-side at the piano time slipped away from them. They argued over lyrics, bridges, harmonies, and it became a work session. They bounced ideas off each other, with the ease of having worked together for years.

Songwriting was a collaborative effort between the brothers. Later, when Micah took a coffee break, Coyote went to his Jeep. He brought a long cardboard tube inside and spread a blueprint out on top of the piano.

"You did it," Micah said, looking at the plans. "It's the

boathouse tower plans. You finally decided to do something with it."

Tess and Macy joined them at the piano. Micah could read blueprints, something he'd learned when he'd helped design his home. He listened, as Coyote went over every detail of his rebuilding, and expansion plans for the boathouse. His plans would demolish the existing boathouse, and the small tower extending from the roof. He would rebuild the boathouse into a larger structure and build a four-story tower with the total dimensions of two-thousand square feet. It would resemble a lighthouse, overlooking the lake.

"Wow," was Micah's reaction. "I like those balconies on the second and third levels overlooking the lake. Using the boathouse roof for a massive deck is a great use of the space. Outdoor living at its best."

"Bikinis and grills," Coyote said, grinning.

"I may have to cut down a few trees, so I'll have a better view," Micah said mockingly.

"Hey! Ouch!" Micah exclaimed as both Macy and Tess whacked him over his remark.

"So, you think it's good?" Coyote asked.

"Yeah, but this is a major undertaking. The foundation of the boathouse will have to support that kind of weight," Micah warned.

"I know, but some of the cost of the boathouse rebuild can come from the family pot. It houses the boats everyone uses, and we've talked about rebuilding it several times. I'll foot the bill for the majority of it. If I'm going to do it—I'll do it right."

When the girls had walked away, and Coyote was re-rolling the blueprints, Micah asked a question he had meant to ask before. "How is that woman doing? The one you moved into Aunt Lydia's apartment."

"Karen is doing fine, so far. She filed a restraining order against her husband, again. She's been trying to divorce him for the last three years. Stan did some investigating. Karen has filed six complaints so far, and none of them have been investigated. Most of them have mysteriously disappeared from the files. She was smart enough that she's kept copies of the reports.

"Stan filed a complaint against the Police Department through the District Attorney's office. There are going to be investigations completed by both the Police Internal Affairs, and the DA offices. Her husband is a real sleaze. He has a history of domestic abuse, with both of his wives, as in polygamy. He didn't bother to divorce his first wife before he married again. She didn't have a clue about him being married before. She's the second wife, so legally she's not married, although Stan is doing some research on Texas statutes.

"Our dear friend Mulclusky has also pulled her medical files and submitted them as evidence. There have been a total of five trips to the emergency room in four different hospitals in the last couple of years. Emergency rooms have to file reports on suspected abuse, and those reports have been signed off and buried without investigation from the Austin Police Department. Stan has the current District Attorney involved, and he's already warned both departments he's not going to allow this investigation to accidentally be buried again.

"Karen's father-in-law is a police captain. He also has two uncles on the force. They have various relatives scattered throughout the police and legal system of Austin. Those guys think they have a private fix going on. Stan and the District Attorney are going to take these people down. Stan loves taking on the bad guys."

They sat on the deck, enjoying the summer night. Long after the steaks were grilled to perfection, and the meal was enjoyed, nightfall fell around them. Katie was carried off to bed when she fell asleep, and Coyote was the first of the adults to call it a night. As he jogged toward Sully's house, Micah cocked his head to the side.

"I wonder what he's doing? He says he's finished with college, but he's gone a heck of a lot."

"He'll tell us when he's ready," Macy said. "You're not the only McKenna who likes to keep his private life private. I'm calling it a night too."

"Lock the doors behind me," Micah said. "I'll walk Tess over to the lodge."

"Stay there, if you want. If something happens, I'll call," Macy said. "Better still, Tess, what would you think of swapping places with me? You can move into Micah's house, and I'll move over to the lodge for the rest of my stay, or I'll move into Sully's house with Coyote. There's plenty of extra space in either place. Max and I will want to spend some time together while he's here."

"Do I get any say-so in this switchover?" Micah asked.

"No," Tess and Macy said in unison.

"It makes sense," Tess said, as they walked down the road toward the lodge.

"Will you be able to finish your papers at my house? It gets noisy," Micah said.

"You have an office designed as a world control center," Tess said. "I think I can make do unless you don't want me to move into your house."

"I didn't say that," Micah said quickly. "I'm all for the idea."

On the walk to the lodge, Tess stopped and turned to Micah. "Do we need to discuss this change? I don't want to push you."

"No, and I wish you would," Micah said honestly.

"What do you mean?"

"Tess, I haven't been a guy who dated a lot, especially in recent years. I'm an old-fashioned man in many ways. I don't sleep with a woman unless I believe there's a future in it. Although I will admit, my brain wasn't working the first time we got together.

"You've been dodging relationships and commitments for a long time. I'm sure it has a lot to do with your parents' situation, but I'm fully committed to you. I don't have a problem with sharing my home, my life, or my bedroom with you. But, I do have a daughter I have to consider. At her age, she won't think there is anything wrong with it. You've been a constant in her life. I need to know if you are even considering taking our relationship to the next stage."

"Marriage?" Tess said, taking a deep breath.

"Marriage," he agreed.

"Of course, I've thought of it," Tess said honestly. "It scares the hell out of me. I've seen what happens when it goes wrong. So have you, and you didn't take that final step."

"I won't do that again," Micah said firmly. "I won't live with a woman indefinitely. Promises are too easily broken. Vows are a binder. Most people don't believe that, but I do. We also have something else to consider. I want more children, and I know you want children. It's time we got on with it. I'm over thirty, and you're getting close to it. Adoption takes time. If we tried in vitro fertilization, that would take time. There's a lot to consider. And, there is your career."

"I won't stop being a physician," Tess said.

"I'm not asking you, to," Micah said. "If you get the fellowship with Dr. Frost, we'll have to move somewhere close to the Naval hospital. I make music and guide singers and musician's careers. You save lives. I can't compare what I do with what you do.

"I've been running McScout remotely for years. It won't make much difference if I'm sixty-five miles away or fifteen hundred miles away. I will be spending more time flying. I haven't done much of that recently."

"You'd do that for me?" Tess exclaimed. "It's asking too much!"

"No, it's not," Micah denied. "I need to know we're on the same page and moving together in the same direction. That direction has to be with a pledge toward forever."

"Marriage," Tess said, taking a deep breath.

"That is how I work," he said. "I can't take that other route again. I won't deny who I am to myself, ever again. I've learned that lesson the hard way."

"I know," Tess said. "I dreamed about marriage with you at sixteen. All those silly dreams girls have at that age. I set it aside, although it was there, tucked away safely, so I wouldn't be hurt by seeing you with someone else."

"I was a fool, and where four years don't make a difference now, the difference between sixteen and twenty is unsurmountable, and illegal. Take a chance with me, Tess," Micah said. "Take a chance on us. We have the next fifty or sixty years to get it right."

"Yes," Tess said, as she was pulled into a tight hug and deep kiss.

With his arm wrapped around her waist, Micah nudged her to keep walking.

"I want the diamond," Tess said. "I'm not willing to relinquish that silly dream. I know you can afford a door knocker, but it has to be small enough so it won't interfere with my work."

Micah smiled. "We'll go out as soon as we can and pick it out. Whatever you want, Tess, I'll make those dreams come true."

## Chapter 16

The switch of Tess to Micah's house, and Macy to Sully's house, required a couple of short trips in his truck. Katie was excited to have Tess with them. A simple explanation that Tess needed to use Daddy's office sufficed without any discussion of where Tess would be sleeping.

"Max is coming next week!" Macy exclaimed, rushing into the house.

"I would never guess that you miss him," Tess teased.

"I do," Macy exclaimed. "You'll like him. He's wonderful!"

"I'm sure we will," Micah said as his phone rang and he looked at the incoming number. "Yeah, Dad, what's up?" He listened for a few minutes. "I'll call you back," he promised.

"What is it now?" Macy asked.

"Dad wants everyone to come over on Friday night. There are a few things he wants to discuss."

"About what?" Macy asked. "We've pretty much settled most of our differences."

"He didn't say. He just said family business," Micah said.

"Which could mean anything," Macy said suspiciously. "It could be an ambush!"

"And, it could be business-related or just something he wants to discuss with us as a family," Micah said. "Mom and Dad aren't the enemy, Sissy."

"Sorry," Macy apologized.

"Friday evening," Micah said sternly. "Don't think you're skipping it, because you're not."

"Are you sure you know what you're doing?" Macy asked Tess. "He's got a bossy side!"

"I know," Tess said. "I also know I've already made a commitment for Friday evening."

"What would that be?" Micah asked.

"I have an interview over at a New Braunfels Hospital at six p.m. I'm going to interview for a resident physician position," Tess said. "The hospital has an excellent rating."

"I thought you were going to try for a small private practice or clinic," Micah said. "Are you going into a panic again?"

"No, but this position would have me working with some very good cardiothoracic surgeons. I've already completed a residency with surgery. This position would help me fine-tune those rusty skills," Tess explained.

"Can I stay over at Granny Nana's, Daddy?" Katie asked.

Micah swung around to look at a calendar. "You have a sleepover/birthday party Friday night and part of Saturday."

"I forgot Cheryl's party," Katie said, but her little face brightened instantly. "I can tell her I have to go to Granny Nana's."

Micah shook his head. "That would be a lie, and you've already accepted the invitation to Cheryl's party. Would you like it if someone promised to come to your party, but then they didn't come? That wouldn't make them a very good friend, would it?"

Katie chewed on her lower lip. "I want to be a good friend. I'll go to Cheryl's party."

"Good decision," Micah agreed.

"Saturday," Micah said when he slid into bed beside Tess.

"Saturday, what?" Tess asked.

"Engagement ring shopping," Micah said, leaning over and kissing her.

Tess closed her eyes, and when she opened them, he was still face-to-face with her. "Do you feel like this has been a long-time coming, but it's still right?"

"Very much so," Micah said. "It does feel right. I feel like I should be apologizing for all those years of trying with the wrong woman."

"You can't change what has already happened. I believe things are meant to happen in their own time. My mind is spinning," Tess said. "All the things I've been thinking about for years are suddenly possible. Ideas and dreams, I'd set aside for years, and now they have flooded to the front of my consciousness."

"Such as?"

"You," Tess said, kissing him, but pointing to her head. "All those little thoughts and wishes that have been floating around tagged with an indefinite *maybe, someday*. I'd more or less given up on men. Children were a dream. The likelihood of finding someone who would be willing to adopt or accept a child that wasn't theirs by birth was a worry. It's overwhelming."

Micah wiped the tears from her face. "It shouldn't be. There's plenty of love in both of us. We have more than enough to share and spread around."

Tess scrutinized her limited wardrobe and finally selected a fern green suit jacket to pair with white slacks. The jacket would bring out the green in her eyes, and she would finally get to wear the expensive shoes she'd bought during their weekend at the Diskill Hotel. She took more care than usual with her make-up and finally passed muster in the bathroom mirror. What mattered was her professional credentials, and there weren't many physicians her age who could match them.

She wasn't sure she wanted to go into a hospital environment full time again. Still, the position would be of a resident surgeon, specializing in cardiothoracic surgery. It would be different from running an emergency department where she had spent the last three years. She had sacrificed her personal life before. She wasn't willing to do it now.

Tess was the last to leave the house. Micah and Macy were on their way to San Antonio for the Friday night family meeting. She was going in the opposite direction. Tess set the house security and made sure to activate the front gate security. She'd been reprimanded twice by Micah because she'd forgotten. The second warning had come with a hard swat across her backside as a reminder.

Living under constant security measures all the time was something Tess found bothersome. However, she knew it had become necessary in his position. She could remember when the McKenna family had lived across the street. When the I-35 band's first CD had hit the music industry charts and kept climbing, the neighborhood had been overrun by rabid fans. While the family had been on a world tour, their home had been nearly dismantled by fans.

Micah arrived at his parents' home and saw Coyote's Jeep pulling in ahead of him. As they were about to enter the house, Macy's phone rang. She answered it, looked concerned, but waved her brothers to go on in the house ahead of her.

When she entered the house, she was tucking her phone away.

Daniel McKenna greeted his children as they came in. Lily ran down the stairs and hugged her siblings.

"How is the new training going?" Macy asked.

"It's hard but exciting and wonderful," Lily exclaimed with a happy smile. "I have to set the table."

As she skipped from the room, Micah turned to Macy. "She's a lot happier than the last time I saw her. Is everything okay? You had a worried look on your face when you took the phone call."

"It was my credit card company. Most people get an e-mail fraud alert. I get that, and a personal phone call. Someone is at it again. This time it was a charge coming in from Seattle. The phone company did some kind of triangulation, and voice recognition on my phone, while they were on the phone with me to make sure I am where I say I am."

Micah nodded. "It sounds like they're on the ball."

Dinner was an unusually quiet meal for the McKenna household. Most of the conversation was between the sisters, or Micah and his father. Noah wasn't present, and Daniel explained he was taking lessons with a local musician who was an industry legend. When the meal was over, Daniel asked Lily to stack the dishes but told her, he and Mom would do the rest of the cleanup later. She was excused because she and Noah had already been told what the meeting was about.

Moving to the family room, Daniel sat beside Carole and took her hand.

"I called this meeting to apologize. Mostly to Macy," Daniel said. "We've already had this discussion with Lily, and Noah, and we will repeat it with Allison, and Sully when we see them next. Your mother has been under some strain over the past several years. Medical tests have confirmed she has a chemical imbalance, and what they call fibromyalgia. We believe it's part of the reason why she has responded to some of our family issues, as she has."

"I have already started a treatment plan which will hopefully alleviate some of the pain," Carol explained. "It will require a special dietary and exercise program, and I am going to be working with a psychologist on some parenting and marital issues. Daniel will join me later in therapy. I do apologize, Macy, for making you feel like your dreams and needs weren't important. I should have seen it years ago, but I didn't!" Carol broke down in tears. "I never meant for you to feel left out. I only wanted what was best for both of you, girls."

"As long as Lily's needs are met, and she's happy, I'll be okay," Macy said gently.

"You'll settle your differences with Allison?" Carole asked.

"Our issues are between us," Macy said with a slight shake of her head. "Please, don't interfere."

"But…"

"Carole," Daniel said firmly. "We agreed it wasn't our business."

Carole seemed to deflate, but she nodded. "I think I need to rest for a while," she said.

"I'll be back," Daniel said, and he walked with his wife from the room.

Macy's phone rang, and she took her cellphone over by a patio-facing window.

"Your bank again?" Micah guessed when she returned to the couch.

"Yes, they said they have a positive lead on the person using a fake or duplicate card, and an arrest is imminent. That's all the information they would give me. They said they would handle it and keep me informed," Macy said. "Why is it this person can steal my identity, but the people in charge of catching them want to keep everything a secret from me?"

"My friend, Karen, who is in hiding right now, is dealing with the same thing," Coyote said. "The laws seem to be skewed to protect the bad guys, not the victims of the bad guys.

Although there is another point of view. If they were to tell the people who had been ripped off or hurt who did it, the victims might go postal, and not wait for the law to do its job. It's sort of a paradoxical situation."

"He's a Libra," Macy said. "He sees both sides of everything."

Coyote frowned and rolled his eyes.

Daniel returned to the family room. He continued the discussion with his adult children. He explained a regimen of hormone replacement their mother would be taking, and the sessions they would both be attending with the psychologist.

"Dad, if the situation doesn't improve, maybe Lily should be allowed to board at the Adams Academy," Macy suggested.

"Your mother is already making progress," Daniel said. "I do intend to keep a better watch over what is going on. Not only with Lily, but with Noah and Allison too. Your mother is a strong woman. She'll get past this, you'll see."

---

Tess's interviews were far more extensive than she expected. The discussions were all-inclusive, with tours of the different departments of the hospital. The surgeons were impressed that she was willing to take a step down from heading a hospital department, to work in a resident capacity to update her knowledge. They discussed allowing her to operate without supervision, as soon as her skills were assessed. Doctor Jenkins, from the orthopedics department, was the first to call it a night. Tess was surprised to discover it was after nine p.m. The time had flown by. She shook hands with the doctors, who promised another round of interviews with the hospital administrators.

After leaving the hospital parking lot, she turned onto the avenue that would take her to the interstate and to the lake property. She was five blocks away from the hospital and accelerating because the stoplight had turned to green. Glancing in her rearview mirror, she saw a large pick-up truck driving far too fast behind her. There wasn't a second lane, and the curbs on the right were lined with parked cars.

Tess steered as close as she dared to the right, but she knew she was going to be hit. She looked to the left, and a scream formed in her throat, but never made it to her lips. The truck slammed into the side of her car. She screamed, but the sound she made was part scream and part FUCK, and she was struck hard when the airbag deployed in her face. In what felt like slow motion, she felt the hit and heard the screeching of metal bending and contorting around her. She couldn't see it, but she heard it. There was a sudden jolt as the movement stopped.

Tess could hear voices around her, but she was fighting to breathe against the airbag, and she tasted blood.

"Ma'am!" a young man shouted at her. "Don't move! There's glass everywhere! Are you hurt?"

"Puncture the airbag!" Tess shouted although she wasn't sure her voice could be heard around the plastic.

"Ma'am, we've already called for emergency help," the young man said. "We can't get this crushed door open, but nothing seems to be leaking from the car, so you should be safe enough. You shouldn't be moved until the emergency people get here."

Tess was trapped. She could feel the warm blood flooding from her nose, and she did a quick self-assessment for injuries.

"I'm a doctor," Tess shouted. "I'm not hurt! Puncture the airbag!"

There was a pop, and the bag deflated.

"Ma'am, you shouldn't be moving around, until the emergency techs get here!" the young man insisted.

"Break the rest of the glass from this window, and lay a jacket or something over it," Tess said. "I'll climb out the window."

It took a few minutes, as the young man was careful about not wanting Tess to get cut with shattered glass. She was finally helped from her car, and she felt sick at the pit of her stomach at its loss. Someone handed her a towel, and another on-looker gave her a bottle of water. She was about to sit on the sidewalk curb when a man took a chair from a sidewalk café table and offered it to her to sit on. The young man who was helping her accepted another bottle of water, and he tried to help her stem the blood flow from her nose. Traffic was at a standstill around her, and the crowd of people was growing.

"Did anyone see the truck that ran into me?" Tess asked.

"I did," a young girl said, stepping forward. She was in her early teens, and she raised her hand. "It was a white Ford pickup truck, a huge one. I was standing over there, waiting for my mother. She's in the drugstore. The driver had his face covered with a bandana. The first two letters on the tag were AV, the last was a six, I think, but I didn't catch all of it."

"That's terrific," Tess said. "Thank you, you're very observant."

Suddenly there were in-coming sirens, police, ambulance, fire, and rescue. While one set of policemen began to direct traffic, others took control at the scene of the accident. An ambulance double-parked, and the attendants came running.

"Are you the driver?" the police officer asked. "What caused the accident?"

"I am, and I was sideswiped and pushed into the other vehicles," Tess said. "That young lady there saw what happened, and considering the crowd that has assembled, I'm sure you'll be able to find other witnesses."

One of the officers went straight to the girl, pulling a note-book from his pocket.

Tess recognized the ambulance paramedics. "It's okay, Marissa, Ted. I'm fine. I just got a bloody nose and a small cut on my arm."

"She's a doctor," the woman paramedic said to the policemen. She turned to Tess. "You know the rules. We have to check you over."

Tess turned to the young man who had been helping her. "What is your name?"

"Danny Monroe," he said. He nodded toward the paramedics. "They'll take care of you from here out. I've got an application in to take the paramedic training."

"Ted, get this young man's name, and information," Tess ordered. "I want to put in a recommendation of my own for his training."

"Yes, ma'am," Ted said, pulling out a notebook, and writing down the information.

Tess walked with Marissa to their vehicle. She did know the rules.

She was checked over, and her arm was bandaged. She was given an icepack to hold on her nose. She'd already checked, it wasn't broken, and it had stopped bleeding, but it was already swelling. By morning, she'd have two black eyes.

Her little compact car hadn't gone far. The truck had pushed her into vehicles that were already parked along the street. One of the cars had been shoved into a light pole. A small truck had been rammed into the car ahead of it. It was resting against a steel mailbox bolted to the sidewalk. From what she could see, four, maybe five vehicles besides her own, had been damaged. There wasn't any part of her car that wasn't bent or destroyed.

"Do you want us to run you over to the hospital?" the paramedic Ted asked.

"No, I'll call someone to come get me," Tess said. "Thanks."

"Ma'am, we've called for a tow service. We have taken statements and are trying to locate the owners of the other vehicles," the police officer said.

"I need to get my purse, and my medical bag," Tess said. "I want the stuff from the glove compartment, too. The only time I had a car towed, it was stripped of everything in it before I got it back."

"I'll take care of it," the officer said. "Why don't you stay seated. Keep icing your nose. It's going to hurt like hell."

"It already does," Tess admitted.

The officer went over to what was left of Tess's car. She could see him stretching through broken windows and handing off her things to the paramedics, who carried them over to her. A saleslady from the shop behind where she was sitting, offered merchandise bags to stow her stuff. She asked if Tess needed help.

"Is your phone working?" Ted, the paramedic asked, while Marissa was wiping an antiseptic cloth over Tess's face.

Tess checked it. "It's working." She turned, looked at her reflection in the window behind her and grimaced. "I've changed my mind. I look like I've been chewed on and spit out. Would you take me over to Resolute? I don't need the emergency room, but I'm going to borrow one of their chairs. I don't think hanging around on the sidewalk is a good idea."

"Sure," Marissa said as they gathered her bags and took them to the ambulance.

Tess walked over to the police. "Am I clear to leave? Do you have all the information you need?"

"It's a clear case of hit-and-run, ma'am," the officer said. "Although there were a dozen witnesses, no one got the full tag number. Most of the stores are closed now, but we'll return in the morning and see if anyone uses surveillance cameras. It's becoming more the norm. We'll send notices to the repair shops and the rental agencies."

"Why do you think it was a rental?" Tess questioned.

"AV could mean Avis rentals," the officer said. "It's standard procedure. A hit and run causing this much damage must have damaged the truck too."

"Oh," Tess said. "I didn't catch that."

"Maybe you should be checked over at the emergency room," the police officer said kindly. "I've heard doctors are their own worst patients."

"True," Tess admitted. She tried to smile, but it hurt. "I'm on my way there. If I fall flat on my face, someone will pick me up. Thanks for your help. Do I need a copy of the police report?"

"Your insurance company will take care of it," he said. "You do need to call the accident into your insurance carrier ASAP. You weren't at fault, and we'll be looking for the person who was driving the truck. Even with a partial tag number, we should be able to trace it."

Micah was home, and he was becoming concerned. Tess had a six o'clock interview appointment, but now it was half-past eleven. Surely they weren't still interviewing. He had called twice, and she hadn't responded. He didn't want to be a pest.

When his phone rang, he jumped on it. "Tess! Are you okay?"

"Calm down," Tess said. "I'm at Resolute. My interviews are over, but I need you to pick me up."

"What's wrong?" Micah demanded. "Something is wrong! I can hear it in your voice."

"That's blocked nasal passages," Tess said, diagnosing herself. "The interviews went great. I'm okay, but I had car trouble. It's after visiting hours, so the front doors will be locked. I'll be waiting in the emergency area."

"I'm on my way," Micah said, moving as he searched his pockets for his keys. He was halfway to the garage before he remembered, jogged back, and left a note for Macy. He activated the house security.

It was a thirty-five-minute drive, although Micah pushed the speed limits. He parked and ran to the emergency room. Finding Tess in green hospital scrubs, surrounded by several large shopping bags, was a surprise. When she turned to face him, he sucked in his breath.

"Dear God, what happened?" he demanded.

"There was an accident, a hit and run," Tess said. "Anyway, my car was totaled a few blocks from here."

"Are you okay!" Micah exclaimed, his eyes searching her face.

"I know it looks bad. I'll look worse tomorrow," Tess stated calmly. "I'm okay. My nose isn't broken, just bruised, and the rest of me is okay too. I can't say the same for my car. I'm afraid it's totaled."

"I don't care about your car!"

"I do," Tess complained. "I finally made the last payment on it!"

"We'll worry about that later," Micah said. "Have you been released?"

"I was never checked-in," Tess said. "The nurses were nice enough to loan me these scrubs."

"Dr. Foster?"

Tess turned to a physician in surgical scrubs. "Hello, Dr. Mitner."

"I was just informed you were here. What happened?" the doctor demanded, already reaching over and taking her chin gently in his hand.

"I was in a car accident. I was using the emergency room as a place to stay until my ride could get here."

"Were you examined by one of my staff?"

"No," Tess admitted. "I'm okay."

"I want to make sure of that," Dr. Mitner said. "Come with me."

"I'm fine," Tess protested.

"Once you walk through that door, you're on my turf! You're not leaving until I am satisfied that you are fine or not," Dr. Mitner said gruffly. "This isn't your ER, Dr. Foster, it's mine. Don't argue! As anyone on my staff will tell you, it won't do you any good!"

"I'll wait," Micah said, glad that Tess was being outranked.

## Chapter 17

Micah closed his bedroom door quietly, making his way to the kitchen, and poured coffee into a large mug.

"Is she okay?" Macy asked.

"She says she looks worse than she feels, but I doubt it," Micah said. "She's been popping headache tablets when she thinks I'm not looking. The doctor gave her a prescription last night, and I'm going to drop it off at the drugstore on my way to get Katie. Remind Tess to call Druckman's Pharmacy and tell them it's okay for me to sign for her prescription. Dr. Mitner said that although she wasn't hurt badly, her muscles would be tightening and aching. It will only be for a couple days. She was lucky."

"I'll stay close," Macy said.

"She hasn't told Lauren," Micah warned Macy. "She doesn't want her sister to worry, so if she calls, tell her Tess isn't here."

"Does it hurt?" Katie asked when Tess joined them in the family room later that afternoon.

"It does, but I'm not seriously hurt," Tess said honestly.

"I'm being very, very quiet," Katie promised in a whisper. "Daddy said to use my inside whisper voice."

Tess smiled and winced. "That's very sweet. Thank you."

She looked over to Micah. "Stop scowling at me. I need to move around."

"Sit down," he suggested.

"Let Daddy kiss and make it better," Katie suggested.

"Does it work?" Tess asked.

Katie nodded.

Tess crooked her finger at Micah. "I seem to need your 'kiss and make it better' cure."

"Any time," Micah said, gently laying his lips on her forehead because he didn't want to touch anything that was bruised or swollen.

"Is it better?" Katie asked loudly, and then she whispered. "Is it?"

"I do believe it worked," Tess said, leaning over and kissing Katie's cheek. "Thank you very much!"

"Why don't you go, and play for a while," Micah suggested.

"I know," Macy exclaimed. "Let's go upstairs and have a tea party."

"Yeah!" Katie exclaimed, forgetting her inside voice again.

"I could really use some caffeine," Tess exclaimed. "Where's my phone?"

"On the kitchen island. I didn't want it disturbing you," Micah admitted. "Do you want soda or tea?"

"Tea."

Tess looked toward the kitchen, and Micah retrieved her phone. She checked her incoming messages, reading them.

"There are several messages from the police, with a phone number, so I need to see what that's about," Tess said, ambling slowly outside to the patio.

Micah began brewing a cup of her favorite tea. Although his first instincts were to protect, Tess wasn't someone who would allow herself to be coddled. When he finished, he took her the tea and waited.

"The truck was rented at the Austin airport," Tess said. "The rental agency has surveillance cameras, so they should be able to get a visual identification of who rented it. Right now, all they know is that it was a man named Russell Marks. He has a police record, but nothing too serious–traffic violations and minor altercations. The phone number he gave them has been disconnected. The address from his driver's license wasn't valid, either."

Micah closed his eyes. "Still, he has a record. I'm calling Detective Jamison of the Austin Police Department, and I'm calling Stan. Give me the names and numbers of the policemen you dealt with last night."

Tess handed him her phone. "You think Carla has something to do with this, don't you?"

"I wouldn't put it past her," Micah said. "At this point, I believe she is capable of just about anything. She's gone over the edge before.

"I installed the video surveillance cameras because she drove through the locked gates here at the compound. She totaled a borrowed SUV belonging to one of her friends. She claimed it was an accident. That was before I installed the steel gates and posts. When Carla damages or destroys something, she always claims it was an accident. It's never her fault. It's funny she never seems to destroy anything that belongs to her."

"She wrecked the townhouse, and tried to get to you through locked gates," Tess exclaimed. "She's flipped over to the dark side."

"I'm going to call Stan and have him contact a private investigator to make sure she's still in London. What happened to you may or may not be related, but I'm not taking any chances," Micah said, storming toward his office.

Tess was moving much slower, but she followed him.

Micah was already on the phone with a New Braunfels police detective. He informed the detective of what had been going on for the last four years. He believed Tess might have become a target for his ex-girlfriend. Yes, he considered Carla Mancuso capable of stalking, and of committing physical harm to anyone.

Micah was on the phone for more than thirty minutes. He notified his father and Byron Norfork at the studio of what was going on.

Less than an hour later, the police forwarded a photograph of the man who had rented the truck at the Austin airport terminal. It wasn't anyone either Micah or Tess recognized.

"I still think this is connected to Carla," Micah exclaimed. "He is probably someone she knows and is using. She's real good at that!"

"And, maybe you're a little paranoid," Tess said. "I know she's been a major pain in the ass for a long time, but this may not be related. I agree Carla has mental issues, but it doesn't mean she's behind everything bad that happens. You've dealt with crazy fans before too."

Micah took a deep breath. "Yes, we have dealt with overzealous fans, but that was in our earlier years. Most of our fanbase has grown up with us, as we aged. I've been dealing with Carla and her issues for a long time, and she's been getting worse. She refuses to believe there's anything wrong with her or her behavior. She refuses to take the medication that could help her. That's fine for her and her personal rights, but what about the victims of her behavior?

"I've spent more than four years dealing with the law and the court systems because of her irrational behavior. When does it stop? When is she held accountable? I'm not unfeeling of her problems, but I shouldn't be expected to have my life constantly disrupted by her vindictive behavior."

"I'll know in a couple of hours if she's returned to the US," Micah said. "Stan has some contacts who can get that kind of information. Until we know one way or the other, everyone in the compound is under lockdown! I'm not taking any chances."

"You think she's coming after me because she knows we are involved," Tess said.

"One of her least endearing qualities is that she's jealous of everyone around me. It really came to a head when I refused to accept any of her excuses, and adopted Katie.

"If this is Carla, it probably means she's had a psychotic break," Tess advised. "This isn't my specialty. I need to do some research."

"Hold it!" Micah said sternly. "One, you're not leaving the compound. Two, you are not leaving the house or going online. Dr. Mitner said seventy-two hours of rest. You haven't reached the twelve-hour mark, and you're already testing my patience."

"Micah…"

"No," he said firmly. "You're allowed to sleep, rest, and eat, and that's all. I'll take care of this. I don't need a textbook to tell me Carla Mancuso is dangerous!"

"Micah…"

"No," he repeated. "I blame myself for this. I was advised to press charges a dozen times over, and I didn't. To hell with trying to be the nice guy! Now you have become her target."

"You don't know that for sure," Tess said.

"I do," Micah said. "You can obey the doctor's orders with or without a sore bottom. I'll leave that decision to you. You will not be leaving this house for at least the next seventy-two hours. Got it?"

Tess looked angry, and then she unexpectedly looked amused. "Okay, macho-man. I'll listen, but only because I'm not in top form to argue with you. I have a killer headache, and I'm going to lie down. If you get any results from all those contacts of yours, and Stan's, wake me. I want to know. I'm invested in this relationship too, and I'm the one who was attacked!"

The results of his phone calls were slow in getting answers. Two police departments, and two sheriff's departments, in different counties, were involved. He'd called the security company on the townhouse in Austin. There was a contract on the property, but the purchase hadn't been finalized.

It was several hours later that Micah answered a call from Stan Mulclusky.

"Carla flew into Toronto, and entered the US by way of a northern border entry," Stan explained. "I've seen the airport video and the entry video, although I can't share them with you. I can tell you, I'm impressed by the airport and border face recognition programs. They work incredibly fast. She flew into the Austin Airport. She was met by a man who fits the description of Russell Marks, but the film capture wasn't clear enough for a positive ID. The police already have a warrant issued for him for possible hit and run, and questioning. The rental company has also issued a missing, possibly stolen vehicle report. We don't have proof the two of them are working together, but you can't take a chance that they aren't."

"I'll take your word for it," Micah said, knowing that his friend and attorney, was rarely wrong.

Micah called Bryon Norfork at the studio to make sure extra security was assigned to the building entrances. The employees were notified, and only the new hires needed to be shown a photograph of Carla Mancuso. Photographs of her and Russell Marks were distributed among the employees.

The New Braunfels police discovered a surveillance camera

aimed at the front entrance of the drugstore across the street, and inadvertently at the scene of the accident. The film showed a woman was driving the truck, but most of her face was covered. The hairstyle was the same as Carla Mancuso, but a positive identification couldn't be made. Tess was told if the truck was found, and Carla's fingerprints were found inside the cab, an arrest warrant would be issued. Until the police had more proof, all they could do was issue an order for questioning.

Stan Mulclusky was on the warpath, with the police, and sheriff's departments, and with Micah for letting the situation deteriorate, without taking action before. In his opinion, a bit of preventive jail or psychiatric facility time would have taught Carla that she couldn't get away with her aggressive behavior patterns. It also might have convinced her to stay on her prescribed medications.

Tess walked in on the tail-end of a blistering tirade from Stan. Micah had his phone on speakerphone.

"Sorry about the profanity," Micah said when he terminated the call.

"I worked in an ER, I can swear in a dozen languages," Tess said. "Bottom line, what happens if they catch her?"

"At this point, she can be questioned. I don't know what else," Micah said. "Until she's caught, we are going to have to use extra caution. The police advise that we travel in pairs, and since you were the target, you have to be even more careful."

"I'm not going to allow her to make me a victim," Tess huffed.

"I was afraid you were going to resist," Micah said. "Let's get past the next couple of days, without arguing about it. Coyote is coming to stay at Sully's house permanently, so Macy won't be by herself. If he has to leave, she'll have to bunk in here with us."

"Do you think Carla would breach the compound? Could she get past all the security?"

"It's a large property to secure," Micah said. "I could claim a lot of things about Carla, but lack of intelligence isn't one of them. It's how she uses that intelligence that's the problem."

---

Four days later, Tess and Macy had gone to San Antonio together, with Coyote as their security guard. Tess was going to retrieve her mail, some books, and additional clothing. Macy was dropped off for her rehab appointment, while Coyote went with Tess to her apartment.

Katie had been sick to her stomach the night before, and Tess's advice was to keep her quiet and watch her for other symptoms. Micah would have been happier if he'd been able to go with them, but what did you do when you had a sick kid? Coyote had volunteered.

When the main gate buzzer activated, Micah reached for his phone to see who was at the gate. He didn't know the man, but he'd seen photographs of Maxwell Barrington-Smythe. After the reveal of his sister's involvement with the man, Micah had researched him thoroughly. His reaction to the man wasn't one of elation, but of dread. It wasn't because he'd found anything negative about Macy's fiancé. It was his reaction to a stranger criticizing his paintings.

He remotely opened the gates, but kept the camera feed running, until he was sure the rental car wasn't being followed, and he closed them.

Micah opened the door and offered his hand to his guest. "It's good to meet you, Mr. Barrington," Micah said. "Macy is very impressed with you."

"I'm at a disadvantage here, and call me Max," a handsome man said, shaking Micah's hand. "Macy talks about her famous brothers a lot. I've bought several of your albums, and I was impressed too. Music is a different bailiwick for me."

"You're into art, paintings, and sculpture," Micah said. "I have visited your gallery in New York City."

"And, you are the mystery artist," Max said, stepping into the house and looking around. He saw very little original art on the walls.

"What gave me away?" Micah asked.

"Paint," Max said. "On your jeans, your boots, and on your fingernails," Max said. "I was impressed with the photographs Macy sent me. Is she here?"

"She went to her rehab appointment," Micah said.

"With protection, I'm assuming from the *mental whack job*," Max asked. "That was her description, not mine. She does revert to American slang when she's upset. She has been keeping me informed about what is going on and her rehab progress."

"My younger brother is with them. He's six-foot, five-inches, and looks like he pumps iron, although as far as I know, he doesn't. No one in their right mind would even try to mess with him."

"That is the problem," Maxwell said. "According to Macy, this woman isn't in her right mind."

"That's true," Micah agreed. "But, she already knows my brother doesn't like her."

"Good show," Max said. "Is he the one nicknamed after a southwestern animal?"

Micah grinned. "Coyote, yes, he's the one."

"While we're waiting for them to return, are you going to allow me to review your work?" Maxwell asked, getting down to business.

"I guess so," Micah said. He walked over to the kitchen and grabbed a baby monitor. "My daughter is sick, and I need to be able to hear her."

Max followed him to the studio and began to inspect the paintings on display.

Micah was surprised he wasn't nervous. His paintings were what they were. Good or bad, he'd done his best. In the last several weeks, his priorities had shifted again. Painting had dropped to a considerably lower rung on the ladder of what was important. He went over to his workstation and sat on the stool he used to hold his painting tray.

Max Barrington said very little. He asked Micah when he wanted to look at the artwork in the stacks. He allowed himself time to inspect each painting. Occasionally, he would remove a canvas and reposition it to the front of the stack. He would study it more and continue.

Micah heard Katie crying, and he jumped to his feet. "I have to take care of my daughter. Take your time."

His daughter needed a children's chew tablet antacid to calm her stomach, a sip of ginger ale, and a clean tee shirt. He settled her on the couch in the family room to watch one of her favorite movies.

Micah looked toward the studio, but he went to the kitchen to make a fresh pot of coffee.

"Punkin, I'm going to the studio," Micah said. "I left the monitor there. Shout if you need me."

"I'm feeling better, Daddy."

Micah found Maxwell still examining the paintings. The art critic turned to face him.

"All the words I used to describe your work to Macy were understated," Max said. "Have you trained under anyone?"

"No. I'm self-taught. I read a lot of books. Some ideas I tried, some didn't work for me, so I went back to the way I was doing it," Micah said, feeling uncertain for the first time.

"Good," Max said. "What you've done was right for your style. Where do you want to go from here?"

"I have no idea," Micah said. "I enjoy painting, but it's not the end-all for me. It's a hobby."

"Many people are multi-talented, in a cross-section of the arts," Max agreed. "Can you see yourself at a showing?"

Micah shook his head. "Not really. I don't mean to sound disrespectful, but most of the art shows I've been to seem to be pretentious. People are wandering around, explaining the *true meaning* behind what is on the canvas.

"I paint what I see. I like wandering around art galleries, big or small, but I like to be left alone to decide for myself what I like and what I don't."

"I agree, but that doesn't make your work any less impressive. I see your work as a show of emotions and passion. The landscapes are good. The portraiture in your paintings displays your true talent. It's all there in the faces, joy, happiness, pain, and sorrow. You have a truly remarkable gift," Max said. "Do you want representation?"

"I've been considering that since Macy sent you those photographs," Micah said. "I wouldn't want my name associated with the art. I'm a known brand in the music industry. I don't want to dilute that recognition. I'm not someone who needs to see my name in lights, tagged on clothing, and everything that crosses my path. Over the years, my brothers and I have refused many offers for that kind of endorsement. I'm also beginning a new phase of my life. I don't know how much time I'll have for painting when the new phase kicks in."

"I can work with an unknown artist," Max said. "It's unusual, but not unheard of by any means. I can exhibit the work without revealing the identity of the artist. It's not going to devalue what you are creating. It will require a mysterious biography and top-secret bookkeeping. We could even do offshore banking if necessary, or the proceeds could go directly to a favorite charity. From how Macy has described you, I don't think money is a motivator."

"I like that idea," Micah said. "My art can remain a secret and support a good cause. That way, I wouldn't feel pressured to produce."

"There might be some pressure from me," Max admitted honestly.

"I think I'm going to like having you for a brother-in-law," Micah said with a grin.

"That's still top-secret. We'll work on the details later," Max said. "When will Macy be back?"

"It's going to be a couple more hours," Micah warned, and he filled in Macy's fiancé on what had been going on."

"Goodness," Max said. "I hope this woman is caught soon."

"So, do I," Micah agreed. "So, do I!"

Macy jumped into Max's arms as soon as she entered the room. He swung her around and gave her a long kiss. Introductions were made again, and Macy dragged Max from the house. They jumped into his rental car, and they drove toward Sully's house.

"Should I follow them?" Coyote asked.

"Leave them alone for a little while," Tess advised.

"Were there any problems?" Micah asked.

"No, and I was watching," Coyote reported. "Except for some really bad burritos I ate while waiting for Tess, everything was good!"

"I told you we could eat after my interview," Tess exclaimed. "Maybe, you've caught the bug from Katie."

"I have an iron-clad stomach," Coyote said, turning to his brother. "What do you think of the English dude?"

"He's exactly as Macy described him," Micah said, turning his attention to Katie, who had come into the room.

"Are you feeling better, honey?"

"I feel better," Katie said. "Can I have a popsicle?"

Micah glanced over to Tess. "The last time she was sick was about four hours ago."

Tess took the child's face into her hands. "You're not running a fever, sweetie." She turned her attention to Micah. "She should be okay. She needs to stay hydrated."

"Yeah!" Katie said, clapping as Coyote reached into the freezer, and handed her a cherry popsicle, and took a grape for himself.

---

"I have something planned for today," Coyote growled as he came into Micah's kitchen, grabbed a mug and snarled when he discovered the coffee wasn't ready yet.

"What's got you in a foul mood already?" Tess asked.

"Little sister sleeping on the other side of the house with her boyfriend!" Coyote snarled.

"Were they loud?" Tess asked with a teasing tone in her voice.

"No, but I knew they were there!" Coyote complained. He gave an aggravated shake of his shoulders. "It's not right."

"She's an adult," Micah said. "She's only a year or so younger than you. You're not going to pretend you're a virgin? I know for a fact when you were sixteen…"

"I'm not talking about me!" Coyote protested. "And, I know Macy's age, but she's still my little sister! It gives me the creeps."

"Grow up," Tess suggested. "Max will only be here for a few days. He has a tight schedule."

Coyote turned to Micah. "Are you going to let him represent you?"

"We've decided on a trial run, "Micah said. "He's going to

take some paintings with him, and show them in the New York gallery."

"Are you signing them?" Coyote asked.

"We agreed on a symbol, and the artist's identity will remain anonymous. I'll decide on an organization I want to sponsor later. A children's hospital for sure, several come to mind right away. We have plenty of time to work on the details, and that's all contingent on the paintings selling."

Coyote took off going wherever he was going. He rarely told anyone of his plans.

Maxwell Barrington stayed at the lake for three days, moving over to the lodge with Macy. He left with a stack of paintings in the rental vehicle. He would have them properly packed for shipping and sent by special courier to the New York gallery.

Macy followed Max to San Antonio, where they spent several days together. She had seen him off at the airport and reported for her rehab session. Later that afternoon, she had gone to Madam Bashlofski's ballet studio. She wasn't able to dance, but she was allowed to do some of the exercises to keep in shape. Madam was quickly becoming a friend and mentor.

---

It had been well over a week, and there had been no trace of Carla Mancuso, or the rental truck found. There wasn't anything to be done except get on with their lives while taking precautions.

The man who had rented the truck had come forward. Russell Marks claimed he was only doing a friend a favor. He hadn't seen any harm in renting a truck and letting Carla use it during a short vacation in Texas. His credentials had been used on the rental agreement. Russell Marks was going to be held accountable for the missing vehicle.

The restraining order against Carla was still in effect. However, Micah had found them to be useless during the previous four years of harassment. Except for the townhouse incident, Carla had been let off with warnings nearly every time she'd been hauled into court. Her lawyers had poured on the poor pity party excuses, and she had walked away with a smirk, knowing she'd gotten away with whatever she'd done again.

Everyone was becoming irritable about having to be on constant watch. Still, everyone was keeping a close watch. There were several empty cabins around the lake. Either Micah or Coyote was checking every day to make sure there were no signs of forced entry or occupancy.

"I'm going to the lodge," Tess said, popping her head around the doorway to Micah's office.

"Hold on," Micah said into the phone. "Tess, I'll be with you in a minute. I'm on an international call."

Tess gave him a wave, and Micah returned to his discussion. She went to the patio and waited and waited. She only needed to run to the lodge to get a research paper she'd left behind. After a thirty-minute wait, she went inside and told Macy she was going to the lodge.

Macy nodded absently, with her head down, her face against her knee concentrating on a painful stretch. Katie said something to her at the time.

Tess jogged down the tiered deck and continued to jog along the graveled road.

Micah left his office looking for Tess. When he didn't see her anywhere, he interrupted Macy's workout.

"Have you seen Tess?"

"Oh!" Macy exclaimed, looking around concerned. "I was concentrating on what I was doing and showing Katie what to do. I think she said something about going to the lodge."

Micah opened his mouth, clamped his mouth shut before

he could voice words in front of his daughter he would regret. He bent to speak in his sister's ear. "I'll go see if I can find her. I don't want to leave the two of you alone, but I don't have a choice. We have to maintain extra measures of security. Keep the doors locked while I'm gone. Do you remember the code to the panic room?"

Macy nodded and went over to Katie. "Hey Punkin, I need a new bracelet, and you promised you'd help me make one with your jewelry-making kit."

"We can make look-a-like bracelets," Katie agreed happily.

"You go ahead. I'll be there in a second," Macy said, following her brother, and locking the door behind him. He didn't take the road around the lake but ducked into the woods, and she was sure he was taking a shortcut.

When the front door opened, Tess startled, her pulse beating faster, until she recognized the silhouette of Micah with the setting sun at his back.

"You scared me!" Tess exclaimed.

"Good!" Micah exclaimed angrily, slamming the door behind him. "What the hell do you think you're doing? I told you very clearly that no one goes out alone!"

"Isn't that a bit overly cautious?" Tess asked.

Micah frowned. "I don't think so. Damn it, Tess, I'm trying to keep you safe." He stepped into her space and pulled her close, his left arm holding her tight, and he circled one of her black eyes with a gentle finger of his right hand. "I don't want to see something like this happening again. She's nuts, Tess, and now she has accomplices. Russell Marks has a criminal record for DUI's and assault! What part of extra precautions don't you understand?"

"I do and can understand your worry, but most likely, she's gone," Tess said.

"She's not gone, she was spotted, but not caught!" Micah growled.

"You didn't tell me that!"

"I didn't have a chance! You can call it whatever you want to call it, a manic breakdown, a clinical crisis. The point is Carla is still out there, and she's dangerous."

"I'm sorry," Tess said.

"That's not good enough," Micah exclaimed. "This has been building, and now it's time."

"What's been building?" Tess asked, and suddenly she understood his meaning. She tried to back away. "Oh, no!"

"Oh, yes," Micah said determinedly. "I wish I was here for other reasons, but you deserve this!"

"Micah, I'm not a kid any longer."

"Then stop acting like one," he growled.

Tess had grown to like being spanked when they were having sex, but this spanking didn't have anything to do with sexual satisfaction.

Micah backed her into a small mudroom, sat on a bench, and upended her over his lap. He spanked her hard with stinging blows that had her crying from the first whack. Micah's callused hand seared an imprint all over her bottom, and the tight leggings she was wearing were no protection whatsoever. Her pleading and crying made no impression on him. Neither did her promise to abide by his security rules. Instead, her words seemed to remind him of how foolish she had been, and he continued whacking her backside with stinging spanks.

"Tessa Foster, I will not let you take chances with your life. You've already been hurt once, and I won't allow it to happen again. I love you, but I will not let your stubbornness put your life in danger. If that means I become your private bodyguard, so be it. If that means I need to set your bottom on fire for not listening, I will do that too! You should know by now that I will not be pushed or ignored."

Micah gave Tess what she would later categorize as another

*big one*. This spanking was on par with several he'd given her as a teenager. She thought his hand would never stop whacking her backside. He finally stood her on her feet and lifted her into his arms. Micah carried her to the room off the kitchen that she'd occupied before.

He set Tess on her feet beside the bed and began to remove her clothing. When he stripped off her leggings, he turned her around to study his handiwork and ran his hand over her reddened bottom. Micah turned her around to face him, and he kissed her.

He stripped off his pullover shirt, and kicked off his boots. His jeans and underwear were quickly pooled at his feet. Stepping out of them, he ran his fingers through her hair and pulled her to him as he bent slightly and pushed his erection between her legs while he kissed her. He plundered her mouth, and when she could breathe again, he laid her on the bed.

Tess had gone weak and wet, the moment he'd touched her. She spread her legs, ignoring that her bottom was still burning like hellfire.

Micah plunged his full length inside with one long, hard stroke. "I need you," he groaned, and when he didn't hear a complaint, he stroked into her hard. He took what was his, thrusting harder and demanding more.

Tess thrust her lower body upward with each of his strokes, desperate to fulfill his needs, and knowing he wouldn't forget she had needs of her own. He didn't, and he took her with him to satisfy their sexual desires.

Micah lay beside Tess, but he didn't withdraw entirely from her. He kissed her, taking his time, and lingering as he moved from her lips to her breasts. He'd been rough, but she liked it that way sometimes. Micah looked at her carefully. She lay sprawled open for him, taking deep breaths, that made her chest rise and fall. She looked sated, a sure sign that she'd enjoyed being ravaged.

"Okay?" he whispered.

Her arms wrapped around his neck, and she pulled him over for a long kiss.

"Okay?" he asked again.

"If this is what happens as a regular result of spanking my ass, I'm all for it," Tess said with a chuckle. "My ass might not agree with it later, but the rest of me sure liked it."

# Chapter 18

Tess looked into the bathroom mirror and grimaced. Her nose was still bruised, black and blue, and both of her eyes were surrounded with the same discolorations.

"Knock, knock!" Macy called as she entered the bedroom. "Are you decent?"

"I'm decent," Tess said, coming from the bathroom. "No amount of make-up is going to cover these bruises, so I'm going naked faced. If someone looks at me funny, I can always stare them down!"

"You don't need make-up," Macy said, honestly. "Even with black eyes, you're gorgeous. You have no idea what I'd give for your height! Everyone in the family except Lily is taller than me, and she's still growing! I'm the runt."

"I'll bet your male dance partners don't complain," Tess said. "There's less weight to lift!"

"True," Macy admitted.

"Are you getting anxious to return to London?" Tess asked.

Macy nodded. "Having Max here for a few days, really makes

me want to go home. I still live at my little bedsitter, but I also spent most of my free evenings at Max's place. We don't want to move in together until we're married. His family is a bit old-fashioned."

"So is yours," Tess said.

"I know. That's why we're not letting either family in on our engagement plans until after my birthday. I miss him!

"Except for the rehab sessions, this has been a great trip. I wish Sully could have been here, but he promised that he'll stop in and see me when he finishes with this movie. I wish I could have spent more time with Noah, but he's already launching his career, and he's at that age where he is totally absorbed with himself. At least Mom's issues were resolved before they affected Lily."

"It's hard when there are bad feelings between children and their parents," Tess said. "Lauren and I haven't had a good relationship with our parents for more than a decade. We have been there for each other, and we're tight as sisters."

"I rarely have a problem with Dad, except when he has his blinders on about Mom," Macy said. "I'm hoping the counseling will help her. If not, I'm ready and willing to go to battle for Lily."

"Where you've had problems with Carole, she was always there for me," Tess said. "When I needed a shoulder to cry on, she was there. So were your dad and your brothers. I can already see a difference in Carole, and Micah has mentioned it too. She's much calmer. I don't think it was your career in dance that Carole objected too. It was the separation from the family. When Lily received the same offer you did from Madam Bashlofski, it was history repeating itself. She didn't want to lose another daughter."

"How she handled my offer, and my goals were what pushed me away," Macy said. "Dance is necessary for me, it's as natural for me as breathing."

"Carole didn't see it that way, hence the déjà vu," Tess said gently.

A loud knock on the door and both women turned to face Micah and Katie. "Are you ready?"

Tess pointed to her face. "This is as good as it gets. The last time I had a black eye, it was from a drug-crazed patient. It took five of us to subdue him and get him in restraints."

"You're still beautiful," Micah said, kissing her. "The Land Rover is stuffed with presents, and it's time to go."

The birthday celebration was a success. The complete family wasn't there, but Daniel reassured Carole, as their children aged and were world travelers, expecting full attendance was unlikely. Sully and his family were in New Zealand, and Noah was playing at a gig. The unspoken question was, where was Allison? No one had heard from her beyond text messages in weeks. Half of the siblings were there, one grandchild, and a future daughter-in-law.

Carole fussed over Tess's blackened eyes and bruised nose. When she discovered Tess had resigned from her job, she had a lot of questions.

"Right now, I'm taking a break," Tess explained. "I'm checking on employment opportunities."

Micah could tell his mother had noticed a personal vibe between them. Still, he steered her attention to the birthday celebration.

Dinner was the usual full-out birthday bash, with all the person of honor's favorite foods. A homemade carrot cake was carried in blazing with candles. After cake, the family retired to the family room, where Daniel opened his presents.

He was thrilled with a new set of golf clubs from Carole. He tried on the vintage leather bomber jacket dating to WWII. Macy had found it in a London shop, although it was an American jacket. Daniel was a WWII history buff, and he loved it. He set it aside with respect and said he was going to have it framed for preservation and displayed in his office.

There were lots of presents that were treated with the same delight. Coyote had found a missing part for a 1956 Chevrolet Bel Air his father was slowly restoring. He hadn't wrapped the gift, but he'd shown his father a photograph on his phone. A collectible pilot's wristwatch had been sent by Sully and his family. They skyped their birthday wishes with their three children, and they showed off Karina's seven-month pregnancy belly. Daniel showed the same appreciation for the smaller gifts from his younger children and grandchild as he did for his specialized gifts from his older children.

When all the presents had been opened, Micah went to his vehicle and carried in the wrapped painting. He propped it on a chair. Daniel unwrapped the canvas, and he stepped back. He covered his mouth with his hand, and his eyes filled with tears.

"I told you," Coyote said, smiling over his shoulder to his oldest brother.

Carole went to her husband, hugged him, and wrapped her arms around him.

"It's them," Daniel said shakily. "I was about nine, and Frank was twelve." He turned and hugged Micah. "You gave them back to me; the way I remember them as a child. They were so full of love for each other and for us, boys."

He turned to the painting and wiped his eyes. He peered at the signature, but it was hard to make out, as it was a stylized symbol of three letters. "Who painted this?"

Micah cleared his throat. "I did, Dad."

"No…" Daniel exclaimed, shocked. "Where did this talent come from?"

"I've been painting for several years now," Micah said. "It was something to do to take my mind off of other problems. I kept it private, probably because I'm a perfectionist. I didn't want anyone to see my goofs and failures. When I painted this, I knew it was for you."

Daniel hugged his oldest son and tried to control his emotions again. He looked around to his children. "All of our children are so talented." He took his wife's hand and kissed it. "We are so proud of all of you! We've always had music, then dance, and now art! God blessed all of you with such amazing talents!"

"Uh, Dad," Coyote interjected with a grin. "Don't expect me to start painting or dancing!"

"You have more than your fair share of talents, son," Daniel exclaimed.

All cell phones had been turned off during the celebration. Still, as the adult children were giving their final birthday wishes and goodbyes, they were pulled from pockets and purses to check for missed calls or messages.

"Oh, no," Macy said, walking to the Land Rover.

Micah and Tess stopped.

"What is it?" Tess asked.

"Another message from my bank," Macy said, but she smiled and pumped a fist in the air. "Finally! They've caught the person who was stealing my credit identity."

The front door opened, and Carole called out. "Would you come back in, please!"

Micah tried to get Coyote's attention, but he was already at the end of the driveway. He and everyone with him hurried to return inside.

"What's wrong, Mom!"

"I don't know," Carole said. "Daniel asked me to stop you, and he went into his office."

"Do you want me to call Coyote?" Micah asked.

"Has Karina gone into premature labor?" Tess asked.

"No, and no," Daniel said from the doorway of his office, but he went inside and closed the door.

They waited twenty minutes before Daniel reappeared. He called Carole first and closed the door. A few minutes later, Carole rushed from the office. She was crying.

"Okay, this is scaring me," Macy said, and she wrapped her arms around Lily."

Micah got to his feet when his father came from his office. "What's going on, Dad?"

"I just got a call from a court-appointed attorney in Seattle," Daniel said. He looked around the room. He faced his children with regret. "I'm sorry, Macy. Allison has been arrested for credit card fraud."

*"Allison! It's her? The bitch!* How dare she!" Macy exclaimed. "My sister! Do you have any idea how long I've been going through this crap?"

"Calm down," Daniel said. "I've already called our attorney. He's going to fly to Seattle to see if he can get her bonded to him, and a change of venue."

"Why bother?" Macy snapped. "She has stolen thousands and thousands of dollars using my name and my credit! Whatever the banks do to her, it is deserved! She's tried to ruin my credit and my name."

"She's your sister," Daniel said.

"She's a lying thief!" Macy exclaimed. "Don't call her, my sister! I want nothing to do with her. You and Mom keep after me to reconcile with her, well what about what she's done to me!

"Allison stayed with me in London for three weeks. She stole money and jewelry from me. She ripped off my friends and flat mates and told lies about me to my friends. When I caught her stealing money from my eighty-three-year-old landlady, she shrugged it off like it was of no consequence. I threw her out, banned her from the premises, and told her to go to hell!

"God knows what she told you, but you accepted it as the

Gospel truth, and I was the one at fault! Well, maybe now, you'll see the true Allison, and make her pay for the harm she's caused!" Macy stormed from the house and slammed the door in her wake.

Macy was silent on the trip home. She went straight to Sully's house, saying she had to finish packing. She only had one suitcase, because she had sent a box ahead with Max to be shipped to his gallery in London.

"Should we try to talk to her?" Micah asked Tess.

"Let her be," Tess advised. "Call Coyote and tell him what happened. He's a good sounding board. She's angry, and she has a right to be.

"Macy's smart. If Allison has stolen from her before, she might have suspected but didn't want to believe it. If she wants to talk, she'll come to us. She's leaving in the morning, and I'm sure she's dreading having to deal with the bank representatives. Having to admit the fraud was committed by a family member isn't going to be easy. They might not believe that she wasn't in on it."

Macy was somewhat subdued on the way to the Austin International Airport the next morning. She was talking with them. Mostly, she was thanking them for supporting her during her rehabilitation and for letting her stay at the lake."

"You're not a guest, honey," Micah said. "You're family. Expect something extra special on your twenty-first birthday."

"I already have it," Macy said, tapping her engagement ring inside her shirt. "What are we going to do for the next two hours? Having to get here so early for an international flight is a pain in the butt. I wish Coyote could have come, but he said he was due in court as a witness. He couldn't cancel or postpone it."

With only twenty minutes of wait time left, Micah received a telephone call that he walked away to answer.

"Allison is out on bail. Dad's attorneys are already working with the bank to repay what she has stolen. Dad says her trust fund is history. She has already appeared before a judge. It will be a couple of days before the Seattle legal system decides on transferring the case to Texas. If they do, Allison will be wearing an electronic monitoring device as part of the deal. It will be up to the Texas authorities to decide how they are going to charge her."

Macy nodded at the update. "I can't feel sorry for her right now. She did this to herself. I hate leaving all this turmoil behind, but it is what it is. Mom will take Allison's side, Dad will buy her way out of trouble, and she won't learn a damn thing."

"Don't be so sure of that," Micah said. "The first thing Dad is doing is having her tested for drug and alcohol abuse. I don't believe she's going to get off this time. The folks have just gotten a major wake-up notice."

She hugged Micah and Tess and bent to hug Katie. "I have to go. Thank you for everything, big brother, and I'll stay in touch. I'd like to be at your wedding, but it will depend on my schedule. I will see you at the opening of the Parker-Barrington Gallery in Los Angeles, in December."

"We understand, and we'll be at the opening," Tess said, hugging her, and they watched her being processed by security.

"When will we see Aunt Macy again?" Katie asked.

"I don't know, baby," Micah said. "But, it won't be as long as it was the last time.

---

"Is she asleep?" Tess asked as Micah joined her bed.

"Out like a light," Micah said. "I keep thinking of those old lyrics, *'He ain't heavy, he's my brother'*. In Macy's case, it's her sister. It's a heavy load for her to carry, although she's not guilty of anything."

"I know you've been a little disappointed with how your parents have been reacting to responding to the twins, and Lily. I hope you don't ever forget how special they are," Tess said.

"I don't," Micah said.

"Compared to mine, yours are saints," Tess said.

"They're not saints, but they are great," he said. "How are you feeling?"

"Like I've been neglected lately," Tess teased.

"I can fix that," Micah said, pulling her nightshirt over her head, and kissing her. He worked his way around her body, feasting on her soft skin while being careful to avoid a few bruises that had appeared after the accident. When he reached her sex, he claimed her with his tongue.

Tess felt herself rising as she moaned and became impatient as he teased her for a long time. Micah was a terrific lover, and he enjoyed playing with her. Sometimes, though, she just wanted to be fucked hard and taken.

"I need you inside me," she panted.

Micah got the message, and he didn't have a problem with delivering. He entered her in one long thrust, and he wasn't gentle. They had been together long enough that he knew to take his cues from Tess. Micah had to straddle a fine line. He wanted to give her what she wanted, take what he needed, and contain the male beast that arose in him at her beckoning.

He lifted her and plunged into her repeatedly. The rhythm began to build, taking her into an orgasm that had Tess thrashing on the bed. Her responses made him feel powerful and potent.

When she was almost to the edge of letting go, he withdrew, and she grabbed at him, pulling him to her.

"No... I need..."

"I know what you need," Micah growled as he flipped her over on her belly.

Tess sucked in her breath as his fingers entered her and

began a rhythm of thrusting. She knew what he was going to do, and it no longer bothered her. Micah's hand spanked her across her bottom, and then lower and closer to her sex. He rubbed out the sting and did it again. The spanks stung, but at the same time, his hands and fingers were arousing her.

When she reached the point where she was about to cry, he stopped. He pulled her arms into a prostrate position, raised her bottom, and lowered her shoulders. He liked to see her fully exposed, allowing him access to give and take as he pleased.

Tess wasn't complaining. She'd grown to love these extended sessions of lovemaking.

Micah entered her from behind. With a hard thrust, he was in her, buried to the hilt. His hand went under her, finding and working her clitoris.

Tess gasped. She could feel the heat building from her stinging bottom.

He rode her, thrusting, pounding, his balls slapping against her buttocks when he couldn't bury himself into her further.

Tess was motivated by pure lust, her body was responding in waves of need. She was so close to coming, and every stroke and thrust brought her closer.

Micah withdrew, flipped her over, and reentered her. Her legs raised around his back, climbing higher on her back. Their coupling was rough and becoming a battle of who wanted what.

Tess exploded inside, but he continued to ride her hard. He knew she had more to give, and he was taking it. She arched her back to allow him more access, as wave after wave of her orgasm rippled over her, making her feel giddy.

Micah ground into her pumping, grinding and giving her everything he had, and finally flooding her with his release.

They dropped together on the bed, wrapped in each other's arms, trying to catch their breath. Neither of them spoke as Micah gathered her into his arms and tucked her in close to his body.

"Sleep," he crooned.

Tess nodded, but her eyes went to the clock on the nightstand, and she took a deep breath. They'd been having sex for three and a half hours. There wasn't any part of her that hadn't responded in sexual fulfillment. Parts of her stung, tingled, and ached. She knew his handprint would be on her ass, and she didn't care. Micah was her man. He'd given her what she wanted, and she knew she was going to have a lifetime with him.

Tess looked into the bathroom mirror and grimaced. Her nose was bruised, and there was still a residue of the dark circles under both of her eyes. They were slowly fading. She had a callback to the Resolute Health Hospital in New Braunfels, and she was interested.

She was going to the second interview session. Dr. Mitner had informed the staff of her injuries, so they wouldn't be surprised at her appearance. He hadn't been told the full story behind the hit-and-run, only the police knew the attempt on her life had been on purpose.

"Knock, knock!" Micah called as he entered the bedroom. "Do you need help with anything?"

"My arms aren't broken," Tess said, coming from the bathroom. "What would I have a problem with?"

"I was hoping to help you remove something," he said in a teasing tone.

"I'll bet you were," she said, smiling.

"You're going to wow them in the interviews," Micah promised. "They know you're perfect for the job. We've got to get moving, though, or you're going to be late!"

"I wish I didn't look like a prizefighter who lost the fight."

"You're still beautiful," Micah said, honestly. "You're gorgeous, and I like the outfit. Professional, but not stiff."

"You don't have to go with me," Tess said.

"Like hell, I don't," Micah growled. "Coyote is babysitting. Ready?"

"As ready as I'm going to be," Tess said. She knew it was useless to try to persuade him otherwise. Micah was all-male, over-protective, and macho. He wasn't going to change his mind. He was going so there would be an extra set of eyes on her."

"How were the interviews?" Micah asked later when she had finally finished several hours of interviews. He'd been waiting for her in the hospital cafeteria.

"I really like the hospital, the staff, and administrators," Tess admitted. "I didn't think I wanted to go back to a hospital environment, but I've been really impressed. The administrators have policies in place about not overworking their staff. I like it more than I thought I would. I would have almost nine to five work hours, plus the commuting time."

"We can work with it," Micah said. "We can work with whatever you decide." He whispered into her ear. "How are your parts this afternoon?"

"Tender, but it was a really good night," Tess said, pulling him to her lips. "I'm looking forward to a gentler one tonight!"

"I can work with that, too!" he promised.

---

Coyote had waved his brother and Tess off. He understood Micah's split allegiances between his daughter and Tess. His brother didn't want to leave Katie, but he had to protect Tess. It had been a tough call, but Coyote knew no one was going to get past him to hurt Punkin. His size alone made large men back down. They didn't realize he hated conflict. The youngest of the three older brothers was the peacemaker among them.

Coyote settled his niece in front of the television and plugged in one of the many Disney movies from his brother's DVD collection. He was sitting at the piano, working on a new song when someone called him from the gate phone.

"Yes?"

"Hello?" a male voice answered. "Is this Micah?"

"No, Coyote. Who are you?"

"I'm George Blankenship. Micah said he wanted a repair done to a pump in the boathouse. I called Micah. He said he wasn't home but to come on over. He said you'd open the main gate. I met you before when I was fixing his garbage disposal. I won't disturb you. I'll just fix the pump and leave."

"Hold on," Coyote said, and he checked his messages. There was one from his brother, warning him that George was on his way. "I'll activate the gate. Don't let anyone follow you inside the compound."

"No problem, I'll be in the boathouse," George said.

Coyote watched the large work truck drive through the gates on the camera feed. The gate automatically closed behind it. He laid his cell phone on the piano and went back to work.

George Blankenship entered the lake compound, smiling. The young woman in the passenger seat sat up from where she had been lying across the seat, hidden from the cameras.

"Coyote is going to be real pleased when he sees you," George said.

"Yeah, he will," Carla Mancuso said, as she pulled a gun from her pocket.

"What the hell?" George exclaimed.

"Keep driving," Carla said.

"Hey, I don't want no trouble. You said you were an old family friend of the McKennas!"

"I was until Micah screwed with me," Carla retorted. "Keep driving! Pull into Micah's driveway!"

George slowed on the road. "This ain't going to settle anything!"

"Drive!" Carla ordered.

"Shit!" was George's response, but he pressed his foot on the gas. "Lady, I've got a kid depending on me. Her momma split on us three years ago. I'm all she's got!"

"You won't get hurt if you do what I tell you to do!" Carla snapped.

George pulled into the driveway and stopped.

"Give me the keys," Carla demanded.

George turned off the truck and reluctantly handed over his keys.

"Now, get out," Carla exclaimed. "Go to the door, and remember, I'm standing behind you!" She jammed the barrel of the gun in his back.

George knocked on the door, and Coyote opened it. "Do you need some..." Coyote backed away as Carla stepped from behind George.

"Get inside!" she ordered, waving the gun back and forth between the two men.

Coyote saw Katie looking away from her movie. He saw Carla's arm move in the direction of his niece, and he stepped forward, blocking her. She was forced to step back, and she raised the gun. George made a grab for her, and she pulled the trigger.

George made an *Aweee!* sound and dropped to his knees.

Carla ran, slamming the door behind her.

"Katie! Hide behind the couch!" Coyote shouted. He started to open the door, but a bullet pinged into the wood casing. He slammed and locked the door and dropped to the floor.

Carla jumped into the truck, started it, and careened out

of the driveway. She fired another shot shattering the passenger window, and the bullet hit one of the large front windows. It didn't break, but a spider-web of shattered glass spread out, with a crackling sound, and a vase on the fireplace exploded.

Coyote ducked below the windows and ran across the family room. He grabbed Katie and ran with her to her bedroom.

"Listen to me, sweetie," Coyote exclaimed, opening the closet door. "I'm going to put you in Daddy's special room for a few minutes. Don't be scared, it should only be for a few minutes. We're okay, but I want you to be extra safe." Coyote closed her into the small panic room, he'd ragged on his brother about installing.

He ran back and knelt down in front of George, who was struggling to get to his feet. Blood was spreading over the shoulder of his shirt. Helping the man to his feet, Coyote shouldered the weight of George to get him over to a kitchen chair. He grabbed a kitchen towel and pressed it to George's shoulder, and called 911. He gave the address, and location, explaining why an ambulance and police help was needed.

The lake property was twenty-five miles from the nearest small town with emergency services. Coyote was told the ETA would be twenty to thirty minutes, and to please stay on the phone until someone arrived.

He used Micah's iPad on the kitchen counter, and brought up the live video of the main gate and saw Carla driving out. Entering the compound was secured by passcode or remotes, but exiting was motion-detector controlled. When the gate closed behind the truck, he knew she couldn't get back inside the compound unless she was on foot.

"It's going to take them a while to get here," Coyote warned George.

"I've been hurt worse than this, in a bar fight," George

said. "That was in my younger and stupider years. Does Micah have a gun in the house?"

"A rifle, but I don't know how to use it," Coyote admitted.

"Get it," George said. "I do know how to use it, and I'd rather be prepared in case that nut job comes back."

Coyote went into Micah's office and returned carrying a rifle and a box of ammunition that he passed to George.

"I'll take care of this," George said confidently, beginning to load the rifle with one hand. "You go get Katie, so she won't be scared any more than she already is."

Coyote opened the panic room.

"Uncle Coyote?" Katie's voice was small and scared.

"You can come out, honey," Coyote said, gathering Katie in his arms. "It's going to be okay. You're safe, and she's gone."

"Mr. Blankenship, Carla shot you," Katie said, looking at his blood-stained shirt.

George looked at Coyote, and despite his pain-stricken face, he smiled at the child. "Now, don't you worry about it, Katie girl. She didn't hurt me that bad, and I'll be okay. Me and Julie are coming over here to go fishing this weekend. Your daddy promised to loan us a boat, and we're going to have us a good time!"

"Katie, why don't you get some clean towels," Coyote suggested. When she ran down the hall, he turned to George. "Thank you!"

"I wouldn't want my little Julie to be scared," George said.

"How bad is it?" Coyote asked.

"I'm hurting," George said. "But I'm alive. I met that crazy woman last night at Benny's Tavern. Damn! She played me, and I fell for it. Said she was a friend of the family, and she wanted to surprise you. She's fucking nuts!"

"Certifiable," Coyote agreed. "I'm sorry, I'm not very good at medical aid."

"I served a stint in the Marines," George said. "I took a

first aid course in basic training. Other than padding the wound site to slow the bleeding, there ain't much that can be done. I'm pretty sure it's a flesh wound. That crazy bitch stole my truck!"

"She's gone too far now," Coyote said. "Most of the time, when she does something crazy, they let her go. They can't let her go after shooting someone. This was attempted murder!"

Help came quickly, in the form of an ambulance, and three Sheriff's deputies. Coyote remotely opened the main gate to the compound, and told the 911 lady on the phone to tell the drivers to drive in and he would be outside waving to get their attention.

The paramedics assisted George, although he insisted on giving the police the information on his stolen truck while he was being bandaged. The responding Sheriff's Office deputies scattered and searched the entire lake area for hours. They didn't find anything suspicious. Coyote was assured warrants for Carla Mancuso would be issued, and he sent a copy of the recorded video of Carla driving out the gate to the Sheriff's office.

Coyote waited until most of the commotion was over before he called his brother.

# Chapter 19

It had been a week since what they were calling 'the incident' happened. Micah had two hired guards driving around the lake in a continuous loop, and armed guards standing outside the front and back of his house. Surveillance cameras had been found aimed at the three occupiable houses. The fingerprints found on the equipment didn't match Carla's, but they knew she was behind them being there. George's stolen truck hadn't been located, and neither had the rented Avis truck.

Micah and Tess had taken responsibility for George's daughter for a few days while he was hospitalized. George had contacted his mother in Florida, and Micah had arranged for her travel to Texas.

George Blankenship had given an interview from his hospital room. The local story had caught the attention of many, and a Go-Fund-Me account had been started. George wouldn't have to worry about finances until he was able to return to work. The handyman gleefully said he should have enough left over to start a college fund for his daughter.

Arrest warrants had been issued, and Carla's photograph

had been plastered all over the local news stations. The story had been on the local and then national television news stations. It had quickly been added to the entertainment gossip shows. This time, Micah and Coyote had given interviews.

Micah was barely letting anyone out of his sight. He'd called a psychologist to come and talk to his daughter about what had happened. He'd been assured by the doctor that Katie hadn't been traumatized by the incident. She was actually very proud that she had followed Coyote's orders immediately as she'd been taught.

Micah wasn't the only one who had gone a bit over the edge. The senior McKennas wanted everyone to come home, but their parental worries were deflected. There was no way Micah was giving Carla any reason to turn on his parents. Daniel already had his hands full dealing with Allison's problems.

Allison was currently in a drug and alcohol rehabilitation center. Her legal issues were on hold until she completed a stint in the treatment center.

Everyone was concerned and anxious, but neither subject was discussed around Katie.

"I'm going for a walk! Alone!" Tess declared, coming from Micah's office and pointing a finger at him angrily.

"It's not safe," Micah said wearily.

"Do you really believe Carla is hanging around," Tess said. "She's not stupid. If she shows her face in public, she will be recognized. Her photograph has been plastered over every television station and network. Even the police are saying she's probably left the area."

"I would have preferred that she left the country," Micah said. "The police have blocked that possibility by requesting her name be placed in the passport name-check system. We're not going to be safe until she is caught and put away in an institution or jail."

"She has several arrest warrants filed against her," Tess said. "Personally, I think it's about time she was held accountable for her actions. She's never going to stop the harassment if she doesn't. She also needs psychiatric help."

"I agree," he said. "We also need to take precautions."

"What's the sense of living within a compound, if we don't have the freedom to move around?"

"In pairs, and she managed to get inside the perimeter, and shoot a man," Micah said.

"I don't need a nanny," Tess said.

"You're a target, so is my daughter, so stop being so stubborn. Carla has never made an attempt to go after Katie before. She was foul-mouthed in her opinions of my adopting her. I wasn't surprised when the first psych evaluation revealed a narcissistic personality disorder."

Micah pulled Tess into a hug and sighed. "I understand that you're frustrated. So, am I. Hang in here with me, sweetheart. Consider this a test. If we can get past this, we can handle anything."

Tess rolled her eyes, but she smiled. "What have I got myself into?"

"I know," Micah said. "Let's sit Katie down, and tell her we have decided to get engaged. Then, we can dress like the *Beverly Hillbillies*, and go downtown to J. D. Clines Diamonds. You can select an engagement ring."

"No, way," Tess said, laughing at his nonsense. "That sounds like something Coyote or Noah would do. Knowing my luck, someone would record it on their phone and plaster it all over the internet. Call and make an appointment. We will dress appropriately, considering where we are going. Ask them if we can come in by the back entrance. I don't want any nosy reporters crashing my day."

"I don't usually have to hide what I'm doing," Micah said.

"That's not true. You've been hiding all this crap for years.

You should have let all this Carla mess go public. If you had, we wouldn't be in this situation now."

Micah didn't like it, but he nodded his agreement. "I was trying to spare both of us the embarrassment, but it backfired. "Let's go talk to Katie."

Explaining an engagement to a six-year-old had seemed on the surface, a simple task. In reality, the word engagement had to be clarified, which led to the word wedding, which Katie did understand. She was ecstatic at the idea of Tess living with them all the time. She was excited that she was going to have a mommy in addition to a daddy. That train of thought led to babies. Could she have a baby sister?

"Or, a baby brother," Micah inserted. "Or, maybe you'll have several of each, and they'll come to us as children of different ages and not babies. It's hard to plan babies and kids ahead of time."

"I'll have sisters and brothers, like my friend Tony. He has two sisters and three brothers," Katie said. "Daddy, you have to get those rooms upstairs finished. We don't have enough bedrooms."

"I'll get that started as soon as Mr. Blankenship is better," Micah promised.

"Do I get to call you, Mommy?" Katie asked Tess.

"After we get married, yes," Tess answered.

"Are you going to be a mommy or a doctor?"

"I'm going to be both," Tess said.

Katie accepted that decision. "When do we get married?"

"*We* haven't set a date yet," Tess said. "I think sometime after I decide what job I'm going to take. I still have a few more interviews."

Katie clapped her hands in excitement. "Yes! I'll have a mommy and a daddy coming to parent days!"

"Okay, here's the deal," Micah said. "We need to dress nice and pretty. We're going to a jewelry store, and Tess is going to pick out an engagement ring because that's what a boy does when he really wants to marry a girl. He buys her a ring. It's Tess's choice. Afterward, we'll go to a nice restaurant for a special lunch."

"Can I have a ring too?" Katie asked.

"No, only Tess gets a ring today," Micah explained. "After we get married, Tess will get another ring called a wedding band, and I'll wear one too. This is a grownup thing."

"Okay," Katie said, disappointed. "Can we go tell Granny Nana and Grandpa?" Katie asked.

Micah looked at Tess, and she nodded. "If we have time, yes."

"Can I stay overnight?" Katie asked.

"Not this time," Micah said, shaking his head firmly, and Katie didn't argue.

J. D. Clines Diamonds already had a beautiful selection of rings ready for showing. Most of them were larger than Tess felt comfortable wearing. She explained she was a physician and needed a smaller diamond or one that was recessed into the setting.

"Pick the ring you want," Micah suggested when the store manager went to find smaller diamonds. "The one your heart tells you is right, and pick a smaller one to wear when you're working, or pick a wedding band that has diamonds in it."

"That sounds excessive," Tess said.

"Sully did the same thing with Karina," Micah said. "She accidentally cut baby Angelina, with the big diamond. Every time she saw that little cut, she cried. She wears the ring Sully gave her for special occasions, and she wears a smaller one for everyday use."

"It's your wallet," Tess warned.

"I'm not complaining."

From the selection presented to her, Tess chose a ring with a lower presentation of diamonds. She decided against a second ring saying that if she was continually changing rings, one or the other would get lost.

Micah tucked the jewelry box with the matching wedding bands in his pocket.

Katie wore a heart-shaped necklace with three small diamonds. Buying it was Tess's suggestion to make it a special day for the child, too. The three tiny stones represented them becoming a family.

At the senior McKennas, everyone was excited about the announcement. Daniel took Micah aside for a private talk. On the way home, Micah told Tess, his father had wanted to be apprised on the Carla situation.

"I'd like an update, too," Tess said.

A wobbly voice singing to a cartoon song was heard from backseat, and they smiled at each other.

Tess leaned over and placed her head on his shoulder. "We need to discuss those brothers and sisters, Katie wants."

"Anytime," Micah said, and he glanced in the rearview mirror. "Holy Shit!"

"What?" Tess turned to look, at the same time a large truck slammed into the rear of the Land Rover.

Tess and Katie screamed, and Micah swore again, accelerating and pulling away from the truck. The black construction truck was gaining on them, and this time it pulled beside them and steered into the driver's side.

"Hold on!" Micah yelled, jamming on the brakes. The Land Rover veered onto the shoulder, scraped against the metal shoulder barriers, and came to a skidding sideways stop before they entered a part of the road that was a cutaway through sheer rock.

A loud crash had them jerking around, and looking through the broken windshield. The black truck had driven into the solid wall of rock. It skidded sideways and flipped over twice before landing on its side.

Steam was rising from the hood of the Land Rover. Micah was fighting to release his seatbelt.

"Out!" he shouted. He unsnapped, Tess's seatbelt, and tried to open his door, but when it wouldn't budge, he twisted around and kicked across Tess several times with both feet, and shoved her door open.

Tess jumped out first, with Micah following her. She grabbed her medical bag.

Micah was already fighting to get the back door open. Both sides of the vehicle were damaged. The truck had slammed into them, on the left side, and the right side had hit the guardrails. When he got the back door open, he dove inside, unhooking the safety seat and carried it with a screaming Katie, still in it, from the vehicle.

When he set it down, Tess began inspecting Katie quickly. "She's okay! She's okay!" Tess shouted.

A car pulled over, and a man and a woman came running toward them. The man was carrying a fire extinguisher.

"Is everyone out?" the man shouted.

"Yes!" Micah exclaimed as Tess was running toward the black truck.

"Get away from the vehicle," the man ordered. "I'm a volunteer firefighter!" He turned to the woman. "Marsha, take the little girl to our car and back up another hundred yards to be safe."

"What the hell is she doing?" the man shouted, pointing to Tess running toward the truck.

"She's a doctor," Micah exclaimed, hugging Katie and inspected her from head to toe again. "You're okay, honey. You're okay!"

"Let me take her," the woman named Marsha said. "We saw what happened! We've already called 911!"

The firefighter was running after Tess.

Once Micah saw that Katie was going to be watched over,

he went inside the vehicle, pulled the seats down. He grabbed an emergency kit from the trunk area. He ran toward the black truck. Micah recognized that it was George's truck, now totaled. Looking over his shoulder, he could see the woman helping Katie into the car, and placing emergency flares on the road.

The black truck was blocking part of the right lane, but there didn't appear to be any fluids leaking from it. He set off three flares in the obstructed traffic lane.

The truck was lying on the driver's side. When Tess tried to reach over the hood, it rocked toward her.

"Back off," the man shouted, forcing her to back away. "It could flip over on top of you!"

"I need to see if the driver survived," Tess shouted.

"Emergency services will be here shortly," the man said.

Tess went to the windshield, which was a web of shattered and broken glass.

"Here," Micah said, pulling on a pair of leather gloves from his box. He stepped forward and hit the windshield with a bottom of a fire extinguisher, several times. When there was a hole, he got a grip on the glass and pulled. Once the glass began to tear away, they were able to see the top of someone's head and blood. There was blood everywhere.

When Tess pushed Micah away, the stranger stopped her. "You can't put any weight on the truck frame! If the weight shifts, it might come over on top of us."

Micah placed his hands on the roof. The other man saw what he was trying to do and added his strength against the roof to keep the truck from rocking over on them and Tess.

Tess leaned over the windshield as far as she dared. She didn't dare move the driver, but she got her hand under the neck and felt for a pulse.

"She's alive, but I can't move her without stabilizing her first."

"You can't do that until the truck is stabilized," the man said. "By the way, I'm Doug, and I'm a volunteer fireman. I've had EMT training, but I haven't had to put it to much use."

"Dr. Foster," Tess said. "How long will it take to get the emergency services here?"

"Another twenty minutes, at least," Doug said.

A truck pulling a large horse trailer pulled over in front of the accident and stopped. Two men dressed as ranchers came running. "Anything we can do to help?"

"Services are on the way," Doug said.

The men turned.

"Wait!" Tess said. "Do you have any bales of hay or straw in the trailer? Ropes, too?"

"We have both," one of the men said. "What do you need them for?"

"To raise this side of the truck!" Tess said, motioning with her hands. "If we could tilt the truck in that direction, and put bales of hay under it, it would stabilize the truck, so it couldn't turn over on us. Once we do that, I might be able to get inside to help the victim."

It didn't take long for the men to carry the bales of hay over. It took them less time to unhook their vehicle from the horse trailer and tie ropes to the hitch.

Tess emphasized that raising the vehicle had to be done slowly, and gently, as the victim couldn't be moved.

The truck was pulled backward very slowly, rising until it was lifted about three feet. Micah, Doug, and the second rancher shoved the bales of hay under it. Then the vehicle was gently lowered back into place.

Doug tested the movement by trying to use his weight to pull it down. Another of the men added his weight, but the truck didn't budge.

While the cowmen were hitching their truck to the horse trailer, Micah tried to break and remove the rest of the windshield.

He watched as Tess crawled over to the front seat carefully. She was trying to balance herself so she wouldn't fall on the woman. They hadn't seen a face, but they knew it was Carla. The most Tess could do was place bandages on the huge gashes she could see.

Suddenly they heard the sounds of emergency vehicles arriving: ambulances, a rescue squad, and fire trucks. The EMTs knew Tess and were glad she was on the scene. It was their job to take over and transport the patient. Three county sheriff vehicles pulled in, adding their support. Tess called for a Life Flight helicopter.

Micah and Doug backed off. Micah waved off the police until he'd checked on Katie again. She was sitting quietly in the car, talking with Marsha.

"Okay, baby?" Micah asked, hugging her.

"I'm not a baby, Daddy," Katie protested. "Are the people in the truck okay?"

"Yes, and all these people are trying to help," Micah said, dodging the question.

"Sir," one of the policemen who had followed Micah said. "If we could have your attention."

"Can you stay with my daughter a little longer?" Micah asked of the woman.

"Of course," Marsha responded. "We were talking about what Katie likes the most about school. I'm a primary teacher, so I need to know these things."

Micah turned his attention to the police officer and walked away, distancing himself, so he could speak freely and not be overheard by his daughter. He explained what had caused the accident.

"Do you think it was deliberate?" the deputy asked.

"If the driver of the truck is Carla Mancuso, it was deliberate," Micah said. "Tess said she shouldn't be moved. Not even an inch, unless the truck caught on fire. I do know the truck she's driving belongs to George Blankenship, a man she shot last week!"

"I heard about that," one of the deputies said.

"It's her," Tess said, joining the circle of policemen. "The EMTs are strapping her into neck and back braces. She's unconscious, and she's lost a lot of blood. I don't know how they're going to remove her from the truck, without jostling her. I've already called for a Life Flight helicopter. The physician onboard should be able to provide plasma, and decide how to remove her from the truck." She turned to the policemen as a group. "You're going to have to close the interstate, so the helicopter can land. The victim is going to require a Level I trauma center, either Del Seaton or Military Medical. Again, the Life Flight physician will determine where she goes."

"We're going to have to take you into the hospital to be cleared, and then to the police station for statements," the deputy said. "We'll notify the trauma hospital too. As soon as the suspect is able, she will be served with the current warrants."

"Those warrants are not her biggest problems right now," Tess said.

"What is, ma'am?" the police officer asked.

"Staying alive," Tess said bluntly.

"This day wasn't exactly what we wanted," Micah said hours later, sitting in the sheriff's station. "How many times do they have to hear the same thing?"

"More than once, that's for sure," Tess said. "Did you finally make contact with Coyote?"

"He's on his way," Micah said, and he shifted a sleeping Katie in his lap.

"If you'd like to lie her down, there's a padded bench in the office," a police officer offered.

"We're okay," Micah said. "Our ride should be here any minute."

Coyote literally skidded into the police station, he was moving so fast. He looked around panicked.

"We're okay," Micah said. "Just take us home."

Coyote lifted Katie from his brother's arms, searching everyone with his eyes for injuries.

"This is where it happened," Micah pointed when they were driving past the scene of the accident. The vehicles were gone, even the flares had been removed from the roadside. There were still black skid marks across the pavement.

"We stopped there," Micah pointed. "She slammed into the rock face, and rolled over twice, before stopping."

Coyote slowed. "If she'd skidded another ten feet, past the rock formation, she might have flipped over the embankment. That's a forty, or fifty-foot slope."

"She did stop, and we were lucky," Micah said. He tapped his brother on the arm, and shook his head slightly, with a nod toward the backseat. He didn't want to discuss what happened with Katie listening. Sometimes she pretended to be asleep. At the sheriff's office, they had been kind enough to take her from the room and distract her when they were giving statements.

The rest of the trip to the lake was quiet. There were several security company trucks parked in front. The main gate looked like someone had rammed into it. It was damaged but still intact.

"I'm going to talk to them," Micah said to Coyote. "Take Tess and Katie home, I'll walk in."

When Micah came in, he went straight to the bedroom. He came out wearing jeans and boots, and he went straight to the woodpile.

"He needs to work off some mad!" Coyote said to Tess. "Let him calm down. He's good at working through his anger, rather than spewing it all over everyone else."

Tess waited. The rhythmic whack of Micah splitting wood was calming to her, too. She pulled a frozen dinner from the freezer. She made coffee in the regular percolator and a pot of tea for herself.

Coyote hovered and settled Katie in her room reading a book.

"Is this ever going to end?" Coyote demanded in a loud and angry whisper. "Is Carla ever going to stop?"

Tess raised a finger in the air when her phone rang, and she went to the patio.

Micah finally made his way to the patio and sat on the glider beside her. "Are you ready to throw in the towel on us? I wouldn't blame you."

"I don't give up that easy," Tess said. "Dr. Hutchison, from the Military Medical Center, called me. It was a courtesy call between ER physicians. I've worked with him before."

Coyote had been standing in the patio door. He slid the screen closed behind him and joined them.

"Carla is still unconscious," Tess said. "It's going to be a slow recovery if there is a recovery. Until she awakens, there's no way to tell how much brain damage has been done. What they can diagnose is that she has severe spinal cord injuries in both her neck in the upper and lower cervical sections. There's a 90% chance she's going to be a paraplegic or a quadriplegic. Before you ask, no, there isn't a cure. There's lots of technology to help, but the spinal cord is like the brain. They are still, in many ways, a mystery to medical science. She will most likely spend the rest of her life in a care facility unless someone is willing to take care of her full-time."

Tess climbed the spiral staircase and found Micah in the studio. He was painting a smaller version of the painting of Coyote and Katie on the Ferris wheel.

"Which one are you keeping?" Tess asked. "The larger one, or the smaller one?"

"The larger one, I think," Micah admitted. "If you don't mind, I would like to hang it in the family room."

"Thanks for asking," Tess said, looking around at the stacks. "I love this house, and the best part is—I wouldn't change a thing. Except, you should have your paintings all over the house."

"There's something on your mind," Micah said.

She smiled. "You read me like a book. I have another appointment with Dr. Frost next week. I haven't made a hotel reservation, and I was wondering if you'd like to come. Even if I'm interviewing, there will be time to see the sights. If I'm interviewing, you could be taking Katie to places that I could skip."

"Such as?"

"There's a Doll House and Toy Museum. I've been there, and it was wonderful."

"You don't strike me as a doll person," Micah said. "When you were a kid, you had crossed hockey sticks on your bedroom wall for décor."

"I have my girly side," Tess said, smiling. "The truth is I got lost roaming around D.C., and I ran into the museum by acci- dent. When that happens, and I'm not on a schedule to be somewhere, I think its providence telling me I need to stop and chill out."

"Have you gone to many museums based on this provi- dence theory?"

"Quite a few," Tess admitted.

"I can clear my schedule," Micah said. "I'd like some

distance between us and what is going on here. I've already received thirty-some calls from reporters."

"I was a part-time reporter for years," Tess said. "They have to jump on the story right away. It would be best for you to give a few more interviews and put the onus on Carla, so some dickhead doesn't claim you are to blame for all her problems."

"True enough," Micah said. "Any word from the Military Hospital?"

"She's conscious, but she's not responding. She has no long-term memory, and she can't retain any short-term memory. She has no movement in her legs and only in one arm, but the doctors don't believe she is controlling it. It's probably involuntary muscle response. What have the police said?"

"They're waiting for full medical reports on her condition," Micah said. "The law enforcement agencies are in contact with the hospital. They discovered a stepbrother, which was news to me. I've never heard of him. The stepbrother refused any responsibility for her. He lives in Australia, and part of his reason for going there was to get away from Carla. She kept interfering in his life and deliberately trying to break up his marriage. The investigator said the brother wasn't surprised by her behavior.

"The court has assigned an adult public guardian. The guardian will make the decisions for her health care, shelter, or other needs. It's such a waste."

"It wasn't your fault," Tess said. "We have to try to regain our normal lives."

## Chapter 20

"Whose idea was it to tour Washington, D.C., in late August?" Micah asked, wiping his brow.

"We could have taken a bus tour," Tess said.

Micah looked over to the gridlock of traffic surrounding the Washington Mall area. "It's faster to walk. Once we get inside the Air and Space Museum, we'll get some relief from this heat and humidity."

"As long as I can get to the hotel and take a cold shower before going to my interview, I'll be okay," Tess said.

Katie came running across from a grassy area where she'd been playing with a small dog.

"Daddy, when can I have a puppy?" Katie pleaded.

"We can discuss it after school starts," Micah said, and she ran ahead of them. "Are kids impervious to heat? She's been running full blast ever since we got here."

"If I remember correctly, we were too at her age," Tess said.

"I did some research on housing and schools near the Naval Medical Center," Micah said. "It's an expensive area."

"I still have to buy a new car," Tess said. "Or I can drive the Mini Cooper."

"The Mini Cooper is less than two years old, we can trade it in for something more substantial," Micah said.

"You really don't like small cars, do you?"

"No," he admitted. "The less vehicle you have around you, the more likely you will be seriously injured, if there is a crash. I think we both know how that works. I'd rather not take that chance, although if you go to work at the Naval Medical Center, you could get around by the metro system or taxies."

"I'll know more after the interviews today," Tess said. "I have already been warned that today's interviews would be intense."

"We're going to a special dollhouse exhibit at the museum on 44th Street," Micah said.

"Excuse me!" a young woman exclaimed, running to Micah. "Would you sign an autograph for me?" She flashed her breasts. "Just sign across my boobs!"

"I think not!" Tess exclaimed, yanking the woman's shirt down to cover her. "That's highly inappropriate!"

"But..."

"No!" Tess and Micah said together, and they walked away.

"I wouldn't have signed," Micah said, laughing.

"Does that happen very often?" Tess demanded, glancing back at the girl angrily.

"Occasionally. We're getting too old to garner that kind of attention, and we know better. I don't want to be accused of inappropriate behavior, even if it was her idea. Someone that brazen wants attention. None of us want to be accused of something we didn't do!"

"It's called paranoia," Tess teased.

"It's called covering our asses," Micah said, chuckling. "Let's go to the National Museum of American History. There's an ice cream parlor in the basement."

"Now that's the best idea you've had in the last couple of hours," Tess admitted.

---

Micah was sitting at his laptop, writing a song when there was a knock on the hotel door. He opened the door to Tess, with her arms full of carry-out bags. He grabbed as many bags as he could get without throwing her off-balance and carried them inside to the small kitchenette area. "I take it we are eating in?" he said

"Everyone at the Naval Hospital was raving about the deli, and it was only a block from here. It was getting later and later, and you weren't answering your phone," Tess said, diving into the bags.

"Sorry," Micah exclaimed, pulling out his cell. "I forgot to turn it on after we left the museums. Damn, I've had seven calls from Stan."

"Daddy!" Katie exclaimed. "That's eight dollars you owe the bad word piggy!"

"So, I do, and I've been very bad," Micah admitted digging into his pocket and handing her two five-dollar bills. "Take this and put it in your suitcase. When you get home, you can put it in the bad word piggy! It's bedtime for you, kiddo, so scoot."

Katie ran off to the bedroom she was using in the suite.

"I've already listened to my messages," Tess said. "Don't panic, everyone in your family is okay."

"Has anything changed?" Micah asked.

"Carla has lapsed into a coma. Her vital signs are deteriorating, and if she continues the downward spiral, she'll be put on life support," Tess explained. She grasped both of his hands in hers. "This is not your fault! None of this is your fault. I suspected, as did Dr. Hutchison that this might happen. The injuries she sustained, in most cases, would have been fatal on the scene. The fact she's hung on this long is an anomaly. She did this. She could have killed all of us. We are the survivors, and we are not going to let her actions ruin our lives."

He nodded and took a deep breath. "Right, let me answer Stan's calls. I had dinner sent in for Katie a couple of hours ago. I thought we'd do room service later."

"Okay, but no blaming yourself! We have the best Kosher sandwiches in the Nation's Capital for dinner," Tess said.

"I won't, and I want to hear about the interviews," Micah said.

When he returned a few minutes later, he kissed Tess. "All is good. Stan said Lauren has set a date, and they're going to be married the weekend after school starts. It's going to be a private ceremony. Stan wants us to babysit the girls while they take a short honeymoon."

"Lauren deserves it," Tess said. "She got such a raw deal with Chris. I thought it was going to turn her against men forever. She was bitter for a long time. Justifiably bitter, but he finally got his comeuppance. Stan is the exact opposite."

"How did the interviews go?" Micah asked. "Are we moving?"

Tess unwrapped a sandwich and took her time taking a bite and chewing. "I want it, but I asked them to defer my application until the next cycle. I spent quite a bit of time talking to the doctors who are currently in the program. I can handle the work, but I don't want to take on the hours required. They are averaging sixteen or more hours a day. If I wanted that, I'd stay with Emergency. I've been working at this pace since I was sixteen, school, part-time jobs, intern rotations, and being in charge of the ER department. Exhaustion had become part of my routine, and when we connected, I couldn't turn it off. I was looking for the next thing, the next fellowship—the next challenge."

Micah was watching her from across the table.

"I've given this a lot of thought, and I've decided to take the job at Resolute Health Hospital. I'm a doctor, and that will mean being on call for the tough cases. I can't stop being what I was meant to be. I can stop letting my professional calling take over my entire life.

"If we're going to be together, we need time to become a family. I'll be a wife and a mother, and I don't for a second believe it's going to be a stress-free transition. Our decisions to have children won't be easy either. We have a lot of options to consider. I can't do that and be on-call twenty-four-seven. I know you would support whatever I wanted to do, but it wouldn't be fair to you or our family.

"Micah, you've put a lot on hold having to deal with the Carla situation for so long. I know your views on children. What she did having those abortions without even consulting you, ripped you apart inside. The cold, hard facts are that she was sleeping with other men. Those pregnancies might not have been yours. I don't believe it would have mattered to you, once you got over the initial shock. You have a fantastic capacity for love.

"As a physician, I have to straddle the right of choice, with my personal views and my issues of not being able to carry a child. Sometimes it feels like there's not much fairness in this world, but I've had to learn to live with it. So will you."

Micah opened his mouth to speak, but Tess held up a finger to silence him.

"I love you. I have loved you for a very long time. I admire your loyalty, but now that we are together, that damnable loyalty had better be turned on for me. I want all of it. I want your love, I want marriage, I want kids. I want the next fifty or sixty years with you. I want you to look at me with the same love and devotion that you painted in that portrait of your grandparents. I know I'm asking a lot, but it's my turn!"

Micah shoved away from the table and walked around to

her. He pulled Tess from her chair and into his arms and kissed her. "I'm going to devote one hundred and fifty percent to you and my family. I'm also going to support your decisions as a physician.

"We are lucky that we get to share this experience. We can devote our energies to each other, and whatever children we have, and I don't care how we get them. I love kids, but even if we decide against having children, it won't change how I feel about you."

Tess shivered as he pulled her closer and drew her into another kiss. She knew what was coming and looked forward to it. She returned his kisses as his hands roamed over her. She was still wearing a business suit, and she struggled to remove her jacket. He pulled it off of her, tossed it over to a chair, and continued to stroke her. She didn't want to feel the material of his clothing. She wanted to feel him, skin to skin.

"Let's take this to the bedroom," she whispered.

"Good idea," Micah agreed, and he swung her into his arms and carried her to the bedroom suite. He fumbled with the buttons on her blouse. Quickly tossed it aside, and focused his attention on her bra with a heated gaze. Micah lowered his lips to her breasts and nipples and suckled on them, bringing them to hard peaks.

His hands were roaming again, over her, in her, and it still wasn't enough.

"I need you inside me," Tess gasped.

"I have to be sure you're ready," Micah huffed.

"Trust me, I'm ready!" Tess dragged him on top of her. "I'm ready! Micah, take me! Take me now!"

He didn't need more encouragement. Micah lifted her legs gently one over each shoulder and lifted her off the mattress. He teased her, rubbing his cock against her and plunging into her with a hard thrust. Each thrust into her drew her further off the mattress.

Tess's eyes flew open, and she sighed with pleasure. She seemed to soften and to writhe with pleasure.

He took her hard and fast with a mindless urgency. Their coupling, this time, was all about satisfying their hunger and passion for each other.

Suddenly Tess stiffened, and she made a sound that was part relief and part joy. Her orgasm came first, and he continued to thrust deep into her. When those fleeting sensations rippled over her, she tightened her legs around him, urging him on.

Micah knew he wasn't going to be able to hold himself together much longer. He plunged deeper into her, thrusting harder until he exploded so powerfully it took two ejections to empty himself. He withdrew and collapsed beside her. A sense of pure masculine ego made him smile.

Tess rolled over onto him, not wanting to break the physical contact.

"Was that what you had in mind?" he asked.

Tess smiled at him. "This was just a teaser. I want much, much more tonight. I want a marathon of deviant behavior."

"How deviant?" he questioned.

She giggled. "Let's just say that when I sit on the plane tomorrow, I want to be very aware of what we did tonight. Every stroke, every spank, every orgasm."

"I wouldn't want it said that I'm uncooperative," Micah agreed.

Their next session came less than an hour later. Micah's approach began with seduction and included turning her bottom bright red. These spankings, though, had nothing to do with agreeing to have a D/D relationship. The spanks had more to do with enhancing the experience of sex.

## Epilogue

Two years later.

"Are we ready for this?" Tess asked, looking at her reflection in front of a full-length mirror.

"I am, and you knew it was coming," Micah said, straightening his cufflinks, and turning her around to face him. "You're too beautiful for me to let out in public!"

"I'd much rather had a big bash out at the lake," Tess said.

"It's too late now, and too cold. I tried to float that idea, but I got shut down. The women in our family are a force to be reckoned with. They finally decided on a big fancy Christmas party, and I don't know who came up with the idea of our renewing our marriage vows at the same time."

"Lauren had her small wedding, she got what she wanted," Tess complained. "We all flew over to London for Macy's wedding, which could have rivaled a royal affair."

"And we slipped off and got married and didn't tell a soul about it ahead of time. It was just you and me, and Katie, and we spent our honeymoon at Disneyland."

"Lauren still thinks it was strange to take Katie with us, on our honeymoon, but it was right for us. We're in this together."

"Punkin is proud to call you, mommy. She introduced you to her class, as *My mommy, the Doctor. She helps people who are sick to get better.* All I got was *This is my daddy, he writes songs, and he fixes things.*"

"She's too young to realize the impact your music has had on the industry. And don't call her that," Tess said, straightening his tie. "She doesn't want to be called Punkin. She says she's too old for a baby name, and her description is accurate," Tess said, smiling. "You fixed me. I had almost decided I was never going to be in a loving relationship. I was killing myself with work to compensate for it. I went from being a lonely work-obsessed physician to being loved and cared for. She'll understand more about what you do when she gets older. All her friends are going to want to become rock stars, and guess who is going to be the most popular Dad then."

Micah chuckled. "I am looking forward to seeing everyone. Sully and Karina arrived last Sunday, and he says they're not going anywhere or doing anything for at least a year. I guess filming a blockbuster is hard work.

"When you've got a family the size of his, and you insist on taking them everywhere with you, I guess it is exhausting. They want some time for themselves and their kids. It's hard to believe their youngest is sixteen months old already.

"Scout is the cutest baby in the whole world," Tess exclaimed, and she jumped when Micah smacked her on the bottom. "Ouch! What?"

"You couldn't wait until I was free, so we could go together," he grumbled.

"No, I couldn't! It was my day off," Tess retorted. "Who would have thought I would become a baby nut! Maybe I'll switch to pediatrics."

"You might change your mind after our twins are born," he

teased. "Days without sleep, dirty diapers, night feedings, and everything else that goes with newborns."

Tess's eyes turned misty.

"It's going to be okay," Micah said, deflecting the fear and trying to reassure her. "You know as well as I do, the pregnancy has been textbook perfect so far. We found the right surrogate, and she's been terrific."

"Our babies," Tess nodded, sniffing and burying her face in his chest. "So many women have to try for years, but our in vitro procedure took on the first try. It still scares me."

Micah hugged her. "There's nothing to be frightened of; everything is right on schedule."

Tess laid her face against his chest. "We had to get past some of the awful stuff first. Carla dying was expected, but it was still awful. I know you didn't have any feelings left for her, but it was still hard. I can't imagine living a life so self-absorbed that no one came to the service. Not a single person came forward for her.

"Then I had to take the meds for a couple of months before the eggs were harvested. I know I was a bitch during that time. All those hormone enhancements were bouncing around in me, and I know I was making you miserable. I had to go through it though, we had to try," Tess whispered with a catch in her voice.

"It worked, and it was worth it," Micah said, pulling her in tighter.

"I had to know for sure."

"I know," he said gently. "We'll have our babies soon. Don't fall apart on me now, sweetheart. Then we'll do it again, or we'll go the route of adoption. We'll have our children, Tessa! I won't break that promise."

The family, friends, and coworkers party was more formal than Micah would have preferred. When the idea had first been raised, both he and Tess had tried for a more casual get-together. Their ideas had been vetoed by the women. Instead, it was taking place in a rented ballroom of an upscale hotel in San Antonio. First, there would be a *reenactment*, and then it would be party time. Except, this wedding was nothing like when he and Tess had been married by a Justice of the Peace.

This time he was in a tuxedo, along with his brothers as best men. Tess was in a wedding gown, and she would have Lauren as her Maid of honor, and his sisters as the bridesmaids. Katie and Sully's oldest daughter, Alexa, were the flower girls.

The family would have a formal wedding they had complained about missing. Tess had tried to maintain some control. Micah was glad there would be a photographer this time. They needed photographs to commemorate what he considered the best day of his life—the day he had married Tess.

Everyone was there, including Tess's mother and her *latest* stepfather, her mother's fifth husband. He was the same age as Micah. The new husband tried to corner Micah three times to talk to him about launching a recording career. After the first encounter, Tess had rescued him. The couple had left after the ceremony. Tess and Lauren's mother seemed to be oblivious to her daughter's feelings.

Lauren, Stan, and the kids were beaming with happiness. Micah's large and extended family were all there, as were most of his employees.

They were glad Carole was looking happy and beautiful. With the new diets, hormone replacement treatments, and the psychology help, she was a much happier person. Carole was taking yoga classes, had lost weight, and looked ten years younger. She'd even talked Daniel into joining a gym, and a Latin dancing class, of all things. Daniel was looking fit and spending less of his time at his business, and more on the golf course with his rejuvenated wife.

Everyone was excited to see Sully and his family. Karina was often seen looking around for their latest offspring, a cute little girl, they'd named Scout Maderia McKenna, and were calling Scout. She was being passed around through family and friends. Sully looked fit. He'd been filming a sequel to a spy trilogy, and he'd been working out daily with a trainer. He was claiming he was going to become a couch potato for the next year, to counteract his forced regimen of diet and exercise while he'd been filming.

Karina looked radiant and happy in her role as wife, mother, and real estate, and stock market investor. Sully made at least half of their income with his multi-million-dollar movie roles. Karina was in charge of the investments.

Coyote was at the party with a pretty young woman named Leigh Ann, whom he introduced around. She was a minister of a small church in Luling, Texas. Everyone noticed she called him Riley.

Macy hadn't been able to make it to the party. She and Max had recently moved to St. Petersburg, Russia. Macy was now a Demi-soloist—or Second soloist—with the Mikhailovsky Dance Company, and she was working toward the First Soloist position. They had posted a Skype message that afternoon.

Noah and Lily were at the party. Noah was in high-school and making the grades that would allow him to occasionally join a band on tour when his skills were requested.

Lily had skipped a grade, and she was straight-A status. She was excelling at the Adams Academy, and she was living at home. She also loved her classes with Madam Bashlofski and progressing in her dance skills.

The only person missing from the party was Allison. She had been released from the rehabilitation center. Days later, she had disappeared, somehow removing the ankle bracelet, she was legally required to wear. When she had been found six months later, she had returned to her drinking and drug habits.

She was in a stricter rehabilitation program now, sanctioned by the courts. She had yet to go to trial for her crimes. Stern warnings hadn't done much good, and she'd been warned by the magistrate handling her case, that ignoring recommended treatment wouldn't be tolerated. She wouldn't be given another chance."

They had all tried to talk to Allison, but she couldn't be convinced she was doing anything wrong. She wasn't listening or cooperating, and they didn't know where else to turn. The whole family was afraid she was going to learn a harsh lesson.

As the post-wedding/Christmas party, continued into the late evening, the guests and family members with small children began to leave. Singles and couples began to call it a night. Everyone expressed their congratulations, and good wishes, although Micah and Tess had been married for eighteen months.

The last to leave were the family members. Sully and Karina, with the help of grandparents, and uncles carried their little ones to the family van. They were strapped into car seats and baby carriers.

Sully was giving his brother a hug and suggesting they get together later in the week when Micah's phone rang.

Micah held up his hand to stop all the casual conversation. He wrapped his arm around Tess.

"We're on our way," he said and disconnected the call. He turned and kissed Tess. "Jenna is on her way to Del Seton Hospital. She's in labor!"

"She's three weeks early!" Tess exclaimed.

"She's having twins," Micah reminded her. "Three weeks early isn't unusual for twins. You know that. Let's go!"

"We'll take Katie home with us," Karina offered. 'She can spend some time with Alexa, and have a sleepover."

"I want to go see my baby brothers being born," Katie protested.

"Honey, they won't let you in," Tess explained. "We talked about this before. We'll call you as soon as something happens. It might be a false alarm."

Katie went with her aunt and uncle, as Micah and Tess rushed to his vehicle, amid shouts of congratulations.

Five hours later, Micah was passed a cup of coffee from Starbucks, by Sully as he sat down in a chair beside his brother. "How come you're not in there?"

"It's taking a while. Tess is the labor coach. It's not like Jenna is my wife, although she is having our babies. We had to go to special surrogate counseling, so we would know how she expects us to react to her giving birth to our children. Jenna is still a woman who doesn't necessarily want an unrelated man watching her give birth. It's being filmed, so I can watch it later, but she didn't want me in the room, in person. We won't be given the babies until tomorrow when the final legalities will be signed."

"Have my nephews been born?" Coyote asked, joining his brothers.

"We're still waiting," Micah said.

Two more hours went by, and Jenna's husband joined them. He introduced himself to Sully and Coyote and explained he supported his wife's decision to be a surrogate. After having their children, she had wanted to help couples who couldn't for whatever reason conceive or carry children. The surprise had been when the implanted embryo had divided, meaning she was carrying twins.

Another two hours went by, and Tess finally joined them. She walked straight to Micah, hugged, and kissed him. "The boys are perfect!"

"Finally, we get some boys," Coyote said, turning to Sully. "You seem to be specializing in girls!"

"I love my girls," Sully growled.

"I love them too, but you're four for four, all girls. I'm glad we're getting some boys," Coyote grumbled. "Little boys are tougher! They don't have tea parties, where I have to wear a tiara."

"It will be a while before they're old enough to wrestle," Tess said, smiling. "Come on," she urged Micah. "You can come in and see them. Mr. Hall, you can come in, too. She's tired, but she is an amazing woman!"

"That, I already know," Jenna's husband said proudly.

When Micah came from the delivery room, Sully got to his feet. "Do you want to crash at our place tonight?"

Micah shook his head. "In a few hours, the psychologist, the social worker, and our lawyer will converge here for the final signatures. We want to get that final step over. Jenna can be released tomorrow if her doctor agrees. The babies will be in the nursery for a couple of days, they are a few ounces short of the five pounds they need to be before being released."

"If you want to see them, they'll be in the nursery in about an hour," Tess said. "Since I used to work here, I've been given a little more leeway than most people. I'll stay with Jenna for a while, and I'll call you when the babies are moved."

Tess and Micah were allowed to hold the babies briefly before they were whisked away to the nursery. They left Jenna to rest, as she was taken to a patient room. They walked to the nursery with his brothers and pointed out the two little babies, sharing a crib. They were labeled, Baby Boy McKenna, #1, and Baby Boy McKenna, #2.

"You haven't picked out names yet?" Coyote questioned.

"We have," Tess said. "Benjamin Riley, and William Sullivan McKenna. Their names will be added tomorrow. Riley and Will."

"Cool," Sully said. "One after each of us. Thanks!" He punched his younger but taller, brother in the shoulder. "Let's go home. You can crash at our place. By the way, I like our new neighbor." He turned to Micah. "You'd better call the folks."

"I will," Micah said as he pulled Tess closer, and they stood looking at the two tiny specks of humanity. Theirs, although he was sure Tess was just as anxious to sign those final papers as he was. It was a terrifying, outstanding detail that had to be completed. The babies were theirs, Tess's egg, his sperm, but they'd been brought to life by the generosity of Jenna Hall.

Even more hours later; Micah and Tess were still wide-awake and tense. Waiting for the officials to arrive, they held hands and reassured each other. Finally, when the last signature was signed, witnessed, and notarized, they were congratulated.

They stood in front of the nursery windows looking at their babies. The nurse came in and replaced the name cards with their full names, taken from the birth certificates.

Micah and Tess looked at each other and smiled as they were both spilling tears. This had been a long time coming for both of them. In fact, the actual time from when they'd made the decision to try in vitro, to the present time, hadn't been that long.

For Micah, it was all the wasted years of a doomed relationship. One that hadn't allowed him to have children. Tess's struggle had been worse as she hadn't known if she could produce viable eggs. She'd been told emphatically that she couldn't take a chance on carrying a child. It would have been extremely dangerous.

Now they were the parents of a beautiful seven-year-old and newborn twins.

"I called Resolute, and I'm officially on maternity leave. We prepared for this, and I've already contacted Dr. Frost and canceled my holding position in his program. I'm going to stick with Resolute, and I'll return there as soon as we get everything under control."

"My Tess," Micah said, kissing the top of her head. "Always thinking months and years ahead. Always prepared for the unknown. You're one of a kind."

"Two years ago, I would never have believed this possible," Tess said, leaning into the solidness of her husband. The man who completed her.

"Me, either," Micah said, and he smiled.

"What are you thinking?" Tess asked.

"I keep hearing, the lyrics of Celine Dion's song *The Power of Love*." He brought her hand to his lips and kissed it.

"One of my favorites," Tess said. "Will you sing it for me?"

"I can't hit the high notes," Micah whispered in her ear. "I can live the true meaning of those words of love to you and our children for the rest of my life."

Tess went up on her toes to kiss him. "A woman, a wife, and a mother can't ask for much more than that! You gave me the power to love!"

The End

## Mariella Starr

Sometimes it's hard to pick what I love most beyond my family; I write, paint, renovate and am a voracious reader. The joke in our house about vices is that mine is books. My idea of the perfect house is the public library, just add a kitchen to make my husband happy, and I would be good with it. I live in Nevada with my husband, and two dogs that I adore, and lot of scorpions and lizards that still make me scream and act girly. I love to travel, and I get to travel to visit my grown children who have both chosen to live abroad, one in Ireland and one in England—what could be better.

I love writing; creating the characters and making them come alive. For a short time, while they are directing me through their stories, they are alive for me and I hope they are to my readers. My favorite genres for reading are history, romances, and mystery. Sometimes I think I spend as much time in research as I do in writing, but it is important to me that the time-periods be correct. It also makes me one heck of a good trivial pursuit player.

I'm a casual person, enjoying a laid back lifestyle where dressing up means putting on real shoes and not flip-flops, cowboy boots or running shoes. (The running shoes are not my idea of fun but my husband says if I'm spending all my time on a computer writing, I also have to move—10 miles a day!) Oh, what I put up with because I love that man. I also love receiving e-mail from my readers and can be contacted at MariStarr@outlook.com

*Don't miss these other exciting titles by Mariella Starr and Blushing Books!*

What to Do About Kassie
Those Merrick Women
The Breaking Point
A Different Kind of Woman
Miss Trouble and the Law
Coming Home to Promise
A Widow's Secrets
Violet, A Contrary Woman
Emma Takes a Stand
That's Life: The Patrick and Ivy Story
Simmer Down, Red
The Amazing Maven
A Little Bit of Sass
Heller On Wheels
A Path Worth Taking
Keeping Sunny Safe
Maybe, With Conditions
Posey's Assets
Broken Vows
The Promise
In Search of a Noble Man
Lacy's Rules
Desiree, A Woman of Defiance
Full Circle
Caitlin's Conspiracies
The Awakening of Alexandria
Charlotte's Comeuppance
Teaching Miss Maisie Jane

*The McKenna Brothers*
The Forever Kind: Sully

Holding Tess

*The Overton Saga*
Isabel's Independence, Book 1
Britannia's Blaggard, Book 2
Sweet Sarah, Book 3

*Connect with Mariella Starr:*
MariStarr@outlook.com

## Blushing Books

Blushing Books is the oldest eBook publisher on the web. We've been running websites that publish steamy romance and erotica since 1999, and we have been selling eBooks since 2003. We have free and promotional offerings that change weekly, so please do visit us at http://www.blushingbooks.com/free.

## Blushing Books Newsletter

Please join the Blushing Books newsletter
to receive updates & special promotional offers.
You can also join by using your mobile phone:
Just text **BLUSHING** to 22828.

Every month, one new sign up via text messaging will receive a
$25.00 Amazon gift card, so sign up today!